A DANGEROUS DECEIT

Marjorie Eccles

This first world edition published 2013
in Great Britain and the USA by
SEVERN HOUSE PUBLISHERS LTD of
9–15 High Street, Sutton, Surrey, England, SM1 1DF.

Trade paperback edition first published 2017
In Great Britain and the USA by
SEVERN HOUSE PUBLISHERS LTD
Eardley House, 4 Uxbridge Street, London W8 7SY

British Library Cataloguing in Publication Data
A CIP catalogue record for this title is available from the British Library.

ISBN-13: 978-0-7278-8322-3 (cased)
ISBN-13: 978-1-84751-840-8 (trade paper)
ISBN-13: 978-1-78010-457-7 (e-book)

Prologue

The earth is at last beginning to stir from its winter sleep, the snowdrops under the laburnum by the gate are just beginning to show their pale green sheaths, but it doesn't feel like spring yet. It's the end of February, and it's been one of the longest and coldest winters Margaret can remember. The wind is keen enough to bring tears to their eyes as they walk up Emscott Hill from Folbury to the cemetery.

When the snow first came it had been little more than a seasonal inconvenience, and for a brief spell it had given magic to a workaday world. But by now everyone has had more than enough of freezing pipes and the icy draughts that sneak themselves indoors, through the edges of window frames and under doors, no matter what. The snow has turned a depressing grey, speckled with muck and soot blown miles along the valley from the furnaces and factory chimneys of the Black Country conurbation. Coughs and colds are rife, the shops are running out of Snowfire ointment for chilblains, but the thermometer shows no sign of rising and the ground rings hard as iron where the snow has been cleared.

Only the youngsters are still sliding joyfully on the frozen pond in the park, the children of the well-heeled of Emscott careening down the slope of the hill on proper sledges with runners, their shouts echoing on the frozen air, while the offspring of less affluent parents, lower down the hill, do the same on home-made toboggans or tin trays.

In the cemetery, Margaret bends over the grave while Symon strides further on and into St Chad's, a chapel-of-ease to the main parish church, which serves the cemetery and is one of his responsibilities as curate. She gives a last tweak to the flowers in the metal vase sunk into the stone chips within the grave's surround. They are daffodils shipped in from milder climes and the bitter wind will soon wither them, but she never fails in her weekly duty of bringing fresh flowers to her father's last resting place. She gathers up the dead ones she has replaced, ready to throw them on the heap in the corner of the cemetery, but for a moment or two stands where she is, her eyes fixed on the grave.

Why? Why did you keep so silent? How did you bear the pain for all those years without complaint? Was that the reason you were always so hard to understand? And why you wouldn't allow us to see it, until it was too late? Why?

On the headstone, the letters are sharp, gilt incisions into the mottled dark grey marble: Major Osbert William Rees-Talbot, DSO 1873–1926.

'That's enough,' she tells herself at last. 'Take a grip on yourself, young lady. Isn't that what he would have said?'

Snuggling the fur collar of her coat tighter round her neck, she turns away and walks rapidly to join Symon in the church.

A few miles away, inside the wild woods that make up the forest at Maxstead, the layers of snow are sparser, partly due to the bare, interlacing branches of the closely growing trees that formed some protection. Even so, birds have dropped frozen from the twig, the badgers, foxes and other denizens of the forest have grown lean and hungry, and the chuckling little streams that run through it have become silent and iced over. That is, inside the forest . . .

On its perimeter, with nothing to hinder it, the snow has fallen as thick as everywhere else. Outside a little covert where the trees stop are great drifts blown by the wind, and beneath them lies another grave, this one unmarked, undetected, its occupant safe even from hungry animals, since it is frozen solid under its shallow covering of deep-frozen earth topped by a thick crust of unbroken snow.

One

The hinges creaked on the heavy church door as Margaret pushed it open. Batting her gloved hands together, she waited as Symon strode towards her from the chancel where he had been changing the candles on the altar while waiting impatiently for her to join him.

'Your nose is cold,' he remarked as he kissed her.

'I don't wonder. We'd better get moving or there's every chance my circulation might never get going properly again. But you – you look warm as toast.'

He did, too, a large, forceful young man radiating energy and purpose and looking very dark and dashing in the long, swishing black wool cloak he wore over his cassock. Her own cherry-red wool coat, despite its fur collar and cuffs, didn't offer anything like the same sort of warmth. Out there by the grave her feet had turned to leaden lumps of ice, though her cheeks were pink with the cold fresh air.

Symon would have liked to wrap his cloak around her, and did so for a moment, drawing her into the warmth of his arms – but he had his position to think of and this wasn't the time or place for dalliance. As it was he kept as close to her as he could when they left the church, shortening his stride to accommodate hers as they walked forward in the teeth of the bitter wind.

She wore his ring, a twist of three rather fine diamonds, on the same finger upon which, in the fullness of time, he would place a plain gold band. The fullness of time, thought Symon, his dark brows coming together – whatever that might mean. They had met over a year ago, and he had fallen in love immediately with this bright girl with the glancing gleam of laughter in her eyes. Falling in love had not been part of his plans at that moment, and she was nothing like the young woman his mother had had in mind, but Celia Vise had been forgotten in a moment. All the same, the date for their wedding had only recently been decided. This was partly due to the period of mourning after her father died, of course – his unexpected death had thrown everything into disarray and Margaret's grief for him was natural; she had been as close to that difficult man as anyone could be – but there was no denying she had been ambivalent about leaving him before that. Now, at last, the wedding date had been fixed, though the vexed question of where they were to live still wasn't decided.

Symon Scroope, a young man for whom decisions were not a problem, was finding Margaret's untypical hesitation hard to cope with. Certainly, his own place of lodging would not do for a married man, even for one who didn't intend to remain a curate for long. And although a house was available, in which his predecessor and his wife had been forced to live, it was disagreeable in the extreme, both in lack of amenities and in its surroundings, situated as it was in a dark and dismal cul-de-sac behind Folgate Street, overshadowed by Holy Trinity.

On the other hand, there was Laurel Mount up here in Emscott, on the market and ambitiously described as a gentleman's residence, which they had already seen the previous week and to which they now walked after leaving the churchyard. It was not, unfortunately, in Folbury.

In many ways unique, to some extent still the same quiet market town it had always been, Folbury was now a buffer between the clamour of industry and the gentle, rolling Worcestershire countryside that lay on its far side; an agreeably haphazard sort of place, with interesting black-and-white timbering, crooked streets and little, time-forgotten courts, snickets and alleys interspersed with newer buildings. It boasted the remains of a medieval moated castle and a few elegant period houses surrounding the ancient church of Holy Trinity, while the spread of the mellow stone buildings of a minor public school, the sounds of its chapel bell, and of cricket on summer evenings, added to its attractiveness. Folbury had so far successfully confined its working parts and its meaner housing to its furthest limits, on the Birmingham road, near the canal and the railway.

Emscott, perched three miles up the hill, was considered Folbury's most desirable suburb, although it had only two or three shops and was not yet on a bus route. Tree-lined streets and houses of polite middle-class dignity, of which Laurel Mount was a prime example, now outnumbered the few cottages extant in the village it used to be, and which most of its residents liked to fancy it still was, and would remain.

The agent had only too willingly handed Symon the keys for another viewing, and this time they were free to roam around the empty rooms unencumbered by his eager exaggerations or his glossing over of the house's defects. Together, heels ringing on Minton tiles and bare boards, they completed a second tour, commenting as they did so on the changes and redecoration that would need to be done – should they ever take up residence. Greatly in its favour, Laurel Mount already had electricity and a telephone installed. It was the fifth house they had inspected. But it had been empty for weeks and it was almost as cold indoors as it had been outside.

'We'll have a hot water system put in, of course,' Symon said expansively, pressing the advantage as Margaret folded her arms across her chest and shivered.

'A hot water system,' she echoed. She had lived all her life without one so far. 'I'm used to cold houses.'

For that matter, the Reverend Symon Scroope was no stranger to them, either. Waking up as a boy in his bedroom at Maxstead Court with the windows frosted up inside, scooting along its draughty corridors, through freezing cavernous rooms, most of them not very warm even in summer – especially the great hall, where the heat from a fire big enough to roast the proverbial ox barely extended more than a few feet away from the hearth. An ancient roaring boiler that grudgingly gave out only faint indications of lukewarm heat in exchange for being fed with tons of fuel had once been installed, but not updated. The Scroopes had never been a family directed towards changing what had been thought good enough for hundreds of years, nor to acknowledging the fact that times had moved on. But Symon – Symon with a 'y' because that was the way Scroopes had always spelled it – was of another generation.

'Well, I see no virtue in deliberately seeking discomfort.' When he used it, he had a smile of tremendous charm that quite transformed his features.

Margaret smiled back and refrained from mentioning the expense attached to the fixing of pipes, radiators and boilers. Neither Symon's theological studies nor his family background had given him that sort of insight into the lives of ordinary folk. It probably wouldn't occur to him for some time that central heating was far beyond all but the favoured – unless it were pointed out to him, when he would, to do him justice, be extremely mortified.

Accepting his proposal of marriage, Margaret had also accepted that it was going to be her duty to instruct him on such matters. Coming from a family such as his, and possessed of a private income, he had an uneasy relationship with his conscience when it came to being able to acquire something no ill-paid curate could afford. He had put temptation behind him over the acquisition of a small car, and went around on a push-bike or walked like every other curate – and even his vicar – did, but had succumbed over her engagement ring and had now convinced himself that buying a house would not be going against his principles.

When Margaret thought of the alternative – that horrid little clergy house crouching in the shadow of the parish church – she could not find a reason to disagree. Indeed, it made even more sense to give some consideration to Laurel Mount. True, the dining room was gloomy, but perhaps it was nothing that couldn't be dealt with by fresh, light wallpaper and paint – and after all, how much time out of one's life was spent in the dining room? In any case, they were unlikely to be living here forever, perhaps not for very long. She cast another look around the drawing room. Although it announced the date of its origins in the shape of a simply hideous black marble fireplace and some dun-coloured wallpaper featuring maroon plums, it was well proportioned and had a south-westerly aspect. The garden had a mulberry tree and might be quite pretty in spring.

The French windows were locked when she tried them, but Symon found the key in the bunch which had been handed over and they descended three slippery wrought iron steps to the flagstones outside, his hand protectively under her elbow. The steps had been cleared of snow, no doubt on the instructions of the agent, but bore a thick rime of hoar frost.

They turned in unison and looked in silence at the unpromising red-brick facade. 'What do you think?' he asked.

Margaret avoided an immediate answer by bending to pick a small, somewhat withered slip of rosemary, grey-green and tough, the last surviving sprig of a frost-bitten shrub poking through a snow-covered flowerbed. It gave off its pungent, peppery smell as she held it to her nose but the leaves fell to the ground, dead, after all.

'Well?' Symon prompted to her bent head, her profile just visible under the modishly close-fitting cloche hat, a matching red to her coat. The question came out sharper than he had intended, but she didn't look up.

He put his finger under her chin and raised it so that she had to look at him. Tendrils of soft brown hair escaped charmingly from under the hat's tiny brim. Her eyes were a clear, golden hazel, thickly lashed. A little frown creased her brow. He looked, and suppressed a sigh. He couldn't dismiss the unnerving feeling of – could it be uncertainty that he had sensed in her lately? In Margaret, strong-minded, even wilful at times? Whatever it was, it was something he couldn't get past. At that moment, he felt an almost irresistible desire to crush her in his arms, along with another, almost equally irresistible one, to shake her and tell her she was nearly driving him mad with this uncharacteristic dithering about which house they were to have, that by now he was entitled to expect her to have been getting over her father's death. A forceful personality like his was not accustomed to being gainsaid. He almost lunged forward to grab her, but then controlled himself. 'Margaret,' he said, breathing deep, 'think carefully before you answer . . . do you really want to marry me?'

Had he actually said that?

She stood for a moment in shocked silence. She almost started to say something, then stopped herself. Finally she answered, a smile beginning in her eyes. 'If there's one thing I hate above all things, it's women who keep men dangling on the end of a string – and now I'm one of them, aren't I, poor Symon?'

He looked affronted. 'Don't laugh, Margaret.'

'Dearest Symon, I'm not laughing, I'm *teasing*.' She looked contrite. 'And that's not very nice of me, either. I'm afraid I've been infuriating lately, haven't I? How do you put up with me?'

Relief surged through him. She did tease him, that was true, but she could also make him laugh, which helped him feel less weighed down with the seriousness he felt was expected of him as a man of the cloth. 'Does that mean yes?'

'I don't see why we shouldn't make something of this house.' And indeed, a few minutes ago she had been envisaging her mother's Victorian cranberry glass collection, placed where it could catch the light, and some nice pictures against pale walls. Tradesmen would deliver, and she was a good walker.

It was scarcely the reply he had hoped for but it reassured him. He was sorry he'd doubted her, even for a moment; he should have known by now that once she had committed herself to something, she would never break faith. 'Well,' he said. 'Well, that's a relief.'

'You didn't really think—?'

'I imagined nowhere but Folbury was going to do. I know how attached you are to the place.'

'So much so that I'd refuse to live anywhere else? Symon, not really!'

Symon, who disliked being made to feel foolish, was even more annoyed with himself, to think that he'd allowed himself to believe she wouldn't contemplate living only a few miles away from where her life was presently centred, where her roots were, where all her activities were bound up. It was not only foolish, but disloyal to Margaret. All the same, a weight lifted itself from his shoulders.

It scarcely mattered to him where they lived – well, hardly at all, as long as they were together – barring that miserable clergy house down in the town, which he had no intention of inflicting on himself, or his new wife. Equally, he was determined not to start their married life in Alma House, the large rambling residence where Margaret presently lived with only her brother, and Maisie Henshall, who helped to keep everything in order. In fact he had absolutely no desire whatsoever to live in the same house as Felix – hasty and argumentative, filled with all those preposterous Socialist ideas, forever throwing the place open to those so-called friends of his, some of whom were so left wing they had espoused Communism and given up their jobs to work for the party, and were never averse to a free meal and a bed. Surely he had only imagined that such a suggestion had hovered tentatively in the air? That Margaret, free now of the obligations to her father, was reluctant to hand over the running of the house to Maisie, or to abandon it to Felix and his cohorts? She was overprotective of Felix, when she had no need to be; he was more than capable of looking after himself.

A few months previously, Osbert Rees-Talbot, who had not only lost an arm but had also sustained other long-lasting and debilitating internal injuries many years ago while serving as a soldier in the South African war, had died tragically. That night, he had kissed Margaret, said goodnight and gone upstairs earlier than usual, in order to take a bath before retiring. An hour later Felix had tried the knob of the bathroom door and, alarmed to find it locked, had called to ask if all was well. There was no reply. The key was in the lock and when the door didn't respond to his shoulder against it, he had resorted to slipping a piece of paper in the space beneath and poking the key on to it. The door open, he was met with the sight of his father, face downwards in the bath he had run.

It seemed there were always difficulties in reaching a firm conclusion in such a death, but in this case it appeared to be so obvious that there had been no need to search for under-lying causes: it was evident that Osbert, possibly overcome by an attack of pain or dizziness, had slipped under the water and, one-armed as he was, his balance never very reliable, been unable to save himself, hapless as a fly with only one wing. The verdict at the inquest had been death due to accidental causes.

No one outside the family remarked on the locked bathroom door, perhaps because they assumed that to be the normal procedure when one took a bath. His doctor, however, who had foreseen such difficulties in view of his disabilities and warned him never to do such a thing, shook his head angrily at the folly of patients who thought they knew better than he did. Within the family, none of them spoke of why Osbert, normally so conscientious about heeding this warning, had felt it necessary on that occasion to disregard it.

They had understandably all been deeply shocked by the tragedy, which had thrown their lives into confusion. But now, in the face of Margaret's procrastination, Symon's never too easily held patience was wearing thin. He considered he had been more than generous in allowing it to go on so long, putting it all down to having too much responsibility thrust upon her since her father had died – amongst other things, dealing with his financial affairs.

The fortunes of the present Rees-Talbots, such as they were, had come into being through their great-grandfather, Huw Rees-Talbot. Through his marriage to a young woman of the locality, he had come to Folbury from South Wales and, continuing the trade to which he had been apprenticed, had set up a brass foundry, one more in the mushroom growth of Black Country trades – some small, some not so small – allied to the metal industry, heavy and light, which had already made Birmingham world famous. By dint of unrelenting work and canny investment, Huw's original two-man foundry had prospered and over the years he had expanded it to take in an engineering workshop for the machining of his castings. He had also bought up several smaller concerns, as well as property, both domestic and industrial. By the time he died, he had amassed a respectable fortune.

His son Joshua had outlived him by only a few years, dying of a heart attack while his own son and heir was in South Africa, in the first stages of recovery following the amputation of his arm. Afterwards, back home in Folbury, his army career behind him and faced with finding a new life for himself, Osbert had taken on the management of the Rees-Talbot finances, but it wasn't a task anyone had wished to take on when he died.

'Find a sound man of affairs and turn everything over to him,' advised his brother, now retired from his own military career. A hitherto lifelong bachelor, Hamer had found himself comfortably entrenched in Malvern, unexpectedly and delightfully married to the widow of one of his fellow officers, and had discovered golf. In the end it had been Margaret – always her father's right arm, literally and figuratively – who had stepped in to keep things ticking over until someone suitably trustworthy could be found, Felix having flatly declared himself unwilling to take on the job. In Symon's opinion – though he had so far kept it to himself – it was high time they all looked after their own affairs.

Now, at last, someone had been found, in the person of Mr Bertram Lazenby, an elderly, semi-retired accountant recommended by the bank. He had nodded approval at Osbert's meticulous ordering of the family affairs, and the conscientious way he had looked after the interests of his brother and sister, but Osbert's system had been one of his own devising and Mr Lazenby had still not succeeded in adjusting it to his own satisfaction. He was taking his time and would not be rushed.

'Symon?' Margaret's question as they went back into the house made him blink, suddenly aware that he'd been lost in his own thoughts for too long. 'Darling Symon, I'm so sorry if I've made you think even for a moment . . . How could I? You must know I love you more than—' Her face became quite pink. Such declarations weren't easy for either of them.

'I do know it, Margaret, my love, of course I do.'

'You mustn't get me wrong – it's just that I've been bothering too much with other things that don't really matter one jot, when you have enough concerns of your own.'

'What concerns do I have that aren't yours?' he asked lightly. But he had felt a jump of alarm, and in a moment his eyes, grey that always darkened with emotion, were the colour of slate. Yes, he had his own – not secrets, not at all, but rather worries he preferred to keep to himself, for the time being at any rate, though it seemed he hadn't been as successful in concealing them as he had thought. Not seeing his own lack of logic, he said abruptly, 'Whatever's bothering you, you should tell me, you know. It's what I'm supposed to be for, isn't it? To listen to troubles.'

'Since when have you ever taken Confessions?'

'Perhaps you ought to try me. And I don't mean in a professional capacity.'

'Oh really, darling, there's nothing to bother you with, just bits and pieces of my father's that still need sorting out.' She touched his cheek lightly. 'Haven't you noticed yet? I'm afraid it's my nature to fuss unduly. You'd better marry me quick, before I become a finicky old maid.' She laughed, yet he fancied the shadow hadn't entirely gone from her eyes.

That same night, a slow thaw began, and over the next few days the snow turned to slush, the gutters ran and the Fol, down in the valley, spread its banks.

On the third day, out at Maxstead, two retrievers were bounding forward, joyful to be back once more in their familiar routine, when the bitch, following her nose, suddenly found something very much to her liking. Setting up an excited barking, she began to dig. The other dog was close behind her and soon both were tugging furiously, their teeth into a brown leather boot that stuck up out of the newly softened soil.

Two

'Oof, I've had enough!' Margaret collapsed into a canvas deck chair and threw her tennis racquet down on the grass.

'You could have beaten me easily, if you'd had your mind on the game,' returned Kay, though in fact she was the one who invariably won when she played against her cousin. She was little and dark and fierce, and she had a formidable backhand, but the game, one of the first of that season, had been an energetic one even for her. Flopping into the other deck chair, she lifted the muslin cover from the lemonade jug, peered into it and poured what was left into two glasses, one of which she pushed across the table.

On this April afternoon, with a late Easter just around the corner and the last harsh winter fast receding into memory, the weather was pretending it was already summer, with only a few lazy, puffy white clouds drifting across a limpid blue sky. The sticky buds were fat on the horse chestnut that dominated the lawn between the house and the tennis court, and a blaze of azaleas lit up corners of the otherwise unremarkable garden which surrounded the house on four sides. Alma House, erected by Huw Rees-Talbot in the heyday of Queen Victoria's reign and so named by him after the first victorious battle in the Crimea (rather as the Duke of Marlborough had named Blenheim), wouldn't look the same again after the azaleas had finished blooming, leaving nothing until next year but their slightly rusty evergreen, the garden devoid of interest except for the brief flowering of the laburnum which hung over the front gate. The garden had never been anything to write home about, and the house itself, designed by some architect who had been carried away by his own imagination, was in fact rather ugly and certainly inconvenient, although being accustomed to both, the family scarcely noticed the shortcomings.

Kay looked at her watch then picked up her glass again. 'I'll just finish this then I must scoot off. I have my women's clinic this afternoon.' She made a little face. 'Tired mums and a hundred squalling babies all over the place, pity me! Return match tomorrow afternoon? I might grab a spare hour or two then.'

'Afraid not. Symon has arranged for us to go over to see his mother.'

'Ah. The dowager.'

'Really, Kay. Lady Maude's quite approachable, you know. When one gets to know her.'

'If you say so.'

They had grown up together, Margaret motherless from birth, and Kay, who was three years older, fatherless as well from the age of two. Kay now looked speculatively at her cousin, very attractive today in the white tennis dress with a low waist and a pleated skirt, and for the moment, at any rate, more relaxed than of late.

'So, everything's all right then, love?'

'Oh, I think so. The bridesmaids' dresses are in hand, and the cake's ordered, and I've already chosen the flowers—'

'—and arrangements for getting Laurel Mount ready are going smoothly. I know all that, that wasn't what I meant.' Kay picked up her racquet and held it to the light, squinting through the strings. 'Look, if it was anyone else but you, I wouldn't ask this – but as it *is* you, and as a doctor, I think I'm entitled . . . Are things all right between you and Symon?'

Margaret sat up. Her face, still flushed with exercise, took on an even rosier hue. 'And what exactly does that mean? As a doctor, of course.'

'Darling, it's no use getting on your high horse with me. *As a doctor,* I can't help noticing that you haven't been yourself lately. To be frank, you've looked positively peaky at times. You aren't – well, regretting your engagement, by any chance? It's not too late to back out, you know.'

'I am not,' Margaret said stiffly after several moments had elapsed, 'in the habit of making promises I don't intend to keep.'

'That's what I'm afraid of. That you'll go ahead just because you've promised, even though—'

'Even though what, Dr Dysart?'

Kay looked directly at her and said sternly, 'I thought you two were madly in love?'

'And so?'

'So why all the fuss about the wedding details? There's plenty of time before July. Aren't you in danger of neglecting Symon himself – just a bit?'

Margaret looked as though she was about to stand up and walk away. But she sat on, not saying anything for a long time. She was well aware that certain people thought she had done rather a boring thing, agreeing to marry a clergyman. Well, she thought sharply, they didn't know how *right* it had been, from the very first. What a rock he was. How alight with happiness Symon made her.

Eventually, she said slowly, 'If that's what it looks like, you couldn't be more wrong. You know what I'm like, about getting things done – and I am *not* neglecting Symon, as you so elegantly put it, and what's more he knows that – if it's any of your business, which it isn't really, you know.' Recovering herself, she added with some spirit, 'Leave Symon – and his mother – to me please, Kay.'

'Oh Lord, you're right, it is none of my business, and no, I don't suppose I *did* really think . . . Seems I've put my foot in it, but you know I always speak my mind and actually I'm not sorry I did because *something's* bothering you, love. You're so touchy lately, and that's not like you. Come on, we've never kept things from each other before, don't be cross . . . Is it all that Maxstead tradition? Could be more than a bit overwhelming, I suppose.'

Margaret managed a laugh. 'You think I'm suddenly getting worried about which knives and forks to use? For heaven's sake, Kay! In any case, it's Symon I'm marrying, not his family tradition.'

'Now you're being difficult, as Aunt Deb would say.' Kay sighed and laid her glass against her hot forehead, though it was an hour since it had been brought cold from the cellar and was unlikely to have any cooling effect. 'Well, I'm pleased to see you know your own mind.' She paused. 'If that isn't it . . . it couldn't be that you're still upset about Uncle Osbert, could it?'

'Kay, of course I'm still upset! He was my *father!*' Less tensely, Margaret added, 'But not in the way you mean.'

'Still, maybe you should give it a rest for a bit – typing and sorting out that manuscript.'

Just before he died, having for some reason become pre-occupied with looking back at the time he had spent in South Africa, fighting in the war against the Boers at the turn of the century, Osbert had suddenly been taken with the idea of writing down his experiences with a view to publishing them as a small book or even just a pamphlet, which he thought might offer something to those interested in military history, and perhaps to the general public, too. He had intimate know-ledge of several major battles, and had also played a significant part in the seven-month siege of Mafeking, a victorious demon-stration of true British grit and moral fibre which patriots at home had not yet tired of hearing about. And indeed, had not Lord Baden-Powell, himself the great hero of that historic event, still remembering Osbert after so many years, sent a letter of condolence on hearing of his death, praising him as an outstandingly able and courageous officer?

But halfway through the project Osbert had suddenly declared it had gone sour, and would have abandoned it had not Margaret, who was typing it out for him, pressed him to carry on, which he eventually did, though reluctantly and with diminished enthusiasm. He gave no reason for his change of heart, except to say that reliving that time, seeing it in perspec-tive, had brought home to him how reprehensibly his own side had behaved in many ways. With his brother Hamer, Osbert had arrived in South Africa, a young captain filled with ideals of honour and freeing the Blacks from slavery, but such notions of fighting for justice and freedom became secondary when faced with what he encountered. By the time he was sent back to England after being wounded, he had not been so proud to fight under the British flag.

After a short silence Margaret admitted, 'I suppose you may be right and I did ought to leave it. But it seems a pity when it's so nearly finished.' In a burst of honesty, she added, 'Though I have to admit he might have had a point – about abandoning it, I mean. Maybe no one *will* want to read the sort of opinions

he had about that war, even now. They're not exactly compli-
mentary to us as a nation. But there's more to it than that.'
She frowned. Until the moment when, out of the blue, the
notion of publishing his reminiscences had occurred to Osbert,
never before had he volunteered information about that war
in which he had fought. Indeed, if asked, he had always replied
shortly that it was better not to know. The abrupt change of
heart was very confusing; he had been a man who rarely
changed his mind once it was made up.

'More to it? Like what?'

'Oh, nothing really, I suppose. Only that he wasn't fighting
all the time he was out there in South Africa. There was a long
gap between when he was wounded for the first time and when
he was allowed to fight again, but he says nothing of what he
did or where he was, or even what was happening with the
war at that time. It may not have been relevant to what he was
saying, I suppose, but it seems odd just to leave a blank. I
couldn't pin him down over it. He simply waved me away
when I asked, saying there was nothing important.'

'The sort of things he wouldn't want posterity to know
about, I expect.'

'Why not? That was what he was writing it for, wasn't it?'

'Well, love, he *was* a soldier. And you know what soldiers are.'

Margaret stood up. 'I knew I shouldn't have said anything.
How could you?' Her eyes gave off sparks and she began to bang
together the glasses and the empty lemonade jug on the tray to
carry indoors. 'I expect Felix and Vinnie will be back soon.
They'll be starving hungry,' she said shortly, closing the topic.

Kay attempted no more, though she didn't believe the
thought she'd voiced hadn't previously occurred to Margaret
herself, either, or that she would put her doubts aside. She
always had to do something about any puzzling situation; she
could never leave it and let its own solution present itself. So
she merely remarked, 'Vinnie's coming to lunch?'

'Yes.'

It appeared that Felix had agreed to Vinnie Henderson's
suggestion of a walk as far as The Beacon. It was well worth
the effort to walk up the long hill, beyond the cemetery and
where Emscott's houses left off and the road gave way to a

mere track across several miles of undulating land. The view on the other side was stunning: a panorama of pretty villages such as Maxstead, its forest and its big house, scattered farms and the land gradually increasing in height towards the distant Beacon, where fires had been lit since time immemorial, whether to warn of danger, as in the panic of the threatened Spanish Armada invasion, or to celebrate, in more recent times, the end of the Great War and the signing of the Armistice.

Felix had warned Vinnie it was a twelve-mile tramp there and back, but she hadn't wanted to waste her day off from the job she had as secretary to the headmaster at the King's School. She'd arrived after breakfast, pulled stout boots on to her rather large feet, laughed as if twelve miles was nothing, which no doubt it wasn't to her, and strode out after him, an Amazon goddess with corn-coloured hair and eyes almost as blue as Felix's own.

'It's a long walk but she wanted to see the view.'

'My, he must be smitten if he's taken time off from revolutionary duties merely for that.'

Kay had always had a big-sisterly affection for both her younger cousins, a sense of responsibility, but she didn't trouble to conceal her scorn at Felix making so much of those left-wingers he kept company with, feeling they went too far and that they would sooner or later draw him too deep into their would-be revolutionary plots. Socialist principles were all very well – she leaned to the left herself and passionately believed that the working classes she mostly worked amongst deserved better lives – but this group of his was pathetic. They had half-baked plans about overthrowing the government, put out seditious literature and encouraged strikes among the workers. In fact, they were very much on the periphery of the present struggle going on between the workers' unions and the government. Though goodness knows the plight of many workers, especially that of the miners, was appalling enough – even worse after the debacle of the General Strike last year, a nine-day wonder which in the end had solved nothing. The country, retorted Felix, was in a financial mess, the working man was suffering more than ever and the government seemed powerless – or unwilling – to do anything about it. Should the rest just stand by?

'Smitten? With Vinnie?' Margaret was saying. 'Well, yes, that's fairly obvious, and would it be a bad thing?' A jolly, breezy girl whom Felix had met at the tennis club, he had very soon introduced her to his family in a way that had left no doubt that he was serious about her. Margaret liked her and thought she was good for Felix, challenging some of his more outrageous opinions with a good-humoured laugh and offering a sturdy common sense that didn't seem to have been given to Felix. She liked the idea of her brother and Vinnie together. And she hadn't lost sight of the fact that if Felix was to marry her and bring her to live here at Alma House, it would solve a lot of problems when she herself was married.

On the contrary, Kay answered, she thought Vinnie would be a very *good* thing. 'And how much better than Judy Cash!'

Margaret smiled, but she did not want to think about Judy Cash. Quite violently, she did not want to think of Judy Cash – and Felix – in the same breath.

Good relations restored, they were still smiling when they reached the house where Maisie, who had just put the telephone back on its rest, announced there had been a message for Dr Dysart from the surgery.

'There's been an accident. Henrietta Street.'

'Don't tell me. Aston's Engineering again?' Kay rolled her eyes.

'I'm afraid so. They said Dr Rowlands wasn't available – he'd just left to attend an emergency up at the hospital.'

Kay was in partnership with William Rowlands, an elderly doctor who, despite his age, did not have the prejudices that many of his contemporaries still had – not to mention a large proportion of their male patients – regarding lady doctors working in general practice. She sighed, wishing the calls had been received in reverse order; she would much rather the hospital emergency had fallen to her.

'OK, I'm on my way.' She was already half out of the door, clutching the doctor's bag that went everywhere with her.

As her Baby Austin chugged the familiar route towards Arms Green, the less salubrious part of Folbury, Kay's thoughts wandered back to the exchange with Margaret. Her well-meant intervention had emerged more like interference, and perhaps that was what it was. You couldn't just barge into people's private feelings and expect to be greeted with delight, especially with Margaret, who was too independent to take advice easily. But it had cleared the air. After all, Margaret was grown up, and had gone into this engagement with her eyes open.

And she hadn't exactly condemned herself to poverty by marrying a hard-up clergyman – or in fact one who in any way conformed to the usual, preconceived idea of what the clergy were. In fact, it seemed a point of honour with Symon not to appear weedy, ineffectual, effete, or any other of the misconceived adjectives applied to curates. He was vigorous and determined – he could beat Kay at tennis any day, in fact frequently did – he was very competitive and liked to win. She understood this all too well.

From what she had gathered he worked exceedingly hard in the parish. He didn't suffer fools gladly, but people had, after their initial caution, come to like him and respect his honesty. He'd no 'side' to him, despite his background. In fact, he'd fitted surprisingly well into a working-class parish, placed here with the best of intentions, no doubt, to learn about how the other half lives. She suspected his sights had initially been set higher, and almost certainly still were, and who could blame him? Ordination as a priest didn't preclude ambition – or did it?

Kay might not know much about the priesthood, but she knew all about ambition. She had known that she wanted to be a doctor from the age of twelve, and had been aided and abetted in achieving this by darling Aunt Deb, who had loved and looked after her when she'd been left an orphan as a young child. Margaret, on the other hand, had never settled on a career, which had at one time exasperated Kay, who thought women, especially competent women like Margaret, had a duty to make the most of the opportunities now open to them. But Margaret had seemed perfectly content to forgo a career in order to look after her father, who had become increasingly dependent on her as he grew more frail. She might have been doomed to join the legion of spinsters left adrift because of the war, which had taken a generation of young men into its maw, had she not met Symon. And no doubt about it, she would make a splendid wife for an ambitious cleric, and a wonderful mother to his children. Yet Kay wondered if Margaret had seriously taken into account the other side of the coin – being the daughter-in-law of the formidable Lady Maude, despite the airy dismissal of any pitfalls.

She pulled her thoughts back to the present as she reached Arms Green, a far cry from the attractive town centre, and no longer green. This was Folbury's other face – clamorous, unlovely, a hugger-mugger of industrial and domestic premises, factories and workshops jammed between houses and corner shops, wherever space could be found. Here on Henrietta Street, a row of two-bedroomed Victorian terraced houses faced a large motor repair garage that constantly belched out fumes, set between a small nail-making shop at one end and Aston's two workshops at the other. For the moment everywhere was quiet on the street. No neighbours gossiped on doorsteps, no little girls played on hopscotch squares chalked on to the pavement, and no boys kicked a football in the road. At this time of day, the mothers would be getting the midday dinner and the children would still be penned up inside the gloomy brick-built edifice of Arms Green Mixed Junior and Infants, which loomed up behind Henrietta Street.

The only activity was centred on a towed motor van that was blocking the road as it was being manoeuvred into the repair garage, while a horse and cart, laden with coal sacks, waited to pass. Kay left her car where it was and made her way on foot to the place where she was headed, right at the far end.

Just her luck to be called out to Aston's again! As a small engineering workshop, Aston Engineering employed no more than a dozen or so workers. But no less than its two-man foundry next door – where its products were cast, where the heat was sometimes almost insupportable and the smallest drop of molten metal could burn through to the bone – the machine shop, with work that involved the drilling, machining and finishing of the rough metal castings, was also fraught with potential danger. Flying bits of metal, splinters in the hands or even the eye were commonplace, and familiarity caused carelessness or inattention, but as elsewhere, faulty machines were often to blame, too. Which would it be this time? Kay wondered. Arthur Aston cut corners and maintenance was not all it should be. She had crossed swords with him more than once over this and was not going to let him get away with it much longer.

Was she in danger of letting her dislike of the man get the better of her? she asked herself as she approached the premises. Quite possibly, she admitted grimly, but that wouldn't stop her.

'Well, Stanley, what is it now?' she asked briskly, pushing open the small door set into the large double ones that opened for loading and unloading. Her nose was immediately assailed by the usual metallic taint in the air, the acrid smell of machine oil, but at the same time she became aware of an unnatural silence. None of the machines was in operation, and the only man visible was the normally unflappable foreman, who now looked extremely agitated.

'What's going on?'

Stanley stubbed his Woodbine out on the floor and shoved his hands into the pockets of his brown smock. 'We've sent everybody home. You'd best talk to Eileen, I reckon. She's in the office.' He jerked his head towards the ten-foot square, glassed-in cubicle built into a corner of the shop floor.

Eileen Gerrity, known to all simply as Eileen, the middle-aged woman who ran the office and knew everything there was to know about what went on at Aston's, sat at one of the two desks which, with a big cupboard, a safe and a small table bearing an ancient Remington, a telephone and a spare chair, comprised the only furniture. She was a bossy redhead with a loud voice and a slash of scarlet lipstick, but today her shoulders slumped, her eyes were red-rimmed and her lipstick was smudged. She was smoking furiously and the pint mug of tea in front of her had grown a milky skin on top.

'It's Arthur,' she said. 'He's dead.'

Utterly taken aback, Kay repeated, 'Dead? Mr Aston? Eileen, are you sure?' Stupidly, she looked around, half-expecting to see Arthur Aston prone on the brown lino. 'Where is he?'

'Next door, and of course I'm sure.' Her voice shook. 'I reckon he's had a stroke. Always had that look, didn't he?'

Kay pictured his face, red above a tight collar, redder as he grew older and stouter. Perhaps . . .

'Next door – in the foundry?' Kay asked. Eileen nodded. 'You'd better come with me then.'

'Ask Stanley, I don't think I can – not again.' Her face had grown slack. What remained of her lipstick looked like a wound against her pallor. Kay gave her a clinical glance but she didn't appear to be about to pass out. Kay recalled the rumours she'd heard about Aston and the woman who'd worked for him ever since he'd set up his business. She closed the office door behind her and went to ask Stanley to let her into the foundry.

Corporal Arthur Aston had been Osbert Rees-Talbot's batman during the Boer War. Though born and raised in Wolverhampton, when he had served his time and left the army he had appeared in Folbury and presented himself to his former officer, reminding him of what they'd gone through together. 'Never had a better gentleman than you, sir,' he said, and went on to announce that he had saved a bit of money during his years in the army – never having been a drinking man, and not married, like – and was looking for some little business in which he could set himself up, preferably in Folbury. Eventually, he found a modest machine shop, given over to the production of small valves, with an adjacent foundry, a set-up not dissimilar to the one Huw Rees-Talbot had started all those years ago. He had been apprenticed to the trade before joining the army and so had a basic knowledge, and he confidently asserted that he only needed an experienced foreman, some skilled workmen and a little more capital to be off to a running start.

Osbert shook his head, but lent him the money he needed and, contrary to expectations, the firm did prosper, not unhelped by the war, when his 'war effort' had consisted of contributing to the constant supply of engineering components needed to support the fighting forces. The profits of Aston Engineering shot up, and had so far enabled the firm to ride the growing economic slump.

After so long in Folbury, Aston had dug himself into the business community, married and bought himself a house off Emscott Hill. There were no children of the marriage and he had continued to be a fairly regular, though not popular, caller at Alma House. Felix damned him as a profiteering capitalist, while Margaret confessed she hated the freckles on his pale soft hands, his heavy, jowly face with its pendulous lower lip and his colourless eyelashes, and couldn't for the life of her see why the fact that they had once served together in South Africa should make her not-easily-persuadable father able to tolerate him. Maisie Henshall, who had worked as maid-of-all-work for his wispy little wife when she had first left school, would open the door of Alma House to him with tightened lips: that previous acquaintance hadn't endeared the man to her.

Popular or not, it seemed Arthur Aston would no longer be a bother to anyone.

The same eerie silence hung in the little foundry as in the machine shop. The coal-fired furnace, whose heat usually hit you in the face, was unlit and cold, and the dark gloom of the cavernous space had taken on a creeping chill. Aston lay on his back in front of a bin of foundry sand, a gash on his temple and sand all over his face.

'It was me as found him,' Stanley said, looking distinctly green. 'The furnace hasn't been fired up for two days so the lads haven't been coming in – we've a stockpile of castings and not enough orders to justify making more just now, see. Short time, like everybody else. The gaffer was sure it'd come all right, though.' He looked sicker than ever, obviously struck by the fact that it was highly probable it was not going to come all right now, that he and Aston's other employees looked fair to be joining the thousands already in the dole queues. 'Any road, about a half hour ago, I had to come round here to check . . .' He waved in a vague direction towards the organized chaos of moulding boxes, wooden patterns, rough castings and other foundry impedimenta as if he couldn't remember what it was he had come in for. 'Well, that don't matter now. Got the shock of me life when I unlocked the door and found him lying there. I didn't even know he'd arrived.'

'He was just like this?'

'Not exactly. He'd fallen face down into the bin.' He indicated the big bin of damp-looking sand into which wooden patterns for the castings were pressed to make a mould for the hot metal, in front of which Aston's body lay. 'I thought, bloody hell, and first thing I did, I turned him over and shook him a bit to see if he was all right, but it was no good, he was gone.'

Although head wounds bled copiously, there was no blood to be seen from the wound on the side of his head, though it would admittedly have been difficult to discern any in such a place, when grime and dust from the coal that fired the furnace was thick over everything.

'Well, let's have a better look at him.'

'Half a mo, Doctor.' Stanley glanced at the light coat she'd slipped on over the tennis dress she hadn't had time to change. 'You'll want summat to kneel on.'

He disappeared, and while he was gone Kay looked down at Aston. He was dressed with his usual military precision, in a smart grey business suit, perfectly laundered white shirt with a stiff collar, and a discreetly patterned tie. His shoes shone with spit and polish. His bowler hat had fallen off and rolled some distance. His fist was clenched around a pencil with a broken point and a small, thick ledger with dirty pages was lying open on the floor. He appeared to have fallen on to the brick floor with only his upper half in the bin. Nevertheless, he was a heavy man and the dent in the dense, damp sand where his head and shoulders had landed was considerable.

Stanley was back a moment later with some folded newspapers which he placed on the filthy floor.

Thanking him, Kay knelt, and with cotton wool and a square of gauze began carefully wiping away the sand which had collected around the dead man's light eyelashes, eyes, his thick, nearly white eyebrows, his nostrils and the heavy, slack mouth. Though the dead could feel no pain – and she had not liked Aston – she worked gently, with respect as well as by ingrained habit. She noted the marks round his mouth and his bloodshot eyes, and eased down the lower lids with her finger. She decided the gash on his temple didn't look either serious or new. There were no other abrasions or contusions on his nearly bald head. Finally, having completed her examination, she stood up. 'This will have to be reported to the coroner.'

Stanley was a small man with greasy hair and a habit of adjusting his glasses by scrunching up his face. They stayed slipped down his nose now, unheeded, while his eyes bulged. 'Coroner? How's that?'

'I can't sign the death certificate without being sure how he died, and that's not immediately obvious. He'll probably order a post-mortem.'

'Eileen thinks he had a stroke and fell against the side of the bin.'

'Well, it's just possible,' Kay said drily, 'that for once Eileen might be wrong.'

More than possible, she thought. Something definitely didn't add up here.

Three

The trail became steeper as Felix and Vinnie climbed the last incline to the Beacon, Felix lagging, while Vinnie forged ahead with undiminished enthusiasm. She had never made this pilgrimage before and that made achieving her object all the more desirable – she was an earnest person, Felix knew by now, who always seemed to feel it necessary to go that bit further, travel the extra mile . . . in everything.

Was that why he was hesitating at this last moment? What an irony, when there were no longer difficulties and objections to their being together.

'Buck up, Slowcoach!'

Absorbed in his thoughts, he had not realized just how far back he had fallen and that Vinnie, demonstrating her ability to outwalk any man, even Felix with his long legs, was fifty yards ahead of him. 'There's no race to get to the top,' he called back, not increasing his pace.

Vinnie laughed over her shoulder and strode on, thrusting forward like a ship's figurehead, her hair blown back by the light wind. She was the sort of girl he had always admired – strong, independent, unflappable in a crisis – but for once he didn't dwell on her attractions. He walked on, hands in pockets, unseeing of the lovely day all around him: the grass springy and tussocky beneath his feet, the red sandstone outcroppings growing more frequent towards the bare, rounded top of the hill, the freshening breeze, the smell of the earth and the sound of a lark ascending, the sun finding clumps of gorse glinting like prospector's gold.

He'd been pulled awake that morning with a tremendous jerk, hot and sweaty, still in the toils of one of those recurrent dreams about his father. Specifically, last night, the memory of that last quarrel when he had told Osbert he was intending to ask Vinnie to marry him, all mixed up with that other appalling, unbelievable happening not two weeks later – the sight of his body in the bath. It was a double nightmare that came back with sickening regularity to haunt his waking thoughts and night-time dreams . . .

He had hardly expected his father to jump for joy at the prospect of him wanting to marry Vinnie, but neither had he anticipated the long, cold silence after his announcement, eventually broken by an equally cold, 'And how do you propose to support a wife?'

'I know I don't have much in the way of prospects, not just at present, but I'm determined—'

'Have I not heard this somewhere before?'

Felix was taken aback by the unaccustomed sarcasm. He had not anticipated that, either. Osbert was not given to intimidation, verbal or otherwise. He had never been easy to approach, not a father to show his affection openly, but he had always been just.

'I will not permit such a thing, Felix. Are you out of your mind? Someone like that!'

Felix had felt a red mist coming over his eyes. '*Permit?* Well, I suppose I might have known! She's not good enough, of course. She doesn't have any money, or position.'

In his heart he had known the accusation wasn't justified. Osbert had never been overly concerned with materialistic matters, but at the same time it had always been his contention that his children should marry what he called 'decently', and Vinnie's family, on her own admission, possessed neither wealth nor position, but even so . . . He should not have said those things.

Felix's nails bit into his palms as he tried to control himself. 'I think that's my business and, well, I'm sorry, but I'm of age, so there's not a thing you can do to stop it, Father. But I would have appreciated your blessing,' he finished bitterly.

'That's something I am not prepared to give.' Osbert's face was rigid.

'I suppose I should have picked someone like Margaret has chosen, someone with—'

'That will do. Margaret has nothing to do with this.' They faced each other, neither willing to give in until, after a moment, the rigidity left Osbert's face and he said in a tone more like that of the father Felix had respected and looked up to in his boyhood, 'It won't do, Felix, my boy. You can do better than that.' He surveyed his son in silence. 'She is an attractive young woman – but as a wife? You must not even contemplate this.'

'Must not? Of course I must!' Felix answered, further infuriated. 'And I'm afraid that whether you like it or not, there's nothing you can do about it.' Though he knew there was. Osbert could withhold funds, and without money . . . Felix had never been extravagant, he was like his father in that money was not an overriding priority with him – all right, he might have overspent his allowance occasionally, and written cheques towards what Kay and Margaret were pleased to call the revolution – but to be without altogether . . . 'You won't stop me. I love her,' he countered defiantly.

'And she?'

'Well, of course.'

Felix was not unaware that women had always been attracted by his rather louche good looks, his lanky height, those vivid blue eyes and the boyish flop of dark hair over his forehead, and he would not admit, much less to his father, his aggrieved astonishment that Vinnie hadn't exactly fallen at his feet – but that was only a matter of time.

'No,' Osbert repeated, white to the lips now, 'you've sprung this on me, but I'm warning you, it must not go ahead. You've disappointed me before, but this you will not do. I shall move heaven and earth to prevent it.'

And however extreme and outrageous that was, however totally unfair, Felix had believed him.

The contretemps had taken place in the garden, where he had happened to come across his father and had blurted out his intentions without having planned what to say. Perhaps, he reflected bitterly, he ought to have submitted a written request to talk to him in his study. Yet oddly, as Osbert rose abruptly from the garden bench and left, typically turning his back and putting an end to something he would rather not continue with, leaning heavily on the cane he had recently come to need, Felix had watched him go back into the house with a feeling of unutterable guilt.

And now, paradoxically, the opposition to his marrying Vinnie having gone, the whole thing no longer seemed so very urgent – or even, maybe, desirable. What if Osbert had been right – that he and Vinnie did not yet know enough about each other to commit themselves to a lifetime together? Had her reluctance only served to egg him on? He didn't think she was the sort to play hard to get, but you never knew.

And then, as it was inclined to do only too often, the image of Judy Cash popped into his mind. Judy, a small sprite with dancing grey eyes and a straight blonde bob, whom everyone else thought so smart and brittle, yet who followed him around like a stray kitten that wanted to be loved, despite his giving her little encouragement. Well, except for . . . He ground his teeth and pushed aside those insane moments under the great chestnut by the lake in the park the other night. The devil of it was, he was not sure whether he even liked her, but she excited and intrigued him. Perhaps because, despite her willingness, she was a bit of an enigma. There were even times when he had a feeling of danger around her. Unlike Vinnie, who was an open book and lived in the present, seemingly enjoying every minute.

As a boy, Felix had hero-worshipped his father. The hand on his shoulder that was like an accolade, Osbert's rare smiles, had been prizes to strive for. Right up until later adolescence, he had revered him as a man of integrity who had fought for his country and found honour in battle, losing his right arm in the process, along with the life of a soldier which up to then had been his whole raison d'être. Felix had pitied him from the bottom of his heart, though he had learnt not to show it. Osbert had never admitted to disappointment, or even to feeling pain, would swat away any questions about the state of his health with an impatient flap of the hand. No one was allowed to feel sympathy for him. No doubt sobered by his experiences in South Africa, on his forced return to civilian life he had become a devout churchman and had served many years as churchwarden of the parish church of Holy Trinity; he had been a trustee for a charitable foundation for widows and orphans, a governor of the King's School, and served as a JP. His life had been ruled by Christian purpose. It was a hard act for anyone to follow, and Felix knew he had ultimately deeply disappointed his father.

By the time he reached late adolescence it had become increasingly apparent that their views were diametrically opposed. The arrival of a new master at his school who was a member of the Fabian Society and an ardent pacifist had hugely influenced Felix, always susceptible to new ideas. Roger Curtis became the hero to be copied – but pacifism was not admissible in a patriotic country in the midst of a war with Germany. As the conflict dragged on, it became a question for Felix of whether, when he was old enough, he would have the courage to tell his father he must refuse to fight. His fears were resolved when the Armistice was signed before he became eighteen and liable for conscription.

He went up to Cambridge to read law, which failed to live up to his expectations. He was contemplating chucking the whole thing when in his second year he was sought out by another undergraduate and drawn into a set with like-minded ideas. Those people who, like his father, thought pacifists namby-pamby, should have been present at those heated, passionate evening debates that often went on through the night and into the next morning, fuelled by beer, cigarettes and their own rhetoric. They fired Felix with enthusiasm but did not help him find the impetus towards buckling down and taking his studies seriously. Instead of the good degree which had been expected of him, he left Cambridge with a mediocre one and his head stuffed with nothing but socialist principles, according to his father.

He had shrugged off Osbert's displeasure and looked around for something else to occupy his time now that Cambridge and his friends were left behind, but nothing satisfactory presented itself and he had let himself be caught up in the oddly assorted group of left-wingers who met in various places in Folbury, and occasionally in Alma House now that Osbert was no longer there.

He began to walk very fast, and reached the top of the hill only a stride or two behind Vinnie. She had flung herself to the ground and sat with her hands cupped around her knees, hardly out of breath. Felix lowered himself to sit beside her, and with backs to the distant Black Country smoke stacks that were now even further beyond, they faced the bird's eye view over rural pastures, farmlands and distant villages. They didn't speak until Vinnie said at last, 'Penny for them?'

Felix shook his head as if to clear it and endeavoured to be more sociable, pointing out the various landmarks and their associations.

'So that's where that man's body was found, in the snow?'
She was looking towards the wild woodland beyond the big
house below.

'Lord, yes, I'd forgotten that. I suppose it must have been
somewhere down there.'

Vinnie followed the sweep of his hand, which encompassed
Maxstead Court in the foreground, its outbuildings, extensive
gardens and the acres of forest that adjoined it, its Home Farm,
the lane leading to the village, the church and the Scroope
Arms . . . all owned or under the patronage of Scroopes past
and present, he informed her.

'My!' she said.

As well she might. She and the Comrades. How they would
spit on all that! Felix bit off Kay's scornful 'Comrades' epithet
even as he thought it. Damn it, the nickname was catching – and
it was not even very appropriate. They were neither comrades
nor friends. They were separate individuals who had struck up
an acquaintance during the General Strike, when a Council of
Action had been organized by local trade unionists, aided by the
Communist Party. After the dismal failure of the strike they had
formed themselves into what they called the Workers' Support
Group, for reasons, Felix was beginning to suspect, that were
more like a class vendetta than the wish to alleviate suffering.
Much of what went on in the group was no more than head-in
the-clouds agitating; nothing was ever achieved. They're a hundred
miles away, he thought, from what we envisioned at Cambridge:
international socialism, the League of Nations . . .

'Did they ever find out who he was?'

'What? Oh, no, I don't think so. It was Judy Cash who
reported the murder. Ask her, she would know.'

Vinnie shrugged, plucked a stem of grass and began chewing
it. 'It's not important, just something that occurred to me.'

She didn't seem to have a high opinion of Judy, although
she hadn't even met her, just heard of her. She was not alone.
The women in the group, three of whom were ex-suffragettes,
were convinced she had no moral fibre, that for all her useful-
ness as a journalist, the articles she sent out to the nationals,
she was only in it for what she could get.

'Not full of the joys of spring today, are we?'

'Sorry, Vinnie. Truth is, I've had a bit of a spat with my sister – well, actually, more of a row.'

'With Margaret? Good heavens!'

'Afraid so.' If any argument with Margaret could ever be classed as such. Normally, encounters with her were almost as frustrating, in a different way, as those he'd had with his father, for she infuriatingly refused to rise to the bait. Last night had been different, though.

She had known straight away, eyeing his disreputable flannel bags, his old check shirt, both in a more deplorable state than usual, that he hadn't got the bruise on his chin by walking into a door, and he hadn't even bothered to drum up an excuse. He knew what he had done was indefensible after their previous conversation, their promises to each other. He stood nearly a foot higher than she did, he was a year older, but she still had the power to reduce him to a sulky schoolboy. 'It's nothing. Don't fuss, Sis.'

'How much have you had to drink?'

'Not much, but he was bigger than me,' he answered, summoning up a rueful grin. He never got anywhere with Margaret by sulking.

She wasn't amused this time. She took hold of his wrist, hurting him, surprising him with the strength of her slender fingers. One glance at her face – not beautiful, Margaret, except maybe for her eyes – and he'd seen that she'd guessed everything. Her usual amiability had deserted her. 'I'm ashamed of you,' she had said, before letting go of his wrist, giving him a withering glance and leaving.

'Not as much as I am of myself,' he'd replied to the door she closed behind her, meaning every word.

He was suddenly aware Vinnie had said something he hadn't answered. 'What?'

'I said you're not much company today. Come on, we might as well get back.'

He apologized and stood up to offer his hand but she was already on her feet. In a moment, she was going down the hill, five strides ahead of him.

Four

In the red-brick Victorian police station at the corner of Town Hall Square and Market Street, Sergeant Joe Gilmour faced the detective inspector sitting opposite with a cautious respect. Not that he, with his six-foot frame and a sturdy independence, was easily overawed by anyone, and certainly he had no need to feel in awe of Herbert Reardon. Principally because they went back some way, from the time when Joe had worked under Reardon on a tough case out at Broughton Underhill, involving a girl who had drowned. At that time Reardon had been a mere acting inspector, and he himself a young constable in uniform, but unlike many more senior officers, Reardon had had time for a bright chap like Joe, showing him the ropes and encouraging him to use his initiative. Joe had always put his early promotion to sergeant down to the advice and support Reardon had given him in the raw days of his youth.

Soon after that case Joe had moved back to his home town of Folbury in order to keep an eye on his elderly mother, and since then had done his stint as an ordinary, small-town bobby: intervening in domestics, stopping fights after closing time, catching lads scrumping apples and generally keeping the peace. But new avenues were opening up – most of the larger towns and cities now had dedicated detective departments and Joe wanted to be part of it. He was raring to go, ready for more demanding work, and if God had given him any brains, the chance to use them. When his mother had died six months ago he had applied for a transfer to the regional detective department. It hadn't come through yet but he was still hopeful. Crime generally was increasing, and the nature of it changing. Wars were costly: the last one had nearly bankrupted Britain – and most of Europe – of its money as well as its youth, and in the economic slump that had followed even petty criminals were putting their minds to more sophisticated ways of getting

money to feed, clothe and house hungry families. There was
nothing like necessity for sharpening the wits.

'Right, Sergeant, let's have the latest,' Reardon was saying,
getting down to brass tacks.

In the absence of the senior station officer, Inspector
Waterhouse, who had taken a week's leave to attend his daughter's wedding up in Newcastle, to be followed by a holiday in
Whitley Bay, an officer from the detective department in Dudley
had been dispatched to oversee enquiries into the sudden and
unexpected death of Arthur Aston, and Joe had been more
than happy to find it was Reardon. He was a decent bloke,
tending to the unorthodox, and maybe that was why he hadn't
gone further up the ladder than detective inspector. Or maybe
he favoured his independence more. He was still riding his
motorbike; Joe had seen it that morning in the station yard.

He'd remembered Joe. People did – it was the hair. Joe
cursed it, the dark red hair that went with brown eyes, but
still red enough to be memorable. Perhaps he should dye it if
he wanted to become a detective. On the other hand, he might
possibly grow bald before that became necessary, considering
the time it was taking for his transfer to come through.

'What have we got, then?' Reardon said, flipping the pages
of the post-mortem report on the dead man, which he hadn't
had time to do more than scan quickly. 'Quick work. Like the
mills of God, the path lab usually grinds slowly,' he murmured.

'Yes, sir.' It appeared that time hadn't reduced Reardon's
tendency to come out with these sorts of statements. 'Well, as
you can see, the cause of death *was* asphyxiation, as Dr Dysart
initially suspected from the marks round his mouth, and his
eyes. It was assumed at first he'd probably tripped or come
over dizzy and fallen into the sand, but there were no signs of
a struggle and . . .'

'And?'

Joe cracked a knuckle, a habit he'd somehow picked up and
was trying hard to break because he knew it set people's teeth
on edge. His aunt with whom he now lodged had told him
so often enough. Besides, it annoyed Joe almost as much; he
felt it was all too likely to give a false impression of nerves.
Maisie Henshall, bless her, had never said anything but he

wondered if she'd noticed. They were getting along very nicely, thank you – well, a good bit more than that, he'd reason to hope – and he didn't want her to think he had objectionable habits, not if she was ever to become Mrs Joe Gilmour.

'And what?' Reardon repeated, trying to push his chair back a few inches in order to be able to stretch his long legs. There was barely room for anyone other than the occupant of the big desk that had been wedged into the cramped space found for the temporary DI, never mind Joe's equally solid frame. But Reardon had shown tact in not asking to take over the office of the absent Waterhouse.

Joe frowned. 'I don't know. Stands to reason if you fall head first into a heap of sand and you get it in your mouth and eyes, you find it hard to breathe. But you'd try to get up, wouldn't you, or at any rate roll over to get your face out of the sand? You wouldn't just lie there until you died.'

Reardon was looking over the flash photographs taken at the scene. The victim was lying on his back and the depression where he'd fallen before being turned over was clear. 'Not unless you were stunned by the fall,' he said, and added as Joe shook his head, 'Damp sand can be pretty unyielding. Or if you'd fainted, say, or lost consciousness – there was that wound on his temple, don't forget – and that was why you fell in the first place.'

'How many healthy men do that?' Joe protested. 'Just faint, I mean. There was no sign he *wasn't* healthy, though he was overweight and soon out of puff, according to the foreman, and the Path blokes have agreed with Dr Dysart that the cut on the side of his head was superficial, not much more than a graze, and anyway it wasn't recent and couldn't have anything to do with his death. There was no sign of a struggle, no handprints or anything to show he'd tried to lever himself up.'

'Hmm. Didn't the woman in his office, Eileen Gerrity, seem to think he could have had a stroke, or a heart attack?'

'Yes, but they say no to that as well. Anyway, there's something else – if you read the report further, sir, you'll see there's a bruise on the back of his neck, right at the base, that can't be accounted for.'

'A rabbit punch?'

'Not that sort of bruise. It's possible he could have been

held down with something heavy.' He paused. 'A foot? After he fell – or was pushed.'

Reardon considered. Twirling his fountain pen between his fingers, he gazed at the map of Folbury and its environs that he'd already managed to dredge up from somewhere and pinned to the wall. His chair was sideways to the window, which faced a brick wall only feet away, and the hideous scars on his left profile were reflected in the glass. Some people found it embarrassing to look Reardon in the face; disrespectful young PCs had been overheard bandying nicknames for the ugly-faced detective inspector when he'd arrived – until they encountered the baleful glance of Sergeant Gilmour, who knew they were honourable scars, acquired during the late war. Joe knew himself to be lucky, as they were, to have escaped the trenches. He'd been conscripted but done no more than his basic training before the Armistice was declared and he'd been sent home. But Reardon's scars didn't seem to bother the man himself, or if they did he concealed it, and the more you got to know him, the less you noticed them.

'Besides,' Joe continued, 'there's the matter of the key to the foundry. That's a puzzle.' He explained that Stanley Dowson, the foreman, had told them the foundry door was locked when he went in, but there'd been no door key on Aston's person, and despite a search, it hadn't turned up anywhere else.

'How many keys are there?'

'Just two it seems, one that's kept in the office next door, and Aston's own.'

'Is it a Yale lock?'

'No, that's just it, it's a mortice. The door couldn't have locked itself behind him when he went in, and there seems no reason why he should have locked it himself. If someone was in there with him, they turned the key and took it with them when they left. Why?'

'Panicking at what they'd done, or giving themselves a bit of time, who knows? I gather the foundry hadn't been working for a day or two, but somebody from the machine shop next door was bound to go in and find him, probably sooner rather than later.' He threw a sharp look at Joe. 'So what are you thinking, Sergeant?'

'Looking less and less possible that it was an accident, isn't it, sir?'

Reardon made a non-committal sound which Joe took to be agreement.

Murder. Manslaughter, at least. A serious crime, whichever it was. And contrary to public belief, one that could still sicken the police. The taking of a human life brought a pretty sharp reminder that police business was more than just keeping the peace, that it also dealt with matters of life and death.

'Remind me, what time was he found?'

'About half-eleven. Dr Dysart was called straight away and she estimated he hadn't been dead long – three or four hours at most. His wife says they left the house for work at about half past eight.'

'They?'

'Yes. He gave her a lift as far as the shops and then took his car on to the garage where it was booked in to have the brakes adjusted. Walking from there would have taken about twenty minutes, so he should have arrived at the office before half nine at the latest, but nobody was unduly worried when he didn't turn up – he was the boss, he didn't have to clock in.'

'All right, Sergeant.' Reardon squared his notes together. 'Usual procedures, then.'

Usual procedures. That meant summoning up the fairly limited resources open to Folbury's police, who were not accustomed to dealing with murder or the routine that went with it.

'I'll do my best to get extra manpower if it's needed, but I warn you we probably won't.'

This was likely to be true, but it shouldn't be a long drawn-out business – probably solved by the end of the week if they were lucky. This wasn't detective fiction, just a small-town murder. Likely as not, the culprit would turn out to be someone who'd been known to have it in for the victim and seized his chance when Aston had stumbled and fallen into the sand, or had knocked him down in a fight begun in the heat of the moment. But then, more deliberately, had held him down until he stopped breathing. Somebody who knew him, where he worked, what his routine was. Unlikely they'd be looking for a stranger, anyway. Most murderers were known to their victims, and it was more than possible that someone else, who knew that bad blood had existed, would come forward and say so.

Reardon was staring at the map again, as though making Folbury and its environs part of his inner landscape, 'Houses on the opposite side of the road in Henrietta Street, aren't there?'

Joe was able to tell him he'd already sent a couple of lads door-knocking, asking if anyone was seen going into the foundry, or coming out, anybody acting suspicious lately.

'And?'

'Nix – from those they've managed to talk to so far, anyway. Nobody saw anything, but we haven't caught up with everybody yet. Sure as eggs, some old biddy will have been nosey-parkering through the curtains, and if he was followed, or whoever it was went with him into the foundry, they might have been seen – unless they were waiting for him inside when he arrived.'

And if they'd let themselves in and been waiting there long, good luck to them, he thought, recalling the bone-cold, almost windowless black hole, with only naked bulbs from the ceiling, that comprised the foundry; there were a couple of boxes to sit on and another for a makeshift table where the two foundry men employed there could eat their sandwiches at dinner time – though when the furnace was lit, like enough it would have been hot as hell's kitchen.

'OK. We'll also need to find out whether anybody was likely to have had a grudge, disaffected employees or such, and what his habits, friends and/or enemies were . . . talk to the employees . . . well, I don't have to tell you, do I? You know the form. Good luck.' He turned back to the file, but Joe made no immediate move to leave. 'Is there something else, Sergeant?'

Joe hesitated. He was sometimes impulsive. Maybe he should keep his mouth shut this time until he'd spoken to Waterhouse. The inspector was a thorn in Joe's flesh, suspicious of one he regarded as a whippersnapper with a probable ambition to overtake him and who routinely put every obstacle he could in Joe's way. He might well choose to believe Joe had gone behind his back. On the other hand, the idea was bothering Joe . . . He plunged.

'The thing is, it's all put me in mind of something that happened at the end of February. A body that was found under the snow near Maxstead, a mile or two out of the village. Not far from Maxstead Court – that's the house belonging to the Scroopes – they're the big name around here.'

Reardon thought for a moment or two. 'Found when the thaw came, skull wounds, still unidentified. What about him?'

Reardon hadn't changed, Joe thought. As usual he'd made it his business to have everything at his fingertips so that he was on top of the job, though he'd done his homework pretty quick to have obtained the details of a cold case that was no part of his present remit. But it had been the only unexplained murder in Folbury for decades; maybe that was why he recalled it almost straight away.

'DI Micklejohn's case, just before he retired. The Snowman, wasn't it?'

'That's what the local paper called him, sir. Gross, somehow . . .' That was how it had seemed to Joe at the time – to dub a brutally murdered man with such a playful nickname – and still did.

'He was dead, Gilmour.'

The need to be reminded that there was no room for sentiment, even – or perhaps especially – when you were investigating a murder, embarrassed Joe. 'Yes, sir. Well. There was nothing at all to identify him, apart from a foreign coin in the lining of his jacket – and swarf on the soles of his boots.'

And that had literally been all there was. A well-built, youngish man with his skull caved in, wearing a brown serge suit in good repair, except for where a few seam stitches had given way in a jacket pocket, through which a coin had slipped into the lining. A pair of worn but still good brown boots, with a lot of tiny, sharp metallic fragments embedded deep into the leather soles: swarf, the fine metal residue from cutting and grinding machines.

'Perhaps not quite a gentleman, then.'

'Sir?'

'The brown boots. No gentleman wears brown boots, unless with tweeds.'

'Oh.' Joe couldn't decide whether Reardon was being tongue

in cheek or whether it was a joke he'd missed, or just another of his obscure remarks. His wife was a teacher and he himself was reported to have a passion for books. 'Well, I'm just wondering if there could be a connection between that killing and this one.'

'The swarf, of course.'

'His boot soles had to have picked it up somewhere, but we went round every brass foundry within miles and came up with nothing. The coin in his pocket was a South African shilling, so it seemed possible he'd been a potential customer from there, being shown around one of the workshops. We started with Arms Green and spread out as far as Birmingham. No shortage of machine shops or foundries, brass or otherwise, but none of the managers or owners had ever had any South African visiting them – and there was no reason why any of the men working on the shop floor would have taken particular notice of any stranger being shown around. Happens all the time.'

'The coin might have been in his pocket for all sorts of reasons. Maybe he collected foreign coins. Maybe he'd visited there at some time. Doesn't necessarily make him South African.'

'That wasn't ruled out.'

'And the assumption was that he'd been killed and buried just before the big freeze, before the ground got too hard to dig?'

'The ground was hard before the snow came. We'd had some heavy frosts and that must have been why he wasn't buried so deep. Waste of energy trying.'

'And since he wasn't wearing an overcoat, nor a scarf or gloves, come to that, in that weather, he was likely killed indoors and transplanted there.'

'Right. Though why out at Maxstead is anyone's guess.'

The place where he'd been found was at the edge of a small covert well off the beaten track, though accessible – just – by vehicle. The grave had necessarily been shallow due to the hardness of the ground at the time, covered by an insufficient layer of what loose earth the killer had managed to remove. Scavengers would have found him earlier but for the freezing temperatures; it was only when the snow began to melt and caused the disturbed earth to settle that the corpse's boot had been revealed.

'Someone who had access to a vehicle of some sort put him there,' Joe said, 'a car, or even a van. But we never got anywhere with that.' Every year saw the number of private car owners or van drivers increasing, not least in Folbury, and without anything more concrete to go on, an extended search would have been fruitless. 'Anyway, no one in the area has ever reported a missing man, and no hotel – from here to Brum – ever had a guest, South African or otherwise, who failed to turn up and claim his belongings when he should have done.' Joe watched Reardon as he added, 'By the way, I – er – went out to Maxstead Court only yesterday. Inspector Waterhouse asked me to let Lady Scroope – sorry, Lady Maude, they say she must be called – know that the enquiries were being suspended.'

'Watch how you go, Gilmour,' Waterhouse had warned sourly. 'No putting your size tens where they shouldn't be.' The inspector had been mortified that he wasn't the one to visit the Dowager Lady Scroope and reassure her that she need give no more thought to the matter of the dead man found on her estate: he was after all the senior officer at Folbury. But the decision had been taken out of his hands by instructions from above that her Ladyship was to be informed immediately, just as he was about to leave to catch the 12.10 for Newcastle.

Considering his reception by the lady and the man called Frith who was with her, Joe could have wished Waterhouse the joy of it. Perfectly polite, of course – thank you very much, Sergeant, good of you to let us know, good afternoon – as if the discovery of the body of a murdered man on the estate had been nothing more than an irritating matter, albeit one best cleared up. Obviously glad to be able to forget the whole business. 'I think,' Joe said thoughtfully, 'she was very – er – relieved.'

For a while Reardon said nothing, thoughtfully tapping his pencil on the desk. 'Then she might not be too pleased if we start making enquiries again. So keep them discreet.'

'So the case might be reopened, sir?' Joe brightened visibly.

'Not at this stage, no chance. Doesn't mean we shouldn't bear it in mind, however, while we look at this other one.' He stood up and stretched his legs. 'Meantime, is there any possibility there might be a bigger room – or possibly a smaller desk – available for me to work from? Since you might be going to have me round your necks for longer than you imagined.'

Joe grinned. 'I'll see what I can do.' Waterhouse is going to love all this, he thought, but managed not to say it. When the DI returned and learnt that Joe had previously worked with Reardon, he would be sarcastic enough and all too likely to believe Joe had taken advantage of his absence to put himself forward. 'Hope I didn't speak out of turn, sir. It *would* be a fairly unlikely lead, I suppose. Until we know why Aston was killed.'

'Detection's full of unlikely leads.'

'But two murders, not two months apart, with nothing to connect them after all, except possibly a brass foundry . . . *might* be just a coincidence.'

'You don't believe that, Gilmour, any more than I do.'

'Not really, sir.'

Reardon smiled slightly. 'In this instance we won't dismiss the possibility that coincidences can be helpful. Stand by your convictions, Sergeant. And meantime, I'll see if I can't get a look at DI Micklejohn's original notes.'

Joe remembered Micklejohn: easy-going, coasting towards retirement after thirty years' service. Not wanting to upset the apple cart at that stage, and not really worried that he'd be leaving with his last case unsolved, either. He'd left with the investigation still continuing. Enquiries had gone on in a perfunctory way, but nothing had ever turned up, resulting finally in the decision by the top brass to wrap the enquiries up.

Reardon asked suddenly, 'You've another sergeant on the strength here? Longton, isn't it?'

'That's right. Just the two of us.'

'Think he could cope, if you were assigned to this investigation?'

Joe fought to keep his face from splitting into a grin. 'Yes, sir.' Comfortably ensconced in what was becoming his permanent position on the front desk, Longton wouldn't exactly jump with joy at the prospect of extra work and having to leg it around – unless it was pointed out to him that it might help him to shed the surplus pounds around his waistline.

'Right. Then maybe you should leave the uniform at home tomorrow.'

Even better. Joe turned with his hand on the doorknob. 'Er, there's just one more thing, sir. That reporter from the *Herald* . . .'

'Which one?'

'They only have one – apart from the editor himself and a photographer they hire from the Orthochrome when they need one, plus a young lad. The reporter's a *woman*. Judy Cash. She's always hanging around the station here. She's out for a scoop, and if she connects Aston's death with the Snowman, well . . . She was the one who dubbed him that, for some reason.'

'That's what they do, the press . . . drumming up readers. Beefing up the situation, giving the unknown victim an identity.'

'I suppose so,' Joe said doubtfully. 'She also kept hinting we weren't doing enough to find out who he was.'

'Well, keep her at bay. Don't let her get the idea we're not doing enough this time.'

'Easier said than done, sir. She might look like the fairy on the Christmas tree but that doesn't fool anybody. Keeping at bay a panther on the prowl would be easier.'

'You're mixing your metaphors, Sergeant. Never mind, keep at it.'

> From *the Folbury and District Herald*:
>
> Folbury Police were called in yesterday to look into the accidental death of Mr Arthur Aston, fifty-three, well known in the area as the owner of Aston's Engineering Company, who was found dead in the foundry adjacent to his machine shop on Tuesday morning.
>
> 'A tragic accident,' commented Mr Stanley Dowson, foreman at Aston's Engineering, who found his employer lying dead when he went into the foundry. Mr Aston, though previously thought to be in good health, had apparently collapsed and fallen into a heap of sand some

hours earlier, but as the foundry was not working that day was not discovered until later in the morning. Mr Dowson said, 'He must have tripped and knocked himself out when he fell into the sand. He was a good employer and will be much missed.'

The police, and Mrs Lily Aston, the deceased man's wife, declined to comment. An inquest is to be held next week.

Dearest Plum,

I could scarcely believe my luck when Butterworth sent me to cover the sudden, unexplained death of Arthur Aston – because I didn't exactly clothe myself in glory in his eyes over reporting the Snowman case, did I? I'd raised too many questions for his liking. As editor and owner of the paper, it's in his interests to keep in with the police, and neither he nor they liked my pieces hinting at incompetence in their failure to discover the identity of the Snowman – or the few bits I'd managed to get past Butterworth when he was 'hors de combat'. The police blamed their failure on having had so few clues to work on (which I knew meant none!) and it's fairly evident they've now abandoned all hope of solving the case.

Harold Butterworth doesn't really approve of women reporters – he thinks they have a disregard for deadlines, not to mention slipshod grammar, spelling and punctuation. As if the Folbury Herald *ever had deadlines, and as if his own grammar, spelling etc. is faultless – even when he's sober! But men who do have those sort of abilities don't exactly see the* Folbury & District Herald *as a stepping stone to Fleet Street, so he has to make do with me and young Ernie, who's only just left school and can't be trusted yet to cover anything more than WI meetings and then not always. He's stuck with me and he thinks I'm stuck with the* Herald, *which is true, in a way. Well, of course, I'm a woman, I have to take what I can get and be grateful for it, have I not? Especially when there's something more rewarding in the offing.*

All the same, I have to keep myself thoroughly in hand when he's around. Be a good girl and eat my porridge. There'll be plenty of better things than porridge if things go as we plan – and

*I don't see why they shouldn't. I am more than halfway there
with Felix.*

*And 'stuck' really doesn't cover it, does it? I'm here by choice,
after all. It fits in very well, working on this provincial rag. It's
given me the chance to become friendly with Felix by getting
involved with that group of his, this WSG, Workers' Support
Group – although it amuses me to know that most of them
only tolerate me because I occasionally get the odd article into
the national press and they realize they need support of that
kind more than ever after the colossal failure of the General
Strike last year. They are a joke, really, so pathetic, so amateur.
Except perhaps for Mesdames Evans, Trefusis and Barton-
Smythe, the ex-suffragists. They can't ever forget that they fought
tooth and nail for the vote, chained themselves to railings, were
dragged by the hair to police cells, sent to prison, force fed and
all the rest of it. And I dare say they're prepared to do it again
for what they see as a cause – courageous women! They despise
the men in the group for what they regard as weakness and I
must say I see their point. Most of them seem to have lost the
heart for fighting – just when they ought to see it's more necessary than ever before. But that isn't my problem, since it's Felix
I'm really interested in, not that rag tag and bobtail lot. And
when I say interested, I mean interested, Plum. It need not
affect our relationship. Try to remember, darling, why I'm doing
this.*

*Meanwhile, Arthur Aston, dead in his brass foundry. A
second mysterious death, barely six weeks after the discovery of
the last is juicy, for Folbury, anyway. Harold Butterworth
dithered about letting me cover it, but since he didn't trust me
to 'hold the fort' either – i.e. sit in the office in case something
turned up – and more likely because he obviously had the
mother and father of a hangover, out I was sent. It's more than
time he got a grip on himself. Frank, the old stalwart I replaced,
now retired, was seemingly content to jog along in the same
old rut, but at the same time it's quite evident that he'd been
carrying Butterworth for years.*

*The police have to look carefully into any sudden, unexplained
death and they are crawling all over Aston's foundry, which they
would not be if they were certain this death was natural. I*

attempted to speak to Joe Gilmour, the ginger-haired sergeant on the case, but he was cagey in the extreme. I mean, even more cagey than usual for the police, which makes me think they know something more than they want to reveal. I shall have to tread softly, in more ways than one. I had what amounted to a stiff warning from Butterworth last time. It's in his interest to keep in with the local police – the inspector, Waterhouse, is one of his Rotary Club cronies – and I can't afford to put his back up again. No one is, after all, indispensable, and it's vital that I stay here, isn't it? And not only for the money . . . though let's not forget that by provincial standards, the Herald actually pays surprisingly well, which is a bonus in itself.

I would like to get to know the Rees-Talbots better, but it's not easy. The family (and I include their cousin Kay Dysart, the doctor, and their aunt Deborah) are very hospitable and have heaps of friends – Felix sometimes even throws Alma House open for the meetings of the WSG – but at the same time, they're such a tight-knit family I feel that whatever happens they'll stick together. When anything goes wrong they close their ranks and don't let their feelings show; they are so well-mannered and restrained, even Felix, whom his family sees as a revolutionary. Really, he is quite a pussycat compared to the rest of the WSG. The violent feelings ritually sounded off at their meetings would horrify Margaret and Co.

More as soon as I have anything useful to tell you, darling.

Five

Lady Maude, widow of Sir Lancelot Scroope, stuck her finger deep into the soil of a small terracotta plant pot, making room for the last of the geranium cuttings she and Heaviside, her head gardener, had been bringing on. She despised anyone who imagined they could garden without dirtying their hands. As far as she was concerned, a finger made the ideal dibber for these tiny plants.

Tenderly, she coaxed the sturdy little cutting into the hole and gently teased the loam over the roots before firming it down and placing the pot with those already completed – nearly two hundred – in satisfying rows on the greenhouse bench, ready to plant out in the garden in a few weeks. She had a plan for the large lozenge-shaped flowerbed in front of the drawing room windows – a blaze of massed geraniums, edged with royal blue lobelia and white alyssum, patriotic and cheerful. She and Heaviside were in complete accord: neither had any patience with newfangled schemes that sought to make a garden look like a wishy-washy artist's palette. Or worse, those dreadful all-white gardens that were said to be the latest thing.

Her task finished, she rubbed her hands down the hessian gardening apron she never neglected to wear over her dresses – once expensive though now doubtless thought dowdy and old-fashioned, a fact which bothered her not in the least – and poured some tea from the Thermos prepared by Mrs Jenkins for what she called her Ladyship's 'elevenses', along with a plate of the sweet biscuits she knew Maude loved. Sitting on her stool to drink her tea she began to review the present situation – principally, whether or not it was time to face the disagreeable task of speaking to her son Julian next time he came down to Maxstead.

Lady Maude was small of stature, but what she lacked in inches she more than made up for in presence. She had commanding bright dark eyes and a way of putting her head a little to one side while she considered how best to deal with people or situations. Sir Lancelot had fondly called her his little sparrow, though in fact, running now to plumpness, she more resembled a purposeful thrush, intent upon the juiciest worm for the next meal.

She was a capable woman, and after the shock of Sir Lancelot's death she had taken refuge in attempting to run the estate at Maxstead as he had done, and had found that with the continuing help of their excellent land agent, an ex-army officer, she could do it very well. But Giles Frith had just produced a bombshell. His wife, a domineering Scotswoman, had suddenly found that after twenty-five years away from the grouse moors and glens of her old home, she was homesick for them and nothing would do but that he should accept an offer which had come out of the blue to act as the local laird's factor. Maude was dismayed, but Frith – who was under his wife's thumb but proprietary about Maxstead and did not really want to leave – had negotiated terms with the laird that meant he could stay here until someone had been found to replace him.

Which was all very well, but it would not solve her long-term problems. These were worrying times: increased taxation on land revenues had hit the Scroope finances hard, while the house was showing its age and was in urgent need of attention. Amongst a great number of other things the roof needed drastic repairs: damp was getting in and a horde of squirrels had been found nesting in the attics, and though they'd been summarily dealt with, the basic problem remained. Already, shooting rights and two farms on the estate had been sold off. The pictures and works of art in the house were undistinguished, most of them not worth selling. She couldn't think of anything else she could do alone – her heart was not strong and she had been warned not to overdo things. Scroope blood did not run in her veins, but she loved Maxstead with a passion. In deference to the memory of Sir Lancelot and for those still living, as well as for future generations, the house and estate must be kept up. It would break her heart if Maxstead were to become an insurmountable burden, especially one unshared. It was time – more than time – that Julian gave her some help and faced up to his responsibilities.

Julian, now Sir Julian after the death of his father, had never
expected to inherit, but so it had turned out after Piers, elder
son and heir, had died of wounds sustained at Verdun, giving
his life for his country and leaving his mother bereft. Julian
was a reluctant heir, seldom down here to see to what was
rightfully now his property, preferring to live what Maude
considered an aimless life in London – aimless apart from some
sort of nondescript job in an art gallery, where she assumed
he was valued more for his connections than his knowledge
– and quite content to leave Maxstead Court and its concerns
to her.

As if her restless thoughts had communicated themselves to
Henry, the old dog at her feet, he woke and opened one eye,
not lifting his chin from his paws. He was an ugly old animal
of uncertain ancestry, born accidentally to one of Sir Lancelot's
retrievers and kept because Piers had pleaded for him. She
snapped a chocolate digestive in two and gave him half, but
she didn't encourage his expectations by giving him more. He
had moped and grown suddenly old when Piers left to join
the army, but now he was attached to her like an old shambling
shadow, looking at her with wounded eyes if she spoke a sharp
word to him. She had broken Sir Lancelot's rule of a lifetime
and allowed him to sleep in the house – actually, in her
bedroom. Old and decrepit as he was, she found him company.

Well, Julian . . .

Lady Maude was not given to illusions about her son, known
as Binkie to everyone except her. Binkie, indeed! But it was
the name he had acquired at school and never dropped, since
nearly all his present friends and acquaintances were those who
had bestowed it on him. A slight man with straw-coloured
hair brushed straight back from his forehead, not unhandsome
but with a sleepy-eyed look and a mouth from which a cigarette permanently drooped. One never knew what he was
thinking. Occasionally, those vacant eyes would sharpen and
he would confound her with some disconcerting remark that
showed he had after all taken in everything she had been saying,
but would then pretend he hadn't. He wasn't cut out to be a
landowner and frequently said so. Opal, it went without saying,
was no help at all.

Maude poured herself more tea. There was something very deep about Julian that she did not understand, and wished she did. She also wished she could bring herself to like her daughter-in-law.

Opal was a decorative creature who, if she had any brains at all – which Maude doubted – was not prepared to demonstrate them. Although she had done her duty and given Julian two children, twins who were still little more than babies, and unfortunately girls, she had a silly, self-centred attitude to life and moved in circles her mother-in-law could not bring herself to approve of. She was now Lady Scroope, and it behove her to remember that. It was to be hoped she was not going to go the same way as her mother, who was reputed to have been one of the many favourites of the late King Edward. Maude prided herself on being broad-minded, but to anyone brought up within the strict values and codes of behaviour that were expected in Victoria's reign, as she had been, the behaviour of the succeeding generation, under the old queen's popular but licentious son, she considered shocking, conveniently glossing over certain occurrences in her own youth. And the moral conduct of the generation which had come next, still reeling from the conflagration of the Great War, determined to forget and do nothing but enjoy itself was not, in Lady Maude's opinion, much better, its blatancy in many ways worse.

Opal! Maude gave vent to what, in anyone else, might have been called a snort. Only last week she had attempted to alleviate her daughter-in-law's undisguised ennui with the short duty visit she and Julian were making to Maxstead Court, hoping to stir up some spark of interest in her future home by soliciting her help with the geranium cuttings. Opal had raised her plucked eyebrows and given her a blank look of amazement, then yawned, not very discreetly, behind her hand.

Lady Maude divided people into two classes: those who thought as she did, and those who did not. The first were friends, the others were cast into outer darkness. She knew there were those in this world who did not share her own interests, mainly her overriding delight in gardening, though she was forced to leave most of it to her gardeners through having too many other important things to do. '*Simply* too *primitive, all that earthy dedication to seeds and things, Binkie, darling.'* Maude had once overheard Opal make this remark, patting her sleek and shiny golden hair, cut shorter than some men's, into what they called a shingle, which Maude thought had the effect of making her look as if she wore a metal helmet clamped to her head.

It was all very disagreeable. How different everything would have been had dearest Piers not been so tragically taken, or had Symon been the second, rather than the youngest son! Symon, who was different in every way from Julian, an ideal heir, who had taken the place of her beloved Piers in his mother's heart. Then there would have been no question of the Church for him.

The last thing in the world that Maude had expected was the announcement from Symon that he was to take Holy Orders. Symon, a priest? She had never thought him religious. Could he be serious? He loved Maxstead with the same sort of passion she did herself, with his whole heart and soul, but it would never be his as long as Julian, or any future son of Julian's, lived. Given his elder brother's disinterest – antipathy even – to his ancestral home, she had always hoped they might have arrived at some sort of accommodation. But it was not to be. That last stormy quarrel between both her boys had put paid to that, when Symon had accused Julian of abrogating his duty to Maxstead, and Julian had retaliated with sneers about 'the parson' which left Symon white-lipped and looking so dangerous that Julian had backed down, saying Symon was welcome to take on both Maxstead and its responsibilities and see if *he* could make anything of it. Which he knew, of course, would never happen.

It had been terrible, with undercurrents between her two sons that Maude hadn't understood. One did not have such rows in the Scroope family. But neither did one question Symon's certainties; even as a child he had been single-minded with a streak of stubbornness. When informing her of what he had chosen to do with his life, he had smiled his beautiful, disarming smile and, without discussing his reasons, tried to take the smart out of it for her, 'After all, the Church has always been the traditional role for younger sons. What else is there?'

Nevertheless, she had received it quite badly and hadn't yet recovered. She herself was not of a religious nature. She walked across to morning service at Maxstead church each Sunday, sat in the Scroope pew and enjoyed the hymn-singing; she opened the church fête every year – though she had been wise enough never to have agreed to judge the most beautiful baby competition; and she continued to give as generously as her husband had done to church funds. And that was as far as it went.

However, if the boy had decided he had a vocation . . . As with most disagreeable things one could not alter, Maude had instructed herself to be reconciled to it, even if she could not do so as gracefully as she knew she ought. There had after all been Scroopes before who had gone into the Church, second or third sons. Two bishops and even one archbishop. And Symon, she was sure, had the gravitas to attain either position, in time. Meanwhile, he was still a lowly curate, and had further confounded her, soon after his placement to Folbury, by announcing that he had become engaged to be married.

One of the peacocks appeared on the lawn, a flash of blue trailing its tail feathers arrogantly, like a court debutante. They were a great attraction to visitors at Maxstead, until the night became rent with their shrieks, disrupting sleep, or when they dropped unexpectedly from the trees where they roosted. As she watched, the bird strutted haughtily off. She stared into the space it left behind, several moments that left room for that door in the past to open, something she hardly ever permitted – or had not, until the moment of Symon's announcement, when it had opened of its own accord.

We had a visit the other day from the police, a Sergeant Gilmour, she wrote that night in her firm, black handwriting. Sitting stolidly at the desk in her boudoir, her greying hair in a tidy night-time plait down her back, an old brown woollen dressing gown that had belonged to Scroope wrapped around her plump form, she was penning the latest instalment of a letter to her dearest friend, Adelaide Dunstable. *They have kept to their promise that they would let us know the outcome of their investigations into the body of that man found when the snow began to melt in February. Of course, as Giles Frith, who happened to be with me at the time,*

*was quick to point out, we would expect nothing less than to be kept
informed, since the body was, after all, discovered on Maxstead land.
Now, this Sergeant Gilmour informs us that enquiries have been
suspended, since nothing further has turned up to identify the man,
and resources are needed in other directions (principally, one assumes,
to help in all the unrest that seems to be bedevilling the workforce of
this country). I supposed the dead man was one of those down-and-
outs one sees everywhere – some unemployed person tramping the
countryside to look for work – but the sergeant said no, he didn't
think so. He gave no reasons for this. He was quite a young man,
but he had watchful eyes. I have a strong suspicion he was not happy
about the decision of his superiors to suspend enquiries.*

*However, neither I nor Giles Frith pursued the matter. I believe
he was as relieved as I was to know it had been put to rest. I have
been finding this unresolved affair rather unsettling. You know what
I am like, Addie, I do not care to have anything at Maxstead beyond
my control.*

That was all flimflam, of course; the business had troubled
her far more than that, and with good reason, but it was
certainly true that it had outraged her sense of the fitness of
things, that any man, whoever he was, could have been
murdered, his head brutally stove in, so they said, brought here
on to the estate by his unknown assailant, and buried, not long
before the first of last winter's heavy snow.

'I was almost convinced that he thought we were holding
something back, Giles,' she had said to Frith when the policeman
had gone. He'd replied very briskly that he was sure he hadn't
– why should he have thought the dead man had anything to
do with us? You must put such a thought right out of your
mind, Lady Maude . . .

Henry, at her feet as usual, gave a sudden snore in his sleep.
She laid down her pen and took off her spectacles to rub her
eyes. She was tired, she needed her rest, but these letters to
her dearest friend were a kind of therapy for Maude. They
had known each other since they were pushed in their peram-
bulators around Hyde Park by their nurses; they had shared
music and dancing lessons, she and Addie Fordingham, as she
was then, and had come out together. Addie, who had married
the eldest son of a duke and was now a duchess herself, had

been one of Maude's bridesmaids, and they were godmothers to each other's children. Sometimes they spoke on the telephone, but the general inconvenience of long distance and Adelaide's increasing deafness made this something of an obstacle race for both of them, so they mainly resorted to the correspondence they had kept up all their lives. Maude wrote a page or two each day and when there were enough, she posted them off. Until now, there had scarcely been an aspect of her life which was not an open book to Addie Dunstable.

The lamp on her desk flickered – as the lights throughout the house were prone to do at any time – and finally went out. She sighed impatiently. She still regarded electricity as a newfangled invention, dangerous and unreliable, along with the faintly menacing gas engine which ran it, housed in its own purposely constructed building by the greenhouses. But before there was any need to seek matches and grope for the candles always kept at the ready, the lamp came on again. She picked up her pen, read through what she had written, then continued.

Symon and his fiancée will be motoring over in her family's car for luncheon tomorrow, I am pleased to say. I have to confess, though I had other plans for him, I am not totally disappointed with Margaret, though disappointingly, she does not want to be married at Maxstead, but in Symon's church, with the reception in her own home. I have of course been obliged to accept this. She is not easily biddable – but then, I was never biddable, either, and I don't believe it has done me any harm! I have come to believe that perhaps she will be a good wife for Symon in the life he has chosen.

She paused, then crossed out 'perhaps'.

There is intelligence in her eyes and a firmness in her mouth that I like, she seems sensible and not easily discomposed, an agreeable young woman who will fit in with the family, despite not being brought up to it. What is even better, she will be more than capable, I am sure, of coping with the Opals of this world! I don't know why this should have surprised me. She is the daughter of Osbert Rees-Talbot when all is said and done. Poor child, I think she still suffers from the loss of her father. How little we all knew, that day when she and Symon brought him to Maxstead, that he would be dead within such a short time! Although I was struck, even then, as I told you, by how ill he looked, older than his years – and oh dear, the loss of his arm! In some skirmish after Mafeking, I understand, but he made it very clear he did not wish to talk about that – nor indeed to talk at all about those old times in Cape Town. His manner was as stiff as if we had never before had any previous acquaintance, and in spite of my efforts, the conversation was stilted and difficult.

She sat with her pen poised for several minutes, then quickly finished the letter off, signing it *'Yrs affectly, Maude'*, and sealing it in its envelope, ready to take down for the post, in case she should be tempted to add the part of that conversation she had never told anyone about – not even Addie.

Six

'I hope you didn't get me here just to talk about that old Arthur Aston,' Maisie Henshall told Joe Gilmour.

Since there was more than a grain of truth in this, Joe was flummoxed for moment. He was experiencing what it would be like to be a full-blown detective – basically not all that different from uniformed duties, in that it could be plodding, repetitive work that didn't yield spectacular results, especially in the first stages of an investigation, before it really got under way. It was becoming clear that he needed to cultivate patience, something he wasn't naturally possessed of.

The murder of Arthur Aston wasn't sensational enough to have made headlines, except for a small piece in the *Folbury Herald*, though it might become so if it turned out to be connected with the Snowman case. So far, the resources at Folbury police station, previously never unduly stretched, had coped, though Reardon had managed to requisition from the powers-that-be at regional level an official car and a constable as driver for the duration of the murder enquiry, bicycles not being considered up to what might be required. At present, it was all down to steady, routine police work, though Joe was learning that even this, as far as Reardon was concerned, meant giving it all you'd got. Even so, it was Reardon himself who'd remarked drily that Joe didn't need to feel his evenings, at least at this stage, weren't free.

Joe had taken the hint and used the time off to take Maisie to the Roxy to see *Sparrows,* a heart-wrenching tale about orphans and a kidnapped baby. Mary Pickford had been over-sweet – she couldn't hold a candle to lovely Lillian Gish in Joe's opinion – and he hadn't really enjoyed the film much, except for when the lady pianist, employing the loud pedal over-enthusiastically at one of the most melodramatic parts, had nearly fallen off her stool, to general merriment. But he reckoned it had been worth the two shillings for the seats and the box of liquorice allsorts, her favourites, he'd bought for Maisie. Besides, she had let him put his hand on her thigh in the darkness.

Remembering this, when they were sitting on a riverside bench in the park, he didn't take umbrage at what she'd just said. 'You know me better than that, Maisie. But we *are* in the middle of a murder investigation, love, so anything we can find out about Aston is important – and I know you used to work for them.'

She gave him an old-fashioned look, then sighed. 'All right. What do you want to know?'

'Anything you can tell me.'

'It was a long time ago, straight after I left school, when I was fourteen. I only stuck it for a month or two before I left.'

'Was the work that hard?'

'Heavens, no. It's not a big house, there's only the two of them, and Lily Aston did her share.'

'Why then?'

'That old goat, Aston, what do you think? Couldn't keep his hands to himself. He once . . .' She looked at him sideways. 'He came up to the attic where I slept one night, opened the door without knocking and came straight in – but I kicked him where it hurt, shoved him out and wedged a chair under the door knob.'

Joe grinned. Maisie was no Lillian Gish, but she was a pretty girl when she allowed it, when she laughed or could be persuaded to let her hair down, and he liked her spirit. 'What did you do? Tell his wife?'

'Lily? No use complaining to her. She'd no say over him. Anyway, I reckon she was too miserable on her own account to notice whether anyone else was all right or not. He treated her as if she was another servant. Hardly spoke to her except to ask her to pass the salt, order her about, or complain his dinner wasn't tasty enough.' She pulled a face. 'He might have had a point there, she wasn't much of a cook – though it didn't help that he was so tight-fisted with the housekeeping money. *And* he made her starch and iron all those stiff collars, two a day sometimes if the weather was hot and they went limp. Very fussy about his appearance he was. She had to clean his shoes!'

Joe could see that to a woman like Maisie that would be the ultimate indignity. It seemed like that to him, too. He couldn't envisage ordering Maisie to clean his shoes – or Maisie, sharp as a tack, obeying him even if he did.

'If she didn't do everything just so, he'd give her the silent treatment, say nothing at all, sometimes for days, though she'd try to wheedle him out of it. He was a right bully.'

'Knocked her about, did he?'

'I don't know about that. I wasn't there that long, after all,' she said slowly, 'but I don't think so.' Joe, who had seen enough domestic violence not to be surprised at what could go on between the four walls of a marriage, and knew one type of bullying led as often as not to another, wondered. 'I know one thing,' Maisie went on, 'she won't be sorry he's gone.'

'So Aston was why you left?'

'Yes. I'd have packed it in straight away but my mum needed the money, so I stayed until I'd looked around for somewhere else. Besides, I was sorry for Lily. She was all right with me. Then I heard they wanted somebody at Alma House and I was lucky enough to get the job. And it was all right after that,' she added simply.

Fresh from the hatefulness of working for Aston and his wife, she had stayed for eleven years, first as a housemaid, then as someone who helped Margaret to run the house. She'd used her common sense and been willing to put her hand to anything, made herself indispensable almost from the word go, and it had paid off.

Osbert Rees-Talbot had always been a rather distant presence, but otherwise it was an easy-going household, social distinctions tended to become blurred, and though it took some time to persuade her to leave off calling the girls 'Miss', it wasn't long before she came to be regarded as part of the natural order of things. Aunt Deborah, a daily visitor to the house, had soon discovered that Maisie was a would-be reader, intelligent but starved of education, and did what she could to remedy this. Most days, her cousin Kay walked home with Margaret from the small private school they both attended, and Deborah had encouraged Maisie to join them in their prep and pick up what she could, and to borrow their books. She still wasn't well-schooled but it had stimulated her to join the new public library and save up and buy books of her own.

And now she had Joe Gilmour, this ambitious young police sergeant, and though he hadn't actually popped the question yet, they all kept wondering what they were going to do without her.

She said suddenly, 'He used to come to Alma House sometimes, you know, Aston I mean. To see Margaret's father. I think they knew each other from way back, and . . .' She stopped.

'And what?'

'Oh, nothing really. Just that it was a funny how d'you do, set everyone on edge when he came. Margaret said he gave her the creeps and her father was always ratty with everybody after he'd gone.' She paused. 'No, that couldn't have anything to do with it.'

'With what?'

But she pressed her lips together in an end of conversation way that Joe was learning to recognize. He sighed and then she went on, 'I sometimes pop in and see Lily, just for a few minutes. And you know, it's funny, but I've had a feeling she looked a bit happier lately, for Lily anyway. Nothing you could put your finger on, though. Maybe old Arthur had changed his ways.'

'That's nice of you to say, considering.'

'Considering what?'

'Considering old Arthur had made a pass at you.'

'Well, he didn't succeed, and I took care to go and see Lily when he wasn't there. And he's not there now, anyway, is he?' She went quiet. 'Here,' she said at last, 'have this last sweet – it's a liquorice twist and I know they're your favourites.'

From *The Folbury and District Herald*:

Following the inquest into the sudden death of Mr Arthur Aston at his business premises last week, further developments have led the police to confirm that they are to continue enquiries into his death. Residents in the area are being questioned and Detective Inspector Herbert Reardon, in charge of the case, is calling for anyone who saw or heard anything unusual in the vicinity of Henrietta

Street, Arms Green, on Tuesday morning, the tenth of April, between approximately eight thirty and eleven thirty, when Mr Aston's body was discovered.

Mr Aston's death is the second mysterious death to occur in Folbury. Readers will recall the Snowman, the murdered man whose body was found buried under the snow near Maxstead in February, and for whom an identification has still not been established more than six weeks later, though the police say that any connection between the two is unfounded, and that they are confident that the mystery of Mr Aston's death will soon be resolved.

Dearest Plum,

I spent most of yesterday trying to gather more information about how Arthur Aston died, but without much luck. Kay Dysart – the doctor – must know, but she wasn't giving anything away. I hung about and waited for her outside her surgery, and when she arrived I asked her if she had anything new to tell me but she was very brusque and said she had no intention of providing me with anything sensational for my paper, even if she knew anything, which she didn't. It was out of her hands now. She added she had patients to see to and would I please leave her to get on.

Her rudeness didn't worry me unduly. I've developed a thick skin where things like this are concerned and I don't intend to let a small snub put me off.

Sergeant Gilmour was no better. He told me to go away – very nearly pushed me away, and probably would have done if he'd dared, or if he hadn't been so much bigger than me – and wouldn't say another word.

I was luckier with Lily, Aston's wife. At first she was almost as bad as the others at trying to ward off questions, but I could see she really wanted someone to talk to, so I persisted, as sweetly as I knew how, and after a while she began to latch on to the idea of being presented in the local paper as a grieving widow. 'No photos, though,' she stipulated. Over a cup of tea and a few expressions of sympathy, she began to open up.

Her life with that man must have been nothing short of torture. He got what he deserved, and she is already beginning

to buck up a bit and see the advantages of him not being around.
She was in fact planning to buy herself some expensive new
shoes, she told me, though she was very defensive about it, and
seemed quite relieved when I didn't look shocked that she should
be thinking about such frivolous things so soon after the loss of
her husband. In fact, I managed to persuade her to have her
hair done as well. If ever anyone needs a bit of pampering, Lily
Aston does.

I know what you'll be thinking, so let me just say here that
it's all too easy to feel a little bit ashamed of oneself in these
sorts of circumstances. Too simple, like taking candy from a baby.
But I won't allow thoughts like that to deflect me, and anyway,
there's more to Lily Aston than you might think at first. She's
tougher than she appears, and she's deep. I'm jolly sure she's
hiding something. Lending a sympathetic ear, showing I'm on
her side, had its results. I'm invited to drop in for a cup of tea
any time. Next time, perhaps I might learn something useful.

Seven

When Kay arrived home that evening after a busy day, her Aunt Deborah had already set the small round table in front of the open French windows for their supper, and the sherry glasses and decanter were waiting for their usual aperitif. Deborah did not share the modern craze for fancy cocktails, but she did enjoy a glass of sherry, and looked forward to this time of day when she and her niece gossiped a little and mulled over the events happening in their very different lives.

'What a day!' Kay said, subsiding into an armchair. 'Haven't been able to stir an inch without falling over the police. They're all over Aston's and Arms Green.'

Deborah's gentle face puckered. 'The police are still there? Why?'

'It's not quite straightforward, Aunt Deb. It seems Arthur Aston was almost certainly attacked.'

'Attacked? But how dreadful. For him – and for his poor wife,' Deborah added, her soft brown eyes sympathetic.

'I wouldn't think too much pity's needed there,' Kay returned bluntly. 'I dare say she'll be glad to be rid of him. Now don't look so shocked, darling, it's what everyone who knew them will be thinking. Downtrodden isn't the word for Lily Aston. The only one who's upset is that woman in his office, Eileen Gerrity. Admit it, he was an awful rotter, you know.'

'Your Uncle Osbert never seemed to think so.'

'Didn't he? I'm not so sure. Aston traded on the fact that they'd been together in South Africa, and he'd saved him from a bullet or whatever it was he did, and I suppose that did make for some sort of bond, but I never got the impression that Uncle really liked him.'

'Hmm.' Deborah adjusted her spectacles and picked up the sewing she was engaged on, a peach crêpe de Chine slip she was trimming with coffee-coloured lace, intended as a gift for Margaret for her trousseau. There were rather daring French knickers to match: modern girls like Kay and Margaret laughed at the idea of Directoire knickers with elastic round the legs. Deborah was not sure that she wasn't just a little shocked . . . even she, who wore whatever clothes she felt like wearing, regardless of what anyone thought.

'That's a very expressive hmm, Aunt Deborah.'

'It wasn't meant to be. Your uncle . . .' She stopped and then went on, 'Whatever Arthur Aston was or was not – well, Kay, violence against anyone is appalling.' After a moment she added, 'What a dreadful thing for Mrs Aston. I think I must go and see her. And we must ask the vicar or Symon for prayers to be said for her husband in church.'

Kay rolled her eyes. 'I always suspected you were a saint, now I know you are. Aunt Deb, that man's been persecuting you for months!'

'Pestering yes, not persecuting. There's a difference.'

'All the same.'

Deborah remained silent, putting a hand up to tuck a tendril of her untidy grey hair back into its pins while Kay, glass in hand, stared out through the open window over the long garden, still and quiet, that had once been her aunt's delight but was not as well cared for now as it had been. Soft scents of spring wafted in. Dusk was beginning to fall and the daffodils under the trees showed like pale, sentinel ghosts. A blackbird began to sing.

'Did it ever cross your mind, Aunt Deb, that it might, just possibly, have been better to do as Aston wanted? If you had gone along with the uncles and agreed to sell the Hadley Piece premises to him, you could have moved out of here and bought yourself a nice, modern little house. You still could, you know. This place is far too big.'

'But when you have your own practice, it will make an ideal doctor's house – room for a surgery and waiting room and everything. Unless, of course, you and that nice young patholo-gist . . . Donald Rossiter, isn't it—?'

'Oh, I've no time for all that,' Kay said, brushing the remark aside. 'Don't sidestep, darling. All right, I won't push it, but I just wonder why Aston wanted that old horror of a building so much?'

The premises on Hadley Piece, in effect a large, ugly warehouse, and one of the properties originally acquired by old Huw Rees-Talbot for the fairly substantial rent it brought in, had come down to Deborah and her two brothers. Out of use as a warehouse for several years now, Arthur Aston had been angling to buy it, having outgrown the two separate Henrietta Street buildings and needing larger premises in order to bring them together to – what was it he had said ? – to rationalize his business. Hamer had been willing enough to sell and Osbert, reluctant for some considerable time, had eventually come round to it just before his death, but it had needed Deborah's agreement too and she had steadfastly refused to put her signature to the document which would enable the purchase to go through.

'He said he needed to expand, Kay.'

'I know what he said, but now is hardly the time to be thinking of expansion. I suppose he thought he could buy it cheap and hold on to it until better times arrive.'

Deborah opened her eyes very wide and said calmly, 'No. That was what he wished me to believe – about expanding, I mean – but he only wanted it to knock it down.'

Kay put her glass on the table and stared at her aunt. 'You surely haven't any sentimental attachment to that gruesome old eyesore? Anybody with any sense would be glad to see it razed to the ground.'

Deborah laid aside her sewing – it was getting too dark to see – and contemplated what was left of her sherry. 'My dear Kay, those new houses that the council have built on what they've christened the Walnut Hall estate . . . that's very satisfactory, but more land will soon be needed if we're to believe Councillor Daley's mayoral promises to provide three hundred new homes in Folbury—' She broke off. 'Oh, drat that squirrel! Stealing the bird food again!' Jumping up, she rushed to the open window and clapped her hands. The squirrel remained motionless for a split second, then swung like a trapeze artist to the branch of a nearby tree, poured itself down the trunk and disappeared.

Deborah resumed her seat, switching on a lamp as she did so. The room blossomed and the garden receded into darkness while into the quiet space came the vibrant chimes of the Holy Trinity church clock. 'Now why,' remarked Kay as its echoes ended, 'didn't that occur to me? That Aston didn't want the warehouse but the land it stands on? And also that you,' she added, smiling affectionately at her aunt, 'are holding on to it until the council wants to build more houses?' People were always doing that, herself included, underestimating sweet Aunt Deborah, who was really quite sharp, and could summon up an equally sharp tongue, too, when the occasion warranted it.

'Unlike Mr Aston, though, I shall see it's sold at a fair price.'

'Not, I hope, at lower than the market value. That would be so like you, Aunt Deb, but not a good idea.'

'There's very little spare money in the municipal kitty for new council housing,' Deborah answered evasively, fingering the long, old-fashioned rope of amber beads round her neck. 'But I wholeheartedly support the need for them. I hear they are marvellous. Three bedrooms, electricity and a bathroom! Ask Maisie Henshall what her sister thinks about living there. After a two-up and one-down in Arms Green, three children and a husband out of work, it must seem like a taste of heaven.'

Heaven to Deborah Rees-Talbot, when she was a girl, had always seemed to be a matter of finding Mr Right, living in a nice house and filling its nursery with children. After all, what more could any girl hope for, however clever she was? And she was clever, she knew that without boasting, much more so than her sister Caroline, and at least as clever as either of their brothers. But whereas the boys were sent away to school to learn Latin and Greek and so on, she and Caroline were left at home to be taught by a governess who knew less than Deborah herself, she discovered as she grew older.

It came upon her in later life that other women of her age and class had managed to overcome the same sort of restrictions and gone on to work at all manner of things – but they had been of a different nature to Deborah, not so naturally compliant and with perhaps more courage. And somehow Mr Right had never appeared on the horizon.

When the South African war was over, her brother Hamer's regiment had been sent to India, where he was in fact destined to serve for most of his army life. Her younger sister Caroline was married with a small daughter, and Osbert was also married by then with a son and another baby on the way, living in the old family home, Alma House, which Deborah herself had never left. Even more than usual, she had felt her life was without purpose, a maiden aunt, not exactly an embarrassment but certainly *de trop*, in her own eyes at least.

So that when Hamer wrote to her and encouraged her to join him in India, she had been unable to resist the spirit of adventure stirred in her by the idea. When she arrived, it wasn't the heat and dust, the snakes and the mosquitoes, the relentless sun, the monotonous rains or the constant battle against infections and upset digestions that brought disillusion; it was the knowledge, imparted to her by way of a joke, that she was thought of as just another girl in the hordes of nicely brought up young women who regularly went out to India expressly to catch a husband – the Fishing Fleet, as they were derisively known.

The Fishing Fleet! She was outraged, even though she could not in all truth have denied that at the back of her mind, if unacknowledged, had been the thought that she might at last have met Lieutenant or Captain Right out there. In her contacts with those other young women who had come out to India, some hopeful, painful in their determination to please, others hard-eyed and determined – and especially when she met the men who were on the look out, stationed out there without a woman – her disillusion was complete. She had taken the next available boat back to England and Folbury, knowing she was being tagged with the even more insulting and utterly degrading term: Returned Empty.

But the experience had at least taught her the value of independence, and she had not returned to live at Alma House. With the money left to her by her father she had set up her own household here in Parkside Crescent, a tranquil, tree-shaded curve overlooking the municipal park. It was a very pleasant location, the house was pretty, and at last she began to live as she wanted to live. She began to take an interest in the affairs of the town and became a pillar of the congregation at Holy Trinity. At home she lived in a state of mild disorder, doing a little painting and becoming renowned for her precise and expert needlework, much of it for the church. She dressed for comfort in the old-fashioned clothes she had once packed away, in roomy skirts and hats with large brims from under which her sweet face smiled and her hair straggled. She gardened and also learnt to cook. But none of it made up for the one thing she longed for: a child of her own. A husband, she had firmly decided after meeting those who might have been available to her in India, she could absolutely do without.

Hardly a day passed that she did not look in on the motherless new baby, little Margaret, to make sure she was being looked after properly by the nanny Osbert had procured, but it wasn't the same as having a child in her sole care. She had never envisaged her dearest wish would very soon be granted, particularly not in the way it was, when her sister Caroline had died suddenly and tragically of pneumonia, leaving an only child with a father who proved himself totally unable to cope. The shock of his wife's death was too much for Jack Dysart, always a weak character. He had thereafter walked through life in a daze until one day he stepped out into the road without a glance either to right or left, straight under the feet of the big shire horses pulling a loaded open charabanc on a works outing to the races in Worcester, and was killed immediately.

And that was how little Katherine had come into her life, where she soon emerged into a forthright little person with a bright, quick intelligence. Determined that Kay, as she soon decided to call herself, would not be left in the same position as herself, it became her mission in life to see to it that the child had a sound education, and when she announced her wish to become a doctor, Deborah had done all she could to encourage and support her.

Eight

Inspector Waterhouse had returned from his daughter's wedding, not pleased to find Folbury police station buzzing with excitement and its formerly leisurely pace revved up several notches, a murder having occurred and the enquiry being well underway, a detective inspector previously unknown to him installed as the investigating officer, and all without his permission. On the small side for a policeman, with a toothbrush moustache, Waterhouse liked the sound of his own voice, but this time he had to listen, inwardly fuming, while Reardon brought him up to date. But Waterhouse was a conscientious police officer with long years of service behind him, and he was smart enough to realize that it was in his interests to be cooperative in the present circumstances. At that moment, the investigation hadn't warranted much more than a couple of his uniforms to do the house-to-house canvassing on Henrietta Street and so on, and if it could be kept that way, without Reardon calling for a team of detectives from Dudley, that was all right by him. With as good grace as he could muster, he put what resources Folbury had to offer at Reardon's disposal and decided to make the best of it. Afterwards, he made up for it by chivvying everyone around. And that included sending Joe Gilmour out to interview Lily Aston for the second time.

Lily wasn't in mourning black that day, though she had on her best dress, a dark red marocain with a biscuit-coloured, self-embroidered modesty vest pinned into the vee neck. No apron or dust-cap, never mind that it was Tuesday morning, her day for doing upstairs. When they first moved here, up-and-coming as they were, Arthur had insisted they employ a maid-of-all-work, but after so many had packed their bags and left, Lily had taken on the housework herself. She preferred it that way; she wasn't used to servants and in fact she enjoyed keeping her own house sparkling and polished. And besides, such a routine filled days that otherwise dragged on forever. On this Tuesday, however, the bedrooms remained unswept and undusted, while she sat defiantly downstairs in the front parlour in an easy chair with a pot of coffee and two chocolate biscuits on the table next to her. She wasn't altogether sure whether she liked coffee, not even with plenty of milk and sugar. Arthur would never allow it, said he hated the smell. He liked a strong brew of Lipton's Indian tea, so they had always drunk that. But Arthur wasn't here now.

She nibbled on a biscuit and sat back, contemplating her crossed feet raised up in front of her on a pouffe. Her shoes were round-toed black leather, low-heeled and roomy, with a single bar across the instep, and she regarded them with loathing. They'd never been fashionable and now they were showing their wear. They seemed to sum up everything about her life. They were why she was going to buy new ones this afternoon – the smart, lizard-skin pair with Louis heels and a T-bar she'd coveted in Rayne's shop window for weeks – and risk what they might do to her bunions. She would buy them after her visit to the hairdresser's, where she'd booked for a marcel wave, expensive and daring though it had seemed when that girl from the newspaper had first suggested it to her. She'd warned Lily it would require frequent visits to keep up with it, but she must have guessed that anything would be worth not having to screw her hair up every night into uncomfortable metal curling pins which, no matter how she tried, made it tight and frizzy. She wouldn't have thought of it herself, but it was true what Judy had said: it was time she looked after her own interests.

She took another determined sip of coffee, pulled a face at the unaccustomed bitter taste, then leant back luxuriously in the chair. She was no longer a drudge, a skivvy. Free at last!

Then – oh, drat it, there she went again, overcome by that feeling of guilt. Her new-found confidence wavered. Free . . . for what? Why was she doing all this – or more rightly, who for? Who was going to care, now, what she looked like?

Unaccountably, the tears began to roll. She had never imagined freedom would feel like this. She kept hearing things: Arthur's heavy tread on the stairs, his snores during the night.

She saw him in his long combinations doing the morning exercises he'd never failed to do since leaving the army, folding his trousers at night and putting them under the mattress (an old army trick) before she was allowed to get into bed – though she'd often had to press them again to his exacting standards next morning.

He'd made her life a misery with his hectoring and bullying, his long, moody silences. Although they were married, they shared nothing except a bed, and that she preferred not to think about. She'd longed to be rid of him, prayed for it every single night. She'd thought of leaving him, only for so long she'd had nothing to make that possible, no money and nowhere to go. And now I have money to spare but . . . oh, drat this – blubbing again!

One thing I do know, though, I don't miss *you*, you old devil, she thought robustly, blowing her nose. But something, some glimmer of hope that had entered her life not so long ago was gone, gone for ever. For perhaps five minutes, she had glimpsed a future where even the previously unimaginable might be possible—

A knock on the front door startled her and nearly made her spill the coffee. Visitors were rare at seven, Cherry Avenue. She sprang up and peered through the lace curtains. The police! That Sergeant Gilmour again. Hastily mopping her face with her handkerchief, she went to answer the summons.

The first thing Joe noticed when she let him in was that she'd been crying, poor woman. He'd met her before, when they came to break the news, and she hadn't shown much emotion then. Probably delayed reaction. She stood aside to let him pass her awkwardly in the narrow hall, crowded with unnecessary furniture and dominated by a coat-and-umbrella stand laden with a selection of coats and hats of various kinds – except, of course, for the bowler Aston had been wearing when he was killed; that was still being held by the police. She went before him into the front parlour, just as overfurnished as the hallway, where everything was polished and maintained to such a high degree of cleanliness it made Joe feel as though he ought to have been disinfected himself before setting a foot inside. It was a dull room with varnished brown paintwork and faded, leaf-patterned wallpaper, but there were a lot of cushion covers and chair-backs in startlingly bright crochet-work. A basket sat on the floor next to a chair, filled with a rainbow medley of wools.

After they entered, she stood in the centre of the room; nor did she invite him to sit.

'What do you want?' she asked ungraciously. 'I already told you everything I could last time you were here.'

He trotted out the usual response to that. 'We're following a new line of enquiry, Mrs Aston.'

She put a hand to her scrawny chest. 'What do you mean, enquiry? There's nothing else to enquire about as I see it. You don't have to enquire about an accident, do you?'

'Well, yes, we do. We have to know how it happened. To make certain,' he added carefully, 'that it *was* an accident.'

'Of course it was! What else could it have been?'

'I'm afraid it looks now as though foul play was involved.'

'*Foul play?*' For a moment he thought she didn't understand what that meant, but then he saw that she did. She had gone deathly pale.

'Please sit down, Mrs Aston.' She sank clumsily into a chair, knocking into a small table and causing the cup and saucer on it to rattle against the coffee pot. 'I'm sorry, this has been a shock – would you like me to pour you some more coffee?'

She shuddered. 'No. But you can get me a glass of water.'

He found the kitchen, small and old-fashioned but as spotless as the rest of the house, looked for a glass, and while he left the tap on for the water to run cold, took stock. It was a soulless place, a table covered with oilcloth, in places worn to its backing by much scrubbing, a copper in one corner, a mangle in the other, one single wooden chair painted a dismal green, an ancient stove and an overall smell of carbolic, unpleasantly reminiscent of public conveniences. He remembered what Maisie had said about her cooking. Joe's aunt, with whom he lodged, wasn't much of a cook either, and it wasn't hard to visualize unappealing meals of grey mince, lumpy potatoes and overcooked cabbage.

When he went back into the other room she was sitting

down and had composed herself again, looking much as she
had when he had first broken the news of her husband's death
– stoical and unyielding, her lips pressed together, as if such a
catastrophe was just more of life's slings and arrows thrown at
her which she had no choice but to accept. 'Should've told
you to get yourself a cup if you want some coffee,' she remarked
as he handed her the water and sat himself down opposite.

'That's all right, Mrs Aston.'

She drank thirstily. 'What's all this, then? What's this foul
play you're on about?'

'I'm afraid it looks as though your husband was attacked,
and died as a result.'

She took another gulp of water. 'Killed, you mean? What
makes you think that, then?'

He explained as gently as he could what they thought might
have happened. 'Had he any enemies that you know of, or
friends he might have quarrelled with recently?'

'He didn't have any friends,' she said spitefully.

Joe raised his eyebrows.

'It's true. He never went out, never went anywhere – well,
hardly, except down to the Rotary Club or the Punch Bowl
sometimes, or to see the major.' The major, thought Joe, making
a mental note to pursue this later, as she went on, 'Anyway,
he stayed late at the works most nights.' Her lips pursed even
tighter.

And then came home and ate an unappetizing supper, sat
down and maybe read his newspaper – there was not a book
in sight – while Lily crocheted yet more cushion covers? What
a prospect: domestic boredom personified.

'But there must have been people he knew. Did he never
mention any names . . . business contacts, some customer from
overseas, maybe?'

Her expression didn't alter but something alerted him. He'd
touched a nerve there. He debated whether to press the point,
but decided against it at the moment, knowing full well it
would only elicit another negative response.

'It's like I told that girl,' she said. 'He kept his home life and
his business separate.'

'What girl was that?'

'Her that writes for the *Herald*.'

Judy Cash again, snooping around. She gave him an itch, that girl, like winter chilblains, and like them, you couldn't get rid of her. He knew he should ignore her, but she exasperated him; she was capable of doing a lot of damage, insinuating herself to get information, getting under people's skin. 'You want to be careful with her. What you say will go straight into the paper.'

'Oh, I know that, I wasn't born yesterday,' Lily replied, scornful of his estimation of her. 'But she's promised it won't, you know. She understands.'

Not *understood*, but *understands*, as if they were in the habit of meeting. He didn't much like that. 'All the same, if you see her again, watch what you say to her.'

She shrugged and drank some more water, and when she'd put the glass down, Joe said, 'He had a graze on his temple, your husband. The doctors don't believe it was recent – or at any rate not received at the time he died. How did he get it, Mrs Aston?'

She blinked rapidly, her work-reddened hands twisting together, then looked down at her feet without saying anything. Her shoes were old and shapeless. Lily Aston was not a woman you took to, but the sight of those shoes, contrasting with a dress much smarter than the one she'd worn when he had seen her previously – a sort of bravado, that seemed to him – somehow filled Joe with pity.

'Did you have a quarrel?' he asked more gently.

She looked up at that and gave a short laugh. 'I suppose that means you think I hit him? Me? Look at me! He weighed thirteen stone!'

'You don't look as though you weigh much more than half of that,' Joe agreed. She also looked tough and wiry, but he forbore to comment on that. 'Was it an accident, or a fall, then?'

'Not that I know of.'

'OK, if it wasn't either, and you didn't have a fight with him, do you know how he got that graze?'

'No.'

After a moment or two, Joe said, 'Mrs Aston, I think maybe you do.'

She went silent, her mouth set in a mulish line. He saw calculation pass over her face as he waited, and then suddenly she said, 'All right. It was that Rees-Talbot.'

She waved a hand towards a framed sepia photograph over the mantel, a group of half a dozen uniformed officers, obviously taken some time ago, somewhere under a hot sun: a bare landscape with a tin-roofed building to one side, two or three stunted trees and what looked like native kraals in the background. 'Him on the right,' she said. 'That's Major Rees-Talbot.' Joe looked and saw a young man with nothing in particular to distinguish him from the others. They were all wearing khaki tunics, slouch hats, riding breeches and boots, holding whips and sporting the same type of luxuriant moustache that had been popular at the turn of the century.

'Thought highly of the major, Arthur did. He was his batman during the war in South Africa, they went through a lot together, he used to say, and the major helped him out a bit when he started his business here. He was cut up when he died.'

Joe adjusted his perceptions. 'Then it wasn't the major he had the fight with?'

'Of course not, I told you, he's dead. Months since. It was his son, that Felix.'

The name Rees-Talbot had caused Joe's ears to prick up. It was a familiar enough one in Folbury, but also the name of the people Maisie worked for. The major, of course, was the late father of Margaret and Felix Rees-Talbot, whom Maisie said Aston had been in the habit of visiting. What else had she said about Aston, apart from the fact that he couldn't keep his hands to himself? Something about a nasty atmosphere he'd left behind him when he visited Alma House, wasn't it? 'What was the fight about?'

She shrugged. 'I've no idea. The young fellow came here and Arthur sent me out of the room. They started shouting, and I came back when I heard them begin to scuffle. It was all over by then, but the place was in a right mess, I can tell you. They'd knocked my palm stand over and my aspidistra was on the floor,' she said indignantly, pointing to a narrow, tapering oak stand, now upright, and on its lace doily a leathery potted plant of no great beauty that looked more than capable of surviving such rough treatment.

'And your husband?'

'Oh, him. He was all right, he went to sit in his chair when I came in, and the young chap left. I will say,' she added grudgingly, 'he had the grace to apologize and pick my aspidistra up before he went.'

'Did Mr Aston say what it was all about?'

Lily looked at him. 'What makes you think he'd tell *me*?'

There was a small silence. 'You didn't get on, then, you and your husband?'

'I didn't say that. Just that he kept himself to himself.'

'So you wouldn't know if he had any enemies?'

'Like that young chap, you mean?'

'Well, from what you say, their meeting doesn't seem to have been exactly friendly. Did you happen to overhear anything of what went on?'

She blushed, an ugly dark red that ran in a tide from her chest and throat right up to her hairline. 'What do you take me for? I don't listen at doors.' She stood up and added with a certain dignity, 'If that's it, Sergeant, then I have to go out soon.'

'Another few minutes, please, and then I'll be off, I promise.'

'Be as quick as you can then,' she said sharply. 'What else is it you want?'

You didn't have to read between the lines, Joe thought, to see she was an unhappy woman in what had been an unhappy marriage, but the cowed wife Maisie had known wasn't much in evidence today. She was showing spirit, though anxious to get rid of him. Yet there still remained the somewhat delicate matter of asking permission to go through the dead man's things, papers and perhaps personal belongings. The papers first.

Before making any request, Joe enquired, 'By the way, did Mr Aston happen to keep any duplicate keys for the works?'

'Duplicates? I wouldn't know. Unless there were some at Henrietta Street. He only had the one set as far as I know.'

'He let himself into the foundry that morning but we haven't found any keys.'

She shrugged and said ungraciously, 'Better have another look, then, hadn't you? A big bunch like that doesn't lose itself easy. They were on a ring with his house keys and that.'

'We'll do that, of course. Meanwhile, your husband's private papers . . . I'm afraid I'm going to have to ask for a look at them.'

'You could if you had the keys, but you'll have to find them first, won't you? It's locked,' she said, with a touch of malice, gesturing towards a dark oak roll-top desk with a green opaque-glass nymph displayed on its top.

He gave her a direct look before saying casually, 'Right, well, never mind that, Mrs Aston, I can force it open. No, no, don't worry, I'll be careful not to make too many scratches. Do you have a knife?'

'Don't be so hasty,' she replied like a shot, alarmed for her furniture. 'There might be a spare key somewhere upstairs.'

There was, of course. After some time she came back with it, sucking a bead of blood from her thumb. 'Key slipped – I mean the one to the cupboard where this was,' she said, handing him the very small key to the desk. 'You'd think it was Winson Green, this house, the way things were kept locked up.'

Arthur Aston was certainly emerging as a careful man, secretive even, but keys kept within locked cupboards? Number seven, Cherry Avenue must indeed have seemed like a prison to Mrs Aston sometimes.

But when he looked, Joe didn't find anything that warranted such secrecy. Aston had been an orderly man and his desk was very tidy. No personal diary, though. Evidently the appointment book he kept in his office desk had been sufficient for him, along with what appeared to be a scribbled reminder list on the back of a part-used chequebook, items meaningless to anyone else: *Rates, 16th June; Harrison, painter, Queen's Rd; WIM (several times); Car Licence, June 30th; Timber, £5.17.6.* The cheque stubs all appeared to be for small payments of household bills. There were no bank statements and no cash in the desk – now he came to think of it, Aston had had very little on him when he was killed, just some loose change in his pocket and a couple of pound notes in his wallet. Careful chap, Aston.

Apart from these mundane papers, there was a file containing deeds for the house and a bank passbook with a tidy though not excessive balance, which would need to be checked more thoroughly. His business statements and a preliminary look through the books in the safe at his office had revealed similarly satisfactory figures. At the back of the file was a marriage certificate dated June 1911 for Arthur Aston, bachelor, and Lily Jane Tucker, spinster. There was no will, nor had there been one among his papers at the office, though it would have been surprising if he'd kept it there.

'Did your husband keep private documents anywhere else, Mrs Aston? A copy of his will, perhaps?'

'Will? I don't know of any will.' She shrugged, not seeming too concerned at its absence.

So unless Aston had lodged a copy with his bank or his solicitor, it seemed he might have died intestate. It was possible, with all his assets realized and his business wound up, that when Lily Jane Tucker married Arthur Aston, she might not have made such a bad bargain after all.

Nine

In preparation for Easter, tonight's choir practice was an extra – just the boys, with none of the deeper male voices as a counterpoint to their piercing sweetness.

'*My soul doth magnify the Lord . . .*'

Perhaps because this setting of the Magnificat was as new and unfamiliar to the boys as it was to Margaret, the choirmaster kept making them stop and go back to the beginning, repeating phrases over and over again. Voices echoing in the empty spaces of the church and around the stone pillars, soaring to the vaulting, becoming ragged, dying away. The choirmaster giving them a note. His interjections, his actual words not quite reaching to where Margaret sat . . .

She had lately found herself coming in here on most choir practice nights, just to listen, much as her father had done. Philip Latham, the young and enthusiastic organist and choirmaster, had been a particular friend of his, their shared love of music, particularly sacred music, having brought them together. She had indeed sometimes been tempted to wonder if her father's faithful adherence to Holy Trinity had as much to do with that as his commitment to his faith. Heretical thought! But who could ever tell with Osbert?

'*For he that is mighty hath magnified me . . .*'

Margaret vaguely wondered who the composer was. Her father could have told her. She closed her eyes but that only brought the questions back. For the last few hours, they'd tumbled about in her mind – the doubts, everything that had gone wrong since Osbert's death, the shock at the manner of it . . .

Strangely, tonight she felt closer to him than at any time since his death, as if this new worry that had arisen today had set up some communion with him. But that didn't mean he could tell her what to do now . . . what to do about things being stirred up again, what to do when she tried to face her fears as she knew she should and her own brisk common sense deserted her.

'. . . *and ever shall be, world without end. Amen.*'

Finally, the choirmaster, having let them sing the canticle right through without any interruptions, was winding up the practice, his voice raised enough now for her to distinguish his words. 'All right, that's it for tonight. But I shall expect a better performance on Sunday. Off you go – *quietly!*' he shouted above the ensuing din that immediately broke out as the choir dispersed. Like choirboys everywhere, they looked and sounded angelic, singing like angels and incapable of mischief or naughtiness when dressed in their dark blue robes and short white surplices, but now they were just ordinary, mortal boys in their rough jerseys and shorts, socks at half-mast as they jostled each other rowdily past her down the aisle and shot out of the door like greyhounds released from a trap.

An uncanny silence was left behind until presently the organ began again – toccata and fugue, eclipsing the gentler notes of the Magnificat, rolling and thunderous, the sort of music that always filled Margaret with melancholy foreboding. An agitation gripped her; she could no longer sit still.

She hurried, almost ran out of the church into a green and gold spring evening, into the tranquil churchyard that was no longer used as a burial ground, shaded by lime trees, bisected by flagged paths where the grass between the old graves was now allowed to grow and become studded with wild flowers. This was not a place that gave off melancholy, nor indeed indulged it; the dead here had slept peacefully for centuries, the inscriptions on their ancient headstones indecipherable now, worn by the passage of time. A fragrance hung around the lych gate from wallflowers which had seeded themselves into the cracks of the old churchyard wall, some already in bloom.

Her footsteps gradually slowed; she felt a hand on her shoulder and spun round. 'I saw you in church, my love. I hoped I might catch you.'

'Symon! I didn't see *you*,' she said, still agitated.

'I only popped out from the vestry for a minute. You seemed very . . . absorbed. What's wrong?' In fact he had watched her from the vestry doorway for longer than that and thought, though he could not be sure from that distance, that she might have been weeping.

'I am *so* pleased to see you, Symon!'

'Now that's good. My future wife is pleased to see me!'

'Of course I am.' His teasing irony had missed its mark. 'I need to talk to you,' she said rapidly. 'Something's happened, but . . . oh, I don't know how to begin!'

He waited, his hand still on her arm.

'There's – there's been an accident at one of the factories in Arms Green.'

'Arthur Aston, I know.'

'You know? News travels fast.'

'I went to pay a pastoral call on his wife yesterday. Though they were not church attenders.' He added, with slightly heightened colour, 'She refused to speak to me.'

In fact Lily Aston had taken one look at his dog collar and demanded rudely what business it was of his when he had mentioned the purpose of his visit, and then virtually shut the door in his face.

'I suppose it must be a difficult time for her,' Margaret said.

'Do you know her?'

'I've never met her but Maisie used to work for the Astons. And – I did know her husband, slightly. He was my father's batman in South Africa and used to come and see him occasionally . . .' Now that Symon was here, she began to feel less agitated and made an effort to get her thoughts in better order, rolling a small pebble on the path with the pointed toe of her smart kid shoe.

'Margaret?' She went on pushing the pebble about. 'You're upset because of Aston's death?' he prompted.

'Not really. Oh, I mean . . . well, of course I am, it's shocking news.'

'What is it, then?' She was smartly dressed as usual, wearing a light wrap coat, cut to button on the hip, in some material with a silky gleam to it, its bronze colour bringing out the glow in her hazel eyes, but somehow draining the colour from her face. She was bareheaded, twisting the straw hat she had worn in church round and round in her hands. 'What is it?' he repeated.

Sympathy was always guaranteed to make her cry, but her

natural control was gradually reasserting itself. She made an effort and breathed deeply. 'This afternoon, the police came looking for Felix. They – they believe Mr Aston died after being attacked.'

'What? And they suspect Felix?' To say he was astounded was putting it mildly. 'Your brother Felix?' he repeated, as if she had some other brother. 'What grounds have they for that?'

'My brother Felix,' she answered with a shaky laugh, 'has been making more of a fool of himself than usual.'

This was eminently conceivable to Symon, but his private opinions about Felix did not include seeing him as a murderer, even when Margaret went on to tell him about the scrap with Aston that Felix had apparently initiated.

'That was – foolish,' he said, choosing the word carefully – idiotic, crass and asinine being unpardonable words in the circumstances. 'But he must have had his reasons for picking a fight with the man?'

'He *believes* he had. You see, the fact is – oh, it's too awful – but the fact is, Mr Lazenby has discovered something – well, unusual, in Father's papers.'

'Mr Lazenby? Ah, the accountant.' After a moment he said, 'We'd better find a seat and you can tell me everything. Unless you'd prefer to go somewhere more private? Home, perhaps?'

'No. Here will do – it could hardly be more private, after all; no one here is likely to repeat what they overhear, are they?'

This time it was he who let the little attempt at frivolity pass. It showed she was feeling more herself, but it was not one of the occasions when he felt it appropriate to laugh and relax and say nonsensical things himself. He led her to one of the seats along a side path, sat her down and then gently held her hand and told her to start from the beginning.

She had been immersed in fashion catalogues when the police arrived, although the elegant creations depicted therein were serving only to reinforce the certainty that her trousseau was not going to be enhanced by anything likely to be purchased from the Misses Schofield on the High Street, whose basic stock-in-trade was lisle stockings and liberty bodices. Her wedding dress was no problem: it was being made by one of Aunt Deborah's friends who had learnt her craft at the Royal

School of Needlework. Skirts that year had shot up to barely an inch below the knee, but Margaret had conceded that was a length inappropriate for a wedding dress and had settled for mid-calf, choosing a simple long-waisted deep cream chiffon over a white satin underdress, the bodice and fluted hem embroidered with roses and seed pearls. As for the rest of her trousseau – well, shopping for clothes wasn't normally Kay's idea of a good day out, but perhaps she could be persuaded into a trip to London . . .

Or perhaps she could stay with her chum Barbara (now known as Babs), who, since moving to London, seemed to spend her life driving around with young men in fast cars, dancing with them half the night, wearing very short skirts, drinking cocktails, and generally living life at a hectic pace. They were young, restless, those who had been spared the war, determined to enjoy what the new future held. 'The bright young things', the papers were calling them, making it seem as though the whole post-war generation was gripped with this mania.

But dull as Babs's letters sometimes made Margaret feel, she knew that a visit to her was not the answer, certainly not at the moment. Better than either her or Kay, she thought suddenly, would be Vinnie, who had only ten minutes before arrived with an extravagantly large bunch of white, sweet-smelling narcissus she'd seen on a market stall and been unable to resist. She had begged to arrange them, and was at that moment doing so in the kitchen. Yes, it would be good to have Vinnie shop with her – she was always so sensible and invariably in good spirits. Margaret's mood had lifted at the idea of doing something so intimate and feminine.

The front door bell had rung at that point and an unusually flustered Maisie ushered in Joe Gilmour, the young red-headed policeman she was walking out with, accompanied by another older man in plain clothes and with a sadly disfigured face, who introduced himself as a detective inspector and asked to see Felix. Felix was upstairs and Maisie was dispatched to ask him to come down. Joe looked as though he would rather not have been there, but it was the inspector, Reardon, who spoke briefly to Margaret while they were waiting.

She hoped she wasn't showing the nervousness she felt about

this request to see her brother – though Reardon was less intimidating than she had expected, once you got used to the scars. She offered them tea – which they politely refused – and did her best to keep the conversation going until Felix, who was taking his time, should appear. Seeing the police, her heart had sunk. She had immediately known without question what this visit must be about.

Felix had finally admitted to her what she had already suspected when she had seen his bruised jaw – that he had taken out his frustrations over what they'd learnt from Mr Lazenby by attacking Arthur Aston in his own home, a man old enough to be his father. That he had underestimated his opponent and come off badly didn't make it any better. He was ashamed of himself, yet obviously still felt he'd had justification, and more, for confronting Aston, and had told her defiantly that given the same provocation he would probably do it again. She could see now that in view of what had later happened to Aston, that stupid action of his could have assumed a nasty significance, at least if seen from the point of view of the police.

Presently a door slammed somewhere upstairs and she breathed a sigh of relief. Nobody but Felix slammed doors.

Reardon didn't attempt to break the silence as they waited. She wondered if he had noticed her tension, and deliberately tried to relax. After another minute or two Felix came in, pushing open the door for Vinnie, who was carrying the vase of flowers, her beret still perched on her head, looking breezy and outdoors. 'Oh, sorry, didn't know you had visitors, I'll make myself scarce,' she said with a sunny smile, putting the flowers down on a low table.

'Stay, please, Vinnie. No reason why she shouldn't, is there?' Felix demanded pugnaciously, holding tight to her hand.

'You are Miss—?' Reardon asked.

'Henderson. Vinnie Henderson.'

'Please sit down if you wish, Miss Henderson.'

'Oh, right-o then.' She allowed herself to be pulled down next to Felix on the uncomfortable horsehair sofa that everyone else normally avoided, its recovering long overdue. The sunlight washing the room made its shabbiness even more apparent than usual, as well as showing up all the other deficiencies created through years of careless, comfortable living, so familiar you never noticed them. Vinnie's flowers, fresh and new, looked almost incongruous, but brave in the circumstances. Margaret smiled at her, glad she was there, helping to bring normality to a situation that was growing increasingly bizarre.

'So,' asked Reardon, after he had pressed Felix into confirming, reluctantly at first, then with a certain bravado, the encounter with Aston, which had apparently already been related to them by Aston's wife, 'what was your grumble with Mr Aston, specifically?'

'Grumble?' Felix gave a short bark of laughter. 'Well, if you call cheating my father out of several thousand pounds simply a grumble, I must beg to differ.'

Margaret tried to catch his eye. This sort of attitude was not going down well with the chief inspector, but when he in turn spoke she sensed it was the words rather than the attitude which had caused him to look so sharply at her brother, that he was perhaps alerted rather than irritated.

'Cheating? Would you explain that, sir?'

Felix shrugged and looked sulky and Margaret took it on herself to answer, quickly putting Reardon in the picture as to Mr Lazenby's position regarding the family finances. 'My father died at the end of last year and we've asked Mr Lazenby – he's an accountant – to sort through all his papers for us to see if anything further needs to be done, though it doesn't now seem as though that will be necessary. My father was quite precise in keeping his affairs in order. But . . .' She stopped and took a deep breath, then went on, her colour heightened. 'To be truthful, I'm afraid he's come across something slightly odd.'

It was her turn to receive one of Reardon's sharp glances, but he merely nodded and waited for her to go on. It seemed that according to Mr Lazenby a considerable loan had been made to Arthur Aston several years ago when he started up his business, and had apparently never been repaid. Of course, some unrecorded agreement about this might have been arrived at between the two parties, Mr Lazenby had said, tutting in disapproval at such an unorthodox way of dealing with matters, but it was irregular, very irregular. And there the matter might have been left, had he not gone on to say that Osbert had also written several very substantial cheques to Aston just before his death, and unless these were gifts and not further loans, they had not been repaid either.

There was a long silence when she had finished. They all looked at Felix who now sat with his head in his hands, saying nothing.

It was clearly Reardon who was going to do all the questioning, leaving the sergeant seemingly relieved at the note-taking role assigned to him. 'Did you already know about this?'

Felix muttered something unintelligible and didn't look up.

'A thousand pounds,' he had heard someone say, walking past the open study window, a surprising statement that had made him pause to listen further. A woman's voice, he'd thought. Harsh, grating. And then his father's, shocked: 'Another? That's quite impossible!'

He had turned away then, shocked himself and, yes, ashamed. Ashamed of eavesdropping, but more at the sequence of thoughts the words had immediately, shamefully but unstoppably conjured up: a woman demanding money. His father, still not much above fifty, and a widower for twenty-five years . . .

Ashamed even more when Mr Lazenby had found that a thousand-pound cheque had lately been made out, not once but three times, and not to any woman but to Arthur Aston. Knowing without doubt then that he'd been mistaken – that it had not been a woman's voice he'd heard demanding money from his father, but Aston's, raised and distorted with anger, greed – or possibly menace.

What if he hadn't walked away from his eavesdropping? What if he'd walked into the study there and then and confronted the person he now knew to have been Aston, and told him to clear out and leave Osbert alone? Would that have saved his father? From what? He had clearly been afraid of Aston exposing something shameful. Would it have helped, or given the other man reason to bring whatever it was into the light? Round and round in his mind the questions whirled. In the end, he had persuaded himself he should forget it, it was none of his business, but by then it was too late. Osbert was dead. It was only when Mr Lazenby had brought those payments to light that he'd found the guts to do something. An abortive attempt, and look where it had landed him! In trouble with the police.

He looked up at last and replied obliquely, 'Whatever the reasons, I didn't see any justification for Aston getting away with it. I couldn't stand it any longer and I went to face him and tell him he was honour-bound to repay every penny he owed.' Anger boiled up in him as he pictured Aston's fat, leering face. 'The rotten blighter had the cheek to find it amusing! He told me to go away and actually laughed in my face.'

'And so you knocked him down?'

'He was the one who started it. He suddenly punched me on the jaw and I – well, I hit him back. But it was nothing more than a tap. He fell over backwards on to the fender and knocked his head against the fireplace, but he was all right. I was the one who got the worst of it. He damn near broke my jaw! Things might have got worse, I'll admit, but his wife came in and that was that. He was OK, sitting down comfortably when I left. Not a very edifying scene, I suppose,' he ended with some bravado, 'but I was bloody furious, excuse me.'

'Furious enough to go back next morning and finish him off at his workshop?'

'No,' Felix said shortly. 'I'd cooled off by then. But I'm not surprised that somebody did fix him. He'd been asking for it one way and another for a long time.'

'Hmm.' Reardon said nothing for a while and then he addressed Margaret. 'Was your father normally such a generous man? To part with such large amounts of money?'

'He was generous to a fault with us, his family, and to the church and other charities, yes.'

'But Mr Aston was hardly a charity.'

'He apparently saved my father's life once, when they were serving together in the South African war. I don't know the details but Father was not one to forget such an action.'

'Aston took care not to let him forget it! That's what the cheques were about. It was damned blackmail, nothing more.'

Margaret said, 'He – Father, that is – always felt guilty. He was given the DSO for bravery, you see, but he always said it was Aston who should have been decorated, though I don't know the details—'

'Well I do!' Felix broke in passionately. 'Father would never speak of it, but Uncle Hamer told me the story years ago, when I was a boy. Apparently, Aston helped drag Father back into safety after he was shot when he was leading his men to take an enemy position – successfully, as it turned out. The fellow was brave, no doubt about it, but it was Father who led the men out into heavy fire and lost his own right arm. No one but him ever said he didn't deserve his medal. To think otherwise diminishes his own courage.'

He slumped back in his chair, his face set. Vinnie suddenly reached for his hand and held it pressed between hers. It was up to Margaret once more to answer the few questions the detective inspector still had, though there wasn't much more, thankfully, that he wanted to know. Perhaps, she thought, there was nothing else he *could* ask really.

At a nod from Reardon, Joe Gilmour snapped his notebook shut, slipping it into his uniform pocket. He gave Margaret a small reassuring smile. She liked the look of this young man of Maisie's, and managed a return smile. The other policeman, Reardon, was not so easy to read, but throughout she had sensed a surprising depth of understanding in him. Maybe it was that facial scarring, the evidence of war wounds that one had, sadly, grown only too accustomed to seeing in the last years. He must have had traumas of his own to deal with.

She stood up as they did, but it appeared Reardon hadn't quite finished. On the point of leaving, he turned and said, 'My condolences on your father's death, Miss Rees-Talbot. A tragic accident, I understand?'

'Yes,' she answered with heightened colour, and added more firmly, 'Yes. As you've no doubt heard, he was crippled by the loss of his arm, and he slipped while taking a bath.'

'That was indeed unfortunate. He must have been a brave man, they don't give DSOs for nothing.' He held out his hand. 'Thank you for your trouble. We'll be in touch if necessary, Mr Rees-Talbot.'

Felix and Vinnie left the house shortly after the police had gone. Perhaps, thought Margaret, he needed to be with her in private, to pour out his troubles into a sympathetic ear, though more likely he felt the need to escape, expecting a lecture from Margaret herself. He needn't have bothered. She was in no mood for the big sister role, and anyway, he already knew how fed up she was with him.

But if he wanted a shoulder to cry on, she thought he had picked the wrong person. Kind as Vinnie was, she was too sensible and down to earth to let him feel sorry for himself.

'So that was it?' Symon asked.

'They haven't arrested him or anything, if that's what you mean. But they said they would need to talk to him again.'

'Hmm.'

'Oh, I know Felix is a fool in many ways, and it's time he grew up and used the brains he's been given, but I really think this will teach him a lesson. It's been a shock, to both of us – about Aston and the money, I mean. What could Father have been thinking of?'

'Presumably he had his reasons.'

'Poor Felix, you mustn't think too badly of him, Symon.' She hesitated, colouring deeply. 'He has to have someone to blame for what happened.'

It was the first time she had even hinted, however obliquely, that Osbert's death had left questions with unacceptable answers. He understood that pain and bewilderment made her afraid of admitting this, even to him. 'You have no need to blame your father, Margaret. Such a thing could have happened to anyone.'

'What made him do it, Symon?' The injustice of it all welled up. He understood that it wasn't her brother she was speaking of. *'What made him do it*? It's so unfair, and it makes me feel so – so *helpless*. I feel I ought to do something to find the truth or I'll burst!' She punched her fist down in frustration.

'Margaret, Felix "did something", and look where it's got him.'

'But you know what he's like. He wouldn't – he couldn't . . .' She stopped, her face stricken.

'Couldn't what?'

She shook her head. 'No, I won't even think that! He's my brother, Symon. I would *know* if he'd done something so monstrous. And I'm responsible – I wish I didn't feel that, but . . .' What she was feeling was just too complicated to put into words. 'You can't understand!'

He looked at her, intently and gravely, his eyes dark. 'Oh, but I can, Margaret. A choice between duty and what we wish is never easy.' She realized with a stab of love that he did understand, of course, none better. He had problems of his own in that direction, with his own brother, though he had never shared the burden with her and thought she didn't know.

Ten

The morning after their visit to the Rees-Talbots saw Joe summoned to the new office which he'd found for Reardon. It wasn't much better than the cubicle he'd first occupied, but it was marginally larger, having been cleared of the dusty accumulation of objects deemed unwanted and stored there for years – chairs that were wonky, but still too good to be thrown away, boxes of dead files, an ancient defunct typewriter. No place could be found for the large cupboard where unclaimed lost property was stored, but it had been shoved into one corner. As a temporary office, it would suffice.

Joe went straight away, pausing only to make a tea-drinking gesture to the duty constable who'd conveyed the message, and to grab and take with him the paper bag of coconut biscuits Maisie had baked last night.

As soon as they were settled, Reardon opened Felix Rees-Talbot's folder containing the notes Joe had taken yesterday, now typed up, and wasted no time in getting to the point. 'Chief and only suspect so far – if we can discount the slight possibility of the wife,' he began. 'All right, he's confirmed what Lily Aston told you, Sergeant – that she interrupted the fight he had with her husband – but do we see him as a likely candidate for going back the morning after and finishing him off?'

'Hanged if I know,' Joe said, struggling with the conflicting emotions left over from the brief hour and a half last night he'd managed to dovetail with Maisie's time off. It had been wasted, just sitting on the river bank watching the ducks. Wasted from a personal point of view, at any rate, because their conversation hadn't gone the way he'd intended. The question he had to ask her was beginning to be more important to him than anything else; it kept cropping up when he should have his mind on other things. But in another sense the time they'd spent together had been productive, if only for the snippet of information she had given him about the case. 'To be truthful, sir,' he said, 'it's hard to say. But no, not really.'

'The maid says he had a hangover and didn't get up until nearly nine that morning, which gives him an alibi. If she's to be trusted.'

Joe stiffened. 'She is, sir, absolutely. I can vouch for that. And she's Maisie, her name's Maisie Henshall,' he said, red behind the ears. 'She wouldn't lie, I'll bet my life on it.' He looked down at the paper bag he was still holding, and after a moment he opened it and offered the biscuits. 'She – er – baked these.'

'Did she now? Thanks.' Reardon took two and after an appreciative bite regarded him speculatively. 'Congratulations in order?'

'I wouldn't go so far as that just yet,' Joe said, reddening further. You never knew, with Maisie. She'd come a long way from the undersized fourteen-year-old who had worked for the Aston's, but he still wasn't sure she was ready yet for what he had fully meant to ask of her last night.

There was a tap on the door and the police constable brought in the mugs of tea Joe had asked for and put them on the desk. 'Thank you, Blaydon.' As the door closed behind him they picked up their mugs and Reardon said, 'Tell me more about the Rees-Talbots.'

'Inherited family business, most of it sold off now, leaving them comfortable, but not rich, I'd say,' Joe replied after a moment's thought. 'Very involved in local affairs, especially the church, and well respected, both Osbert and his sister. There's that other brother of course, the uncle that was mentioned last night, but he doesn't live around here . . . Malvern, I think. Osbert was a JP and all that, churchwarden at Holy Trinity. Big funeral when he died.'

Reardon stirred sugar into his tea. 'Drowned in his bath. Unusual.'

'Easy enough to slip and not be able to save yourself with only one arm. That was the verdict at the inquest – accidental death.' Joe paused and the silence lengthened. 'There was nothing to say it wasn't, and it seemed a reasonable supposition at the time.'

'But now?'

Joe cracked his knuckles and then picked up the mug of tea

to stop himself. He didn't quite know how to put what he had to say, but after a moment or two he found the words. '*She* didn't think it was an accident. Maisie, I mean. She – she told me last night that after what's happened – I think she meant us talking to Felix – she thinks it might be important and that I could tell you . . . She believes old Rees-Talbot did it deliberately, and what's more she's pretty sure the family believe that as well.'

Reardon reached for another biscuit. 'What grounds do they have for thinking that?'

'Apparently, there weren't as many pills left in his pillbox as there should have been. And he'd locked the bathroom door while he had his bath, which he never normally did, though the chances of him being found and prevented – well, how long does it take to drown, a few minutes?'

'And nobody has said anything because they don't want it to be known that it was suicide.' Reardon looked meditatively out of the window. It was a better view than his previous one. Instead of an unrewarding brick wall, he now had a slanting view of the Town Hall, and a window where a row of pigeons jostled for space. 'They wouldn't be the first.'

It was a familiar story: relief at avoiding the shame of a suicide and all that entailed, the horror of a loved one having to be buried in unconsecrated ground because to kill oneself was not only a criminal offence, it was also immoral, a sin against God, that of self-murder in the eyes of the Church. And oddly reminiscent of that other case Reardon and Joe had worked on, where the family of the girl who had drowned had faced the same dilemma – accident or suicide? Like that family, the Rees-Talbots had strong connections with their church, and most likely had the same dread of the scandal associated with the taking of one's own life.

Apart from that, it was a tragedy for the family, however you looked at it, and maybe understandable that a hothead like Felix Rees-Talbot should want to find someone to blame, jumping to the conclusion that his father had been driven to it by Aston when they discovered he'd been putting the pressure on. Over what, though?

'All right, then. What we're thinking is: Aston has something on Rees-Talbot so strong he's prepared to square him with a lot of money to stop the beans being spilt. Until the demands become greater and he gets fed up with paying out, but can't face up to the consequences if whatever it was becomes known, so he takes his life.'

'After which,' Joe said slowly, 'Aston is murdered.'

'Hmm. He's far from being the fool he appears to be, that young fellow Felix. He no more believes all that business about his father's grateful generosity to Aston than you or I – nor does his sister, if I'm any judge. He told us he believes it was blackmail. And if he believes that was what caused his father to take his own life, what better motive for killing Aston?'

Could Rees-Talbot's death really provide the reason for Aston's murder, for what up to now had seemed like a motiveless crime? 'If we knew what it was that enabled Aston to blackmail him, in the first place . . .' Joe began.

Reardon drew a triangle on the pad in front of him, with a name at each corner: at the apex, The Snowman, then the other two, Osbert Rees-Talbot and Arthur Aston. He looked at it for a while. 'What links them?'

'South Africa, I suppose,' Joe said after a moment or two.

'But also – since all three of them are dead – there must be another link. The person who killed Aston . . . and maybe killed the Snowman as well. Unless Aston himself was party to that. It seems the Snowman was killed just before the big freeze began. Which was . . .'

'Second week in December.'

'And Rees-Talbot dies round about the same time. Guilt?'

After a moment, Joe said, 'Maybe. But he couldn't have been the one who killed the Snowman. Or at least he couldn't have driven him out to Maxstead and dug his grave. Not with only one arm.'

Out at Maxstead Court, Lady Maude was sitting in her greenhouse, but for once she was idle. She couldn't keep her mind on geraniums. Wayward memories kept drifting down the years, refusing to be banished. She had been plagued with them for days; ever since that young policeman had been to see her the past had refused all her commands to stay in the past, where it belonged. She picked up a pot, put it down again. It was no good. She gave in at last and let them come . . .

That she had been there in South Africa at all was a tribute to her tenacity. As Lady Maude Prynne, only daughter of the Earl of Linsdale, a debutante who had been expected to make a brilliant marriage, she had instead fallen desperately in love during her first London season with a young man who had nothing in the way of assets but his good looks and the glamorous uniform of a lieutenant in Her Majesty's navy. Her parents had other ideas for her, however, and that budding romance had been promptly scotched, despite tears and tantrums. She had wept and thought her heart was broken. For the next two years, she managed stubbornly to resist every effort to see herself married off . . . but then had come release.

A second war against the Boers in South Africa had broken out, and she was taken by her mother to a glamorous fund-raising event at Claridge's, organized by Lady Randolph Churchill, who was hoping to raise enough money to equip and staff a hospital ship and sail out to Cape Town with herself on board – in a fetching white uniform designed by her own hand – and the would-be nurses in slightly less flattering ones. She was also anxious to reassure herself as to the well-being of her son Winston, who was a war correspondent attached to the South African Light Horse and had in fact been taken prisoner of war, although he had managed to escape.

Fired with patriotism, Maude had used her mother's slight acquaintance with Lady Randolph Churchill and begged to be part of the contingent of nurses. She was told that there could be no question of it. Amused, however, Lady Randolph listened to her pleadings: she would do anything, Maude promised, perform any menial task, roll bandages, clean floors, anything. In the end, such were her powers of persistence that she had eventually been allowed to sail as a lowly member of the staff. The Earl had sighed over his headstrong daughter but eventually had given his consent. After all, Lady Randolph had promised to keep an eye on her.

The *SS Maine*, fully equipped with doctors, qualified nursing staff (as well as Lady Randolph and her friends) and the best medical facilities available, having duly arrived in Cape Town, it was soon discovered that the ministering angels of mercy on board were not, as they had hoped, destined to enjoy for long the delights of the beautiful, wealthy, cosmopolitan city, bursting with officers either on leave or convalescing. Not for them attendance at parties, balls and dances at the luxurious Mount Nelson Hotel or the ostentatious houses of the rich uitlanders, foreigners who had made their fortunes in South African gold or diamonds. They were made aware in no uncertain terms that was not the purpose they were there for. In those early days of the war things were not going well for the British, and the hospital ship, they were informed, was urgently needed up in Natal, after a crushing defeat at a place called Spion Kop. Lady Randolph and her team therefore sailed off up the coast to Durban, while poor Maude was left behind in Cape Town, feverish and furious, struck down with – of all things – measles!

There was no question of her being allowed to stay on a hospital ship in the circumstances. It was a humiliating end to her adventure, but her captivity, as she saw it, was at least alleviated by being offered care and accommodation in the house of a moneyed family of Dutch descent whose strict religion bade them maintain a resolutely neutral stance in the conflict. They had two daughters of her own age, and their house in one of the wide tree-lined streets of the town had marble floors, French furniture, and fountains in the flower-filled gardens. Sophie and Bettje were pretty and delightful girls, and in their company Maude recovered her temper. And once she was allowed out, she found herself drawn into the social whirl, and for the first and only time in her life, knew what it was to feel and act a little wild.

All the same, it was a part of her life she had afterwards preferred not to dwell on, until Symon's engagement had forcibly brought it back. Maude, who already had an eminently suitable young lady lined up for him, was dismayed, especially when the name of his intended, Margaret Rees-Talbot, regis-tered and she remembered – had she ever forgotten? – the two handsome young Rees-Talbot brothers, Osbert and Hamer, army officers whom she had met in Cape Town after her recovery from measles.

She and the brothers had been amused to discover that back home in England they had lived within a few miles of one another, and yet had to travel six thousand miles to meet. It had not occurred to Maude at that point that any previous interchange between them would have been highly unlikely, given the different spheres in which their families moved. Out there social distinctions had seemed to matter less. And the Rees-Talbots had agreeable manners; they had been to a good school, and Sandhurst.

Both young officers had shown bravery in battle, Osbert in particular. He was recovering in Cape Town from internal wounds received at the Battle of Colenso, and his brother was spending as much of his leave there as possible in order to be with him; they were very close. Personable Hamer had something of a reputation with the ladies – though he was adroit at avoiding undue consequences – but it was Osbert, a young captain of a quieter and more serious nature, still pale and looking rather ill, but invested with glamour from his exploits, who was surrounded by feminine hero-worshippers. He did what was expected of him, flirted and danced with them as soon as he was able, made them laugh with his unexpected, somewhat sardonic humour, but he was restless in Cape Town, determined to get well enough to rejoin the fighting. Eventually he was declared fit for duty and sent up-country to Mafeking in Bechuanaland, a beleaguered garrison which had been under siege since the very first day of the war, in command of a small company with orders to cross enemy lines into the small township and thus supplement the handful of officers already there under Colonel Baden-Powell. The daring escapade was successful and he remained there, promoted to major, until at last the seven-month siege was raised.

Maude, however, never saw him again. Long before the end of the war, she was dispatched home, and on her return, the dry, common-sense part of her nature that was to become her ruling trait took over. She had had a fling, which was more than most girls of her age had, and must put it behind her. She had not found the romance once denied her and was now unlikely to, and she made up her mind that if she couldn't have her sailor, it didn't matter whom they gave her to. So she had allowed herself to be pushed into marriage with Sir Lancelot Scroope, at heart little more than a bluff country squire, with nothing on his mind other than the custodianship of Maxstead Court, his estate, his horses and dogs and the welfare of his tenants. He in his turn had seen the advantages of a marriage with the only daughter of the Earl of Linsdale. It was not the fairy-tale she had once dreamed of, but it had proved to be a good, sound marriage with true affection on both sides, which just showed that the wisdom of the young when in love was not to be trusted.

Because really, she could now admit, she was too practical and down-to-earth, not the stuff fairy-tale princesses are made of, and Scroope had turned out to be a kindly if unimaginative husband and a good father. He cared not a jot for society and little more for politics. He harrumphed over the newspapers and grumbled that the country was going to the dogs; nevertheless, during the late war, he had done his bit and carried out his duties as Lord Lieutenant for the county in an exemplary and untiring way. Maude missed him more than she could say.

And now, the wheel had come full circle and a quarter of a century later, Symon was going to marry the daughter of Osbert Rees-Talbot. Which, in view of what had recently happened, could put the cat well and truly in amongst the pigeons.

Eleven

Folbury and its town centre wasn't yet familiar territory to Reardon. He was walking through its old part and taking what he hoped might be a short cut to Town Hall Square and the police station, to stretch his legs after his half-hour lunch break and incidentally get the feel of the place where he was presently working.

Preoccupied with his thoughts, he hadn't noticed how very narrow the pavement had become, here where the road, barely wide enough for modern traffic, snaked alongside the ancient timbered Moot Hall – a hazard currently the subject of much heated controversy. On the pavement, Reardon barely avoided collision with the elderly woman much hung about with scarves and assorted parcels who was walking towards him. Just in time, he drew himself against the wall, tipping his hat. She smiled as she passed, but after a few steps she turned round.

'Excuse me, but I believe you're a police officer, are you not?' she asked, peering at him from under a large hat of the type he had not seen women wearing since before the war. 'The gentleman in charge of that dreadful occurrence in Henrietta Street? My niece, Dr Dysart, pointed you out the other day. I am Deborah Rees-Talbot.' She redistributed her parcels and held out her hand.

'Herbert Reardon. Inspector.'

'I would very much like a word with you, Inspector. Come with me, if you will. Just a few minutes, I promise.'

Still slightly bemused by being called a gentleman and a police officer in the same breath, he meekly obeyed. He followed where she led, just around the corner, down a few steps into a small hidden courtyard that was walled on three of its sides, its fourth flanked by the windowless side of a large building.

'Isn't this a pleasant little spot?' she beamed, relieving herself of her parcels and perching unselfconsciously on one of the steps. 'I often come to sit here on my way home from shopping. Not many people remember now what was here behind these walls, you know. There used to be a row of cottages several years ago, very picturesque but frightful slums really. All gone now, thank goodness, except for what's left of their gardens.' She plucked a spike of purplish willow herb that was growing by the step on which she sat and waved it around. 'Charming, don't you agree?'

He saw that indeed there were still a few remnants of a former existence: flowers here and there that he didn't think were weeds – though he was no expert – as well as plenty that were, grass and dandelions especially, bright splashes of colour springing up through the cracks between the paved slabs and along the bottom of the walls. Against the faceless brick side wall of whatever that big building was, supported by a tumbledown trellis, an old-fashioned Dorothy Perkins still ramped, thick clusters of frilled rose pink flowers wafting their scent across the yard. A buddleia sprouted improbably from a crack in a wall. It was very quiet, this hidden little corner, warmed at this time of day by the trapped heat of the sun. He saw what she meant by its charm.

'It won't stay like this for long, of course. There's some talk of a parade of shops . . . which brings me to what I want to talk to you about.' She paused and then said, 'Osbert Rees-Talbot was my brother.'

He had of course marked her down several minutes ago as being the aunt Gilmour had spoken of, who'd been so good to his Maisie when she first went to work at Alma House, as well as being the doctor, Kay Dysart's, aunt. Maisie apparently had a great respect and liking for Aunt Deborah, Gilmour had said. Aware of her watching him from under the brim of that peculiar hat, he could understand why she was said to be eccentric – not mad, but a little fey perhaps. He decided to humour her.

'Forgive me, but what has a parade of shops here to do with your brother?'

'Oh, Osbert had nothing to do with this place – that was just an association of ideas. Though Arthur Aston, as far as I know, might well have been amongst those who are wanting to buy it, for the same reason he was wanting to buy Hadley

Piece from us – to make a profit.' She paused and plucked another of the weeds growing near the step on which she was sitting, while looking at him with guileless brown eyes.

'Oh.' He had a feeling this was going to take more than the few minutes she had suggested if he was to make any sense of it. She made him feel large and awkward, looming in front of her as she perched on the steps, so he seated himself at the far end of the one she occupied. 'What or where is Hadley Piece?'

'I thought you might not know,' she said, nodding her satisfaction, and then went on to explain with admirable succinctness, 'It's a run-down, tumbledown old factory. Arthur Aston had been hankering after buying it for ages. It was originally bought by my grandfather, and eventually came to the three of us jointly, to my brothers Hamer and Osbert, and myself. When Mr Aston approached us to buy it, Hamer was quite willing to sell his share. He lives in Malvern, you see,' she added, as if residence in the spa-town was quite enough to explain everything, 'and has no idea what goes on around here – but Osbert and I were dead against it. I'm afraid Mr Aston made rather a nuisance of himself, pestering us to sell, despite our refusals.'

'A tumbledown building? I'm tempted to ask why you refused.'

'He said he wanted it to expand his business, but that was nonsense. The place is practically derelict, goodness knows what it would have cost him to make it usable again. No, he wanted to buy cheap and sell dear. I'm afraid he was not a nice man, Inspector.'

'Ah. But who would want to buy it from him?'

'The council, eventually. Not the building, but the land. They need land to build more homes, and it's in my mind Hadley Piece should be given to them for that purpose.' At his raised eyebrows, she smiled. 'We all – myself, Hamer and Osbert's children, to whom his share has now passed – have more than enough money for our own needs without the necessity for extracting that bit more from what the sale of a white elephant like that would bring. I shall do my best to persuade the others.'

He thought with amusement that her 'persuasions' might well be irresistible. 'Why are you telling me this, Miss Rees-Talbot?'

'None of it matters any more now, of course, unless . . .'
She paused. 'I have to confess, I am concerned why Osbert,
just before he died, for some reason gave in to Aston's pestering
to sell to him, so that in actual fact I was the only one who
was holding out at the end.'

She was not an old woman – in her mid-fifties, he judged
– but that odd, old fashioned get-up made her seem so, until
you looked at her face, which was still youthful. But now, suddenly,
she did look older, and very sad as she sat on the steps, the
willowherb in her hand. Suddenly she asked, 'How many accidental drownings in the bath have you known, Inspector?'

He met her clear gaze gravely. 'Personally, I have never come
across any. The human instinct for survival is very strong. One
would struggle, unless . . .'

'Unless one were handicapped, unable to struggle. Yes, yes.
But you see, Inspector, Osbert was well able to cope with the
loss of an arm. You would have been amazed at what he could
do. I do not believe for one moment that his disability would
have prevented him from saving himself.'

'I understand that his general health wasn't good. It might
have caused him temporarily to lose consciousness.'

'That's possible. He was often in a great deal of pain. But I
don't believe that, either. Let's not beat about the bush . . . it's
clear that when you spoke to my niece and nephew, they didn't
mention this Hadley Piece business to you – probably because
they didn't think it important. But when Margaret told me
about the other – transactions – with Arthur Aston that Mr
Lazenby has discovered . . . well, put together, it seems to me
very much like a case of what I believe is known as blackmail.'

She kept her eyes on him as he thought about what she'd
said. 'You are a very astute lady, Miss Rees-Talbot. So you
must realize there has to be some cause for blackmail.'

'Well,' she said quite sharply, 'Osbert's life, since he was
wounded and came back to live in Folbury, didn't lead to
opportunities for the sort of activities I imagine would give rise
to blackmail. At the same time,' she added sadly, 'I have to
admit there was always something reserved, secretive even, about
my brother. He never revealed himself, not entirely, even as a
boy.'

She stopped, for so long he thought she might be having second thoughts about approaching him with all this.

'Miss Rees-Talbot, is there something more you feel you should tell me?'

'I'm afraid there is. It pains me to say my brother was not a man who would face up to things. He was not a physical coward – far from it, and his military record will prove that. But he would not always face facts. He preferred to walk away, to shut his eyes. I've thought very hard about this . . . maybe he was being made to pay, not for something he did, but something he did not do. A sin of omission, Inspector.'

'I'm not sure I understand.'

She sighed. 'Well, I don't understand either. Have they told you he was writing a book about his army experiences in South Africa – which he abandoned when it was nearly complete? No? It might be a good idea if you asked my niece for a look at it. He must have witnessed many injustices when he was out there fighting – in fact I know that he did, though he would say little about it – and in the end perhaps he was unwilling to acknowledge certain things, until he saw them put down in black and white. Perhaps he was being blackmailed not to mention them? Perhaps Aston was involved in the same thing, and he was being blackmailed, too? Otherwise, why has he been killed?'

The sonorous boom of the parish church clock reminded Reardon he'd planned to be back at the station twenty minutes since. He stood up and shook her hand, dry and papery in his grasp. 'Miss Rees-Talbot, thank you for bringing this to our notice. I won't forget what you've said.' He smiled. 'We could do with someone with your intuition on the Force.'

'It's only common sense.' She too stood up and picked up her parcels. They were numerous but not heavy and she shook her head when he offered to help her with them. 'I'll just leave you with this, Inspector . . . If Osbert did take his own life, it must have been under the greatest provocation. I believe in the end, despite everything, he would never have done that had it not been to protect his family. He would not have committed the ultimate sin, otherwise.'

Twelve

I could get used to this, better than Shanks's pony any day, Joe was thinking as he stepped out of the police car on the opposite side of the road to Aston's workshop on Henrietta Street – though not if it meant being driven by Stringer, the young constable who had come with the car to act as driver. Joe had taken an instant dislike to him, a moaning minnie with a permanent grievance and a constant gripe about why, when he was so keen, had been to grammar school and had a gift for sniffing out suspects, he'd been unaccountably passed over for selection into the ranks of the detectives. Joe could have told him why.

He had barely stepped thankfully out on to the pavement and shut the car door behind him before he heard a reedy voice summoning him: 'You there – policeman! Here a minute.' He turned in the direction of the call and saw a white-haired woman sitting at an open window in one of the houses just behind him, beckoning. 'Policeman!' she called again.

Joe was over the moon that Reardon had succeeded in having him taken off all other duties in order to work with him on this case, but so much for plain clothes and anonymity! He hoped he hadn't developed police plod. More likely it was the hair that made him a target for anyone who thought they could nobble him to find out what was going on. This woman had obviously seen him previously with the other police and remembered. He sighed and walked over to the house.

The warm weather was continuing and the sash window had been thrown up from the bottom. The old woman sat in a chair in front of it, swathed in shawls. Behind her he glimpsed the sad trappings of an invalid's existence: a table with pillboxes and a jug of water, a white counterpane on a brass bedstead that had been brought downstairs for the convenience of those who had to care for her, a helpless old person who had to be helped from bed to chair.

This particular old person, however, though she looked frail, with lines of pain drawn round her mouth and her face leached of all colour, seemed far from helpless. She was briskly knitting a sock on four steel needles, the heel already turned, her hands moving ceaselessly, without the need to look at what she was doing. Her eyes were bright with intelligence. 'Have you caught who did it yet?'

It was what he'd expected and he didn't pretend not to understand. Aston's death was presently the main topic of excited interest in the whole of Folbury, but especially here, in the street where it had occurred. 'Not yet, Mrs . . .?'

'Ibbotson. *Miss* Ibbotson. Gladys. You never came to ask me any questions.'

'Not me personally, no, but I was under the impression everyone in the street had been approached by one of our officers.'

'The rest of them were, but I wasn't so well the day they came round. I'd had to take to my bed that day, so my niece didn't bother me. She tells me they wanted to know if anybody saw anything funny going on.'

'That's right, but if you were confined to bed, Miss Ibbotson—'

'Gladys. Nobody calls me Miss Ibbotson. See, I wasn't in bed, not *then*. Not the day they say it happened, I mean.' Joe felt a quickening of interest. He perched himself on the stone windowsill, where he could talk to her without having to bend down and not raise his voice too much, though there was no chance of being overheard since the street was deserted at the moment. 'I see most things, you know, sitting here,' she went on. 'Nothing else to do but look out and watch folk.'

Day after day, Joe thought, nothing to see but the mundane life in the street: the comings and goings between the various workshops, children running about, bouncing balls against the wall or playing marbles, neighbours setting out to go shopping must provide the sum total of her day's interest. No view except of Aston's workshop, the motor repair place belching out fumes and the tall Victorian brick-built elementary school looming up behind that. 'So what did you see, then, Gladys? Or maybe who?'

'Well, for a start I saw Vincent.'

'Who's Vincent?' He didn't recall any Vincent being mentioned by the two bobbies who'd done the door-knocking, and he'd been looking through the notes they'd made just before he left the station.

'The milkman. Tompkin's lad.' She was enjoying this, spinning it out. 'I had my eye on him because he *will* leave his blessed float right in the middle of the road while he delivers, don't matter how many times he's told he's obstructing other traffic, and I was going to give him a piece of my mind – until it happened. No thought for anybody else, not like his father used to be. It's only a narrow street and if anybody else comes along it causes a right commotion, I can tell you.'

No one else had mentioned the inconsiderate milkman to the police, but then, his arrival was an everyday occurrence, so familiar no doubt that he'd grown to be part of the scenery – and in any case it hardly seemed likely he'd nipped in and shoved Aston down into the sand between delivering pints of milk. 'What do you mean, "until it happened"? What happened?'

'We-ell . . .' Gladys did not intend to be rushed. 'Somebody did want to get past the float – it was a butcher's van, and the driver got mad and started tooting his horn enough to waken the dead. The poor old horse nearly bolted – would've done, I daresay, if Vincent hadn't come back with his churn just in time to grab the reins before he'd fairly got going. But he nearly ran over that woman that was crossing the road, all the same.'

'You didn't say you'd seen a woman as well, Gladys.'

'Didn't I?' She grinned mischievously, showing an unexpected dimple, then sobered. 'Anyway, I hadn't noticed her till then, you know, what with the milk cart in the middle of the road and all the shemozzle it was creating. But she could have come out of the foundry. I don't say she *did*, mind, I didn't actually see her come out, but she could have.'

What people thought they saw at the time of an incident and what they really did see didn't always hang together. Neither did what different people had seen at the same incident always coincide. But Gladys Ibbotson didn't seem like a person who made mistakes.

'Are you sure it wasn't a man?'

'Not unless he was wearing women's skirts.'

'What sort of woman was she then? Old, young, short, tall? Had you ever seen her before?'

Gladys shook her head. 'I don't know. Only saw her for a second or two, out of my eye corner, so to speak, and the milk cart between us. She didn't try to cross the road again, just jumped back sharpish from the horse's hooves and turned and ran round the corner. I think that was why I remembered her, because she ran.'

'What time would this be?'

'Nine o'clock,' Gladys said promptly. 'The school bell had just sounded and everything went quiet in the playground, like it does. I checked my clock with it. Sometimes Muriel forgets to wind it up, and if there's one thing I can't abide, it's a clock that's not right.'

'Did you know Mr Aston, Miss Ibbotson?'

'Gladys. Only by sight. I used to see him, him and that woman that works for him, but I've never had cause to speak to either of them. Very smart chap, I'll say that for him. Always in a nice dark suit and a black bowler. Shoes polished.'

'He used to be in the army.'

'That accounts for it, then.'

'Well, thanks – Gladys. You've been very helpful.' Joe eased himself from the windowsill, ready to go across to Aston's. 'Don't forget to let us know if you recall anything else.'

'Well, you know, I do remember one other thing, now I come to think of it. I don't suppose it'll be any help, but she was wearing a brown coat, that woman.'

'I'll make a note of that.' Maisie had a brown coat. And how many other women in Folbury owned one? Scores, for all Joe knew.

That women could and did murder was hardly news, but it was an intriguing idea, that a woman might have been responsible for killing a big man like Aston. And yet, it wouldn't have needed much physical strength – a push from behind, Aston perhaps winded as he landed in the sand, and then a foot pressed on his neck – a minute or two would have sufficed.

The workshop was in full operation once more, men standing in front of their machines, the screech of grinding and drilling setting Joe's teeth on edge. Straight away he spotted Stanley Dowson, who lifted a hand in recognition but didn't accompany him into the office, where Eileen Gerrity, in a fug of cigarette smoke, was bent over a stack of what looked like invoices. Her coat was hanging on a peg at the back of the door. It was green, a darkish green, unlike the bright emerald shade of her jumper, patriotic to her native Ireland no doubt but a violent contrast to her hair – much more carroty than his own, he noted.

She made no objection to his request to look through the safe once more, and waved him to the desk which Arthur Aston had presumably occupied, after which she left him to get on with it and disappeared. In a few minutes, she returned with a pint mug of tea, which she placed at his elbow.

'Thanks, Eileen. Very welcome.'

'Sugar?' She held out a blue sugar bag with a teaspoon stuck into it.

'Please. I see you're back in business already,' he said, helping himself and then waving the teaspoon towards the activity beyond the glass. From where he sat, he could see every machine on the shop floor. Aston would have been well placed to keep an eye on the men working for him.

'There's no reason not to for the moment,' she said, 'until we know how things are going to pan out. We still have orders to complete, and the chaps need their wages.'

'And after that?'

She shrugged. 'It'll depend on her, on Lily Aston, won't it? Whether she keeps the place going or sells up.' A shade of vindictiveness coloured the way she said it. Maybe it was a sore point that the business would go to Aston's wife – especially if the rumours about Eileen's association with her boss were true and she suspected he hadn't left a will, and that she herself was therefore unlikely to get anything.

When he had first interviewed her, just after Aston's body had been found, Eileen had been in a state of shock. Now she seemed to have recovered what seemed to be her natural bounce and resilience. She was a war widow and needed to work, she had told him then, her husband had been killed on the Western Front – thank God they'd had no children. A well-developed woman who gave off energy like an electric light bulb – even her orangey hair seemed to strike off sparks – she had worked for Arthur Aston ever since the establishment of Aston's Engineering.

Joe remembered what Lily had told him about her husband working late. Unprepossessing as Aston had been, he had not seemed to see that as a bar to approaching women – and from Maisie's testimony, even young girls – and rumour had it that his association with Eileen had been going on for years. Actually, Joe could see the attraction this woman would have had for him – the utter contrast between her and his lacklustre wife. Eileen Gerrity seemed like the sort of woman who would in other circumstances enjoy a laugh, and not be averse to a drink or two, while poor Lily looked as though she would at the best of times have difficulty in summoning up a smile.

He wondered if she had known what was going on, and that was why she had mentioned all those late nights at the office. She hadn't given any signs that she had, but he was beginning to suspect Lily was a dark horse.

'Anything you want to know, just ask,' Eileen said, returning to her desk.

Joe was here to give closer attention than before to the contents of both the safe and Aston's desk, not the sort of task he relished, but previously time hadn't allowed more than a cursory look at what the safe contained. He didn't expect to find anything he'd missed, though, mainly because there was surprisingly little in the way of paperwork. Arthur Aston, or Eileen, or maybe both, had set up a fairly simple accounting system, which seemed to work well enough for them. There had been the usual stuff, he recalled – the wages book, purchase and sales ledgers, invoice files, bank statements, correspondence files – and that had been about it. Eileen kept the figures neatly and Aston's diary was also kept up-to-date by her, though he'd had relatively few appointments, most of them seeming to be with regular clients. Occasionally, beside a customer's name, Aston had made the same sort of cryptic notes he'd written on the back of his chequebook, and that seemed to be all he had needed.

'Where did Mr Aston meet his customers?' he asked Eileen over his shoulder.

Her desk chair was back to back with Aston's, where Joe
was sitting, and she swivelled round to answer. 'Sometimes for
lunch at the Rotary Club, if he thought they were important,
or else at the customer's place, sometimes here.' She laughed
at his raised eyebrows and pointed to the spare chair in the
corner. 'It was as good as anywhere. There wasn't anything
special that I didn't know about.'

'What about his business relationships, were they good?'

She didn't reply for a moment and then she said carefully,
'It wasn't his policy to make enemies.'

'I'm not suggesting it was, but was there anyone who was
dissatisfied with the way he conducted business? Now, or at
any time previously?'

She played with the fountain pen she was holding without
meeting his eyes. 'Well, I can only think of one, but honestly,
if you knew Frank Greenwood . . .'

'Who's he?'

'Greenwood and Bell. They're the carriers we use to pick
up and deliver orders.' He waited. 'Oh, all right. It was Arthur's
– Mr Aston's – practice to go through the statements sent in
once a month with me, and to see what money we had coming
in, what bills we had outstanding, what needed to be paid
straight away and what could run on for another month. He
liked to play about with the accounts, you know. Keeping the
money moving, he called it. Frank Greenwood's normally
pretty easy-going and he didn't usually press for quick payment,
so we'd sometimes let his account go for another month – but
then it got to two months, and when it reached three, he
stormed in here one day and demanded immediate payment
or else . . .' She frowned. 'It took the wind out of Arthur's
sails, but to be fair, I think it was Frank's partner, Charlie Bell,
who was doing the demanding, and he sent Frank because he's
always been the one to deal with us.'

'"Or else"? What did he mean by that?'

'He threatened the law. He tried to get nasty but, well, it
was just a laugh. He's not that sort, not really. If you're thinking
he might have killed Arthur, you're wrong. He couldn't knock
the skin off a rice pudding.'

'What about his partner – Charlie Bell?'

'I don't know about him, I've never met him. But it would seem a funny way of settling a business dispute. And what would he be doing in the foundry, anyway?'

Privately, Joe agreed, but he said, 'That might depend on whether it was an argument that got out of hand.' He thought for a bit. 'OK, apart from that, what about the men working here? Had there been any trouble with any of them? No one sacked recently?'

She shook her head. 'They've all worked here for years – the nine chaps on the machines in here, and the foundry men. Those two have both been laid off quite a bit lately, I'll admit, but they knew Arthur wouldn't have done that if he'd any choice. He was a good boss, you know,' she added after a slight pause. 'He could be a tight-fisted old devil and he wouldn't tolerate slackness or slovenly work, but he was fair.'

'How did you get on with him yourself?'

It was a loaded question and she knew it, but she answered without a blink. 'He was all right. We had a drink or two in the Punch Bowl now and then.'

'OK. Does WIM mean anything to you, by the way?'

She didn't reply, and after a short silence, he repeated, 'WIM. It was written down several times on the back of the firm's chequebook, and on the back of his personal chequebook at home.'

'It was a habit he had, it used to annoy the bejaysus out of me, the way he scribbled over everything.'

'So you've no idea what it means?'

'No.' She picked up her glasses, fiddled with them and finally put them back on. 'No, I haven't.'

'Well, it's nothing that matters, probably.' He pushed his chair back. 'I think that's as far as I can go for now, but we may have to get someone who knows more about these things than I do to check the books over thoroughly – not that we expect any discrepancies, mind,' he added hastily, seeing she might be about to protest. 'Just routine.'

As he was leaving, the green coat hanging behind the door prompted him to ask her what time she started work.

'Half past eight's my starting time, but my bus gets to the end of the street at quarter past, so I'm always here well before that.'

'Then you wouldn't have seen a disturbance out in the road at half past eight, between the milk float and a butcher's van?'

She laughed. 'Vincent, you mean? There's always some rumpus going on about the way he stops in the middle of the road. But no, I wouldn't have seen it, being in here, would I?'

Not for the first time, it struck Joe how claustrophobic the little office was – no windows, and only the shop floor outside the glass. He wondered what it would be like to be working here in the heat of summer, squashed together as everything was. And this reminded him of something else. 'By the way, what can you tell me about Hadley Piece?'

'That old warehouse? What is there to tell?'

'I don't know, but I gather Mr Aston was negotiating to buy it because he needed bigger premises. I can understand why.' He gestured round the little office, a makeshift sort of place if ever he'd seen one. And the machines that occupied the shop floor left no room for more out there, either, if Aston had been thinking on the lines of expansion.

'I don't know anything about that,' she said, though he thought she did.

He left Aston's, and with Gladys's comments still in mind, went along to make enquiries at the other two workplaces on that side of the street.

Thirteen

Binkie Scroope and his wife were alone in the drawing room of their large, first-floor mansion flat in Belgravia. All the furniture in the flat was modern: the last word in blond wood, glass-topped tables, unframed mirrors. It was decorated in tones of oatmeal, cafe au lait and dove grey, a neutral *de rigueur* colour-scheme of the moment, beloved of Opal and her friends. Binkie had not cared enough to raise any objections when it had been chosen – at least it wasn't all dead white, which it might have been – but by now he thought it exceedingly dull. Its blandness was getting on his nerves. He didn't know which was worse – this, or the faded glories of Maxstead.

A letter from his mother had come for him by the afternoon post. He read it through again, then put it back in its envelope, and put the envelope in his pocket, without making any comment. The best way to deal with Maxstead was not to think about it at all.

His lazy eyes surveyed Opal – pretty and spoilt, quite good-natured on the whole, until it came to Maxstead and money. She was lying back in her chair, wearing black satin lounging pyjamas lavishly embroidered at the hems and cuffs, her bandaged leg up on a cushioned footstool, turning over the pages of *Vogue* while simultaneously playing jazz band dance music on the wireless, smoking a cigarette through an amber holder and dipping into the hideously expensive box of Charbonnel et Walker chocolates he had bought her. It was rare, if not unheard of, for them to be spending an evening in, but Opal had tripped over her carelessly dangling evening stole as they returned home in the grey light of morning after a night out and had sprained her ankle and been ordered to rest it.

She was bored beyond tears. It was only three days since it had happened, but incarceration within the four walls of the flat was testing the limits of her endurance and fraying the edges of her temper. Prolonged association with her toddlers was not the unalloyed pleasure it was supposed to be, and she had already had sharp words with Nanny over their behaviour. No one had called to see her since lunch. Worse, it was windy outside, causing a lot of static on the wireless and making it difficult to listen to Harry Roy. The flowers sent by her friends were beginning to wilt in the central heating.

She said fretfully, 'For goodness' sake take those lilies out, Binkie, darling, they're going off. I can't think why Edmé Porter brought them – she knows I've always detested the smell of lilies. Isn't it time for cocktails?'

Binkie left the room, without taking the flowers. He was away some time. She was looking impatiently at the clock when he eventually returned, carrying by its tall stem a single shallow cocktail glass with a twist of lemon and a maraschino cherry. He had changed into his evening clothes, his white silk scarf was slung around his neck, his coat folded over his free arm. She looked at him incredulously as she took the glass from him. 'You're not going *out*, surely? You can't leave me here on my own! Oh, Binkie-Boo!' Her painted cupid's bow mouth turned down discontentedly.

The use of her private pet name for him, employed in this particular situation, left him unmoved. 'Just for an hour or so. You have that new novel to read.'

'Oh, that – it's frightfully overrated. Couldn't be more boring, in fact. I can't get past the first few pages.'

'It's been very well received. Maybe you should give it another try.'

'Oh, rats to that!' Her gaze sharpened. 'You're not . . . you're *not* going to meet that – that man again, are you? You promised!'

'I told you months ago I wouldn't see the fellow again, and I haven't.'

She stared at him and her voice began to shake with temper as she said, 'This is all because I complained about having to go down to Maxstead next week, isn't it? Because I refused to go with you?' He said nothing. 'It is, I know it is.'

He studied her for a moment, then crossed to the little fumed oak desk in the corner that was reserved for her personal use and extracted an opened envelope from one of the pigeonholes. Holding on to it by its corner he fluttered it in the air.

'What . . . what's that?'

'As you know very well, it's your dressmaker's bill.'

'Binkie, you have no right—'

'I have every right – if I'm to find the money to pay this exorbitant amount. Which I assume you expect me to do.' Without raising his voice he went on, 'I have every intention of going down to Maxstead. And you will go with me. And you'll be nice to my mother. Do you hear me?' Their glances met. 'Don't wait up for me, Opal.'

He went out. The door closed behind him, leaving her speechless with rage. Then she picked up *Mrs Dalloway* and hurled it across the room. It hit the big vase of lilies but it wasn't heavy enough to knock it over. She burst into tears.

Leaving the station for home that night, Joe cursed to himself when he saw the elf-like figure of the reporter, Judy Cash, turning the corner from Town Hall Square and dancing towards him. He was further annoyed to find that she had seen him, and to realize retreat would be undignified, if not cowardly; he wasn't good at fending off people like her.

'Sergeant Gilmour, what luck!' She was bright as a button, and began to walk alongside him. 'I was hoping to see someone and get the latest.'

'Then your luck's just run out, Miss Cash, sorry.'

'Oh, Judy, please! Come on!'

'You know very well I can't tell you anything.'

'There isn't anything to tell, that's what you mean, isn't it? You've still no idea why anybody should have killed Arthur Aston?'

'We don't know that anybody did, yet. Anything else is pure speculation. Your paper will be the first to be told if there's anything the public needs to know.'

A number three bus was trundling down Market Street. It wasn't going where Joe wanted, but he could always nip off when it had turned the corner. At danger to life and limb, he jumped on to the platform, grabbing the pole, and swung himself inside. The conductor shouted, 'Oi, you, that's not allowed!' but the bus was already gathering speed. He felt an unmitigated idiot, paying his fare and jumping off at the next stop.

Dearest Plum,

I long to be able to talk to you, but as that isn't possible, this will just have to do.

I had another disappointing encounter with Sergeant Gilmour a couple of hours ago. He won't talk to me at all. I think he's rather frightened of me, which makes me smile. But he's not the only apple in the barrel. I've managed to strike up an acquaintance with a young police constable, not as useful, but he might do.

He's called Dave Pickersgill, and he's a sweetheart, lovely dark eyes with the sort of eyelashes most girls would die for, but rather shy and very earnest. I let him take me out for a drink the other night – it had to be the Shire, of course. Nice girls don't go into public houses. But next time I must think of somewhere else we can meet and talk. 'A bit posh for me, all this,' he remarked, obviously uncomfortable at being in Folbury's best hotel, as if he felt that people would think he was getting above himself, trying to mix with their upper crust. He's quite sweet, really, but I have to say, a bit naive. He knows, of course, that I'm the press and went all red at one point when it dawned on him I might be probing too deeply about the murder. Poor pet, he doesn't realize what he's giving away sometimes by not saying anything. Though I believe him when he says he really doesn't know much; the extent of his involvement so far has been making door-to-door enquiries in Henrietta Street, and that sort of thing, but I shall keep up with him. One never knows what he might pick up and let slip inadvertently. One thing I have learnt: the police already know it was no secret that Arthur Aston could be a fairly nasty piece of work, and they think it probable that someone has taken the law into their own hands to pay him out for something he'd done, which contradicts what Gilmour said. Rough justice, maybe, Plum, but just deserts.

I only hope they don't believe that person could have been Felix. I went to see Lily Aston again, and this time she told me that he'd had a fight with her husband the night before he died, and admitted that she has told the police about it, too. I could scarcely believe he'd been such an idiot. If he'd wanted to, he couldn't have given them better grounds for suspicion. I'm sorry to say he can be a bit of an ass sometimes, in the way clever people often are. Intelligence, but no common sense. He is so immature, for all his age. One can only hope he must wake up one day and allow himself to grow up and be the person he really is inside.

Apparently the police have been asking Lily about the keys to the foundry, which they believe the killer took away, removing all doubt that Aston's death could be regarded as accidental. How careless! But then, we all make mistakes, darling, sometimes. Anyway, it's unlikely they'll be found. It would be a naive killer, wouldn't it, who kept them, rather than throwing them into the Fol or somewhere.

More later.

Fourteen

Joe, in the somnolent three p.m. after-lunch hour of the afternoon, was rereading the files collected for the Aston case.
They'd been worked over so many times without getting
anywhere it was hard to stop himself yawning. PC Pickersgill's
handwriting on the pre-printed forms he'd filled in looked as
though a fly had crawled across the paper, and reading the
laboured, typewritten answers gained from his doorstepping
duties was even more painful. Hadn't he ever heard that ribbons
should be changed before they were threadbare, that the type-
face should be cleaned occasionally and type bars properly
straightened after they'd jammed? The blocked spaces in the
characters, giving the report the appearance of a bad attack of
black spot, began to dance before Joe's eyes.

He went to fetch himself some tea, came back and ploughed
on. It was maddening. Even at that busy hour of the morning
when Aston had died – children going to school, latecomers
rushing off for work – no one on Henrietta Street had admitted
to seeing anything unusual on the morning of the murder,
with the later exception of Gladys Ibbotson. Aston had arrived,
let himself into his foundry and nobody had seen him. But
the houses were 'through' houses, not back-to-back, with the
front parlour facing the street and the kitchen-living rooms at
the back.

Nor was there anywhere on the street where anyone hanging
about waiting for Arthur Aston to arrive could have stayed out
of sight, not with the two Aston workshops, Dunn's Motors
and the nail-making shop occupying the one side, and the row
of terraced houses on the other. The only possible place of
concealment would have been inside one of the workshops,
but the weedy, self-important youth at Dunn's who performed
roughly the same sort of duties as Eileen Gerrity did at Aston's,
plus odd jobs in the workshop, had sniggered at the idea when
Joe had approached him. A woman venturing into Dunn's? he'd

repeated, wiping oily hands on an oily rag. While men were lying on their backs on the floor beneath the vehicles being repaired, with full view of her legs? Not likely, unless she'd been a tart. More sniggers. Joe had likewise drawn blank at the nail-making shop, where a man and his wife worked alone.

That put paid to anyone identifying the woman Gladys had seen, then, and left only the houses, where none of the occupants had any connection with Aston's nor, as far as anyone had been able to ascertain, with Aston himself. He hadn't been a popular man, yet so far they'd come across no one who had enough resentment against him to want him dead – with the possible exception of Felix Rees-Talbot, and Aston's wife, Lily. But even Lily might have decided there was an easier way of getting rid of an unsatisfactory husband than resorting to following him to the foundry and taking such a risky way of killing him – always supposing she'd known he would go straight in there, rather than into his office, anyway.

All this, of course, applied to anyone who might have done the deed. The crime had none of the marks of premeditation: the killer had not come equipped, or even taken advantage of any of the heavy tools lying about – the hammers, files, spades, iron rods and other nameless potential weapons. No weapon had been required. All that had been needed after a sudden shove, or even an accidental fall, into that pile of sand, was pressure to keep him there. A spur of the moment reaction, made in the heat of a quarrel and regretted afterwards, or just simply that an opportunity too good to miss had arisen for someone whose motives had not yet been made apparent.

Joe finished his tea. He was on his own today. Reardon had made a sudden decision and taken himself off on his motorbike to the village near Worcester where the detective inspector, Micklejohn, who'd been in charge of the original Snowman case, was settling into a small cottage with a shed in the garden for his racing pigeons; a nice place where he and his wife hoped to spend their retirement.

Joe stifled another yawn. He rocked back on his chair, sucking his pencil and contemplating the lists again. There was only one house on Henrietta Street where no one had been at home, either on that first door-to-door enquiry, or at the subsequent follow-up. He let the chair fall back on to its four legs. Since he couldn't see any further way forward at the moment, it seemed like a good idea to take a break, wake himself up, use his initiative and have another go to see if he could catch anyone at home.

This time he didn't make use of the official car, less out of any consideration for the cost of petrol to the police than a reluctance to face yet another of Stringer's complaining monologues. Instead, he hopped on a bus which took him up Victoria Road, to a stop within yards of Henrietta Street. There was still no reply to his knock at number eighteen. He put his hands either side of his face to try to peer into the front sitting room, but heavy lace curtains at the window prevented him from seeing anything of the room inside.

He walked further along to Gladys Ibbotson's house. This time the sash window where she had been sitting was closed and similar lace curtains to those at the other house were drawn across. In answer to his knock the door was opened by a tired-looking young woman in bedroom slippers and a flowered, crossover pinafore. Her first words after he had introduced himself and enquired for Miss Ibbotson confirmed his guess that she was Muriel Hollins, Gladys's niece. 'I'm sorry,' she said, 'they took Auntie Gladys into hospital yesterday.'

'Nothing too serious, I hope?' He was concerned. He'd liked Gladys.

She sighed. 'No more serious than usual. She's always in and out, poor old duck. Chest infection this time.' She looked curiously at him. 'What did you want her for?'

'We've been trying to get hold of the people at number eighteen, but they're very elusive and I thought she might be able to give me some help as to when I could find them at home. She seems to know everything that happens on the street.' He looked at her speculatively. 'Maybe you can help?'

'I don't know about that, but you'd best come in.' She led the way along a narrow hallway, past a steep, narrow flight of stairs and into the large kitchen-living room at the back, filled with too much furniture, some of it no doubt cleared from the front room to make way for auntie's bed. There was a warm smell of baking, a pie cooling on a tray and a large pot of tea already made, a mug and *Woman's Weekly* on the table next to it. She indicated a chair by the table and fetched a flowery patterned cup and saucer from a cupboard, polished it with a tea towel, poured tea into it and passed it over to Joe, taking the opportunity to refill her own mug. 'You've come at the right time. There's just half an hour before the kids come in from school and then it'll be Bedlam, little monkeys.' She smiled fondly. 'How can I help?'

'It won't take that long.' Joe was sorry he'd intruded into what was evidently a snatched precious half-hour or so to herself before the advent of her children – two boys and a girl, by the photos on the mantel – clamouring for their tea and her attention. 'Who lives at number eighteen?'

'I can't tell you their name. A married couple, I think they are. They came here – oh, about six months since, or maybe more, but they keep theirselves to theirselves, you hardly ever see them, especially her. They'll use their back door, anyway, like we all do.' He looked out of the window overlooking a small back yard with an outdoor privy and a washhouse that obscured the view of the alley beyond, which the backs of similar houses in the next street would face. 'I don't think anybody's seen either of them for ages.'

Another blank, Joe thought, but he was interested.

'You could try Wilfred's. Wilfred Smith. He keeps the corner shop and his sister Eva helps. He owns number eighteen and three others on the street as well. His dad bought them as they came empty, when they were going cheap. Like father, like son! I reckon the old man meant them for his family when they married, but none of them ever have. Well, chance'd be a fine thing for *her*, old Vinegar Face.'

Joe grinned. Maybe the sharp observation was a family inheritance, or maybe she'd just picked it up from her Auntie Gladys. Either way, it was honest. He stood up. 'Looks as though that should be my next port of call, then. I'll leave you in peace and pop along now to have a word with Mr Smith.'

'And the best of luck!'

'Thank you for your help – and for the tea, Mrs Hollins, you make a good cup. I hope your auntie will soon be well again.'

'Oh, she will, it'll take more than that. She'll always come back, as she says, like a bad penny,' she told him with a smile.

They were so comically alike they couldn't be anything but twins, Wilfred Smith and his sister Eva, even to the side parting in their greying hair. She wore hers slightly longer, cut in a straight bob and clamped to her head with a fierce hair grip, and he had on a brown smock and she a button-through overall in intimidating black. Apart from that, it would have been difficult to determine their sex.

As the shop bell tinkled, the two stocky figures turned in unison to inspect the new entrant. Eva had been attending to the rows of tins displayed on the shelves and stayed where she was, duster in hand, while Wilfred leaned forward with his hands on the counter, but there was no mistaking the hostility on their faces. Encountering their unwelcoming stares, he wondered if everyone received this sort of reception – hardly customer-friendly – or if it was just because they remembered him, as Gladys had done, as one of the police. He hadn't been the one to question them when the enquiry started, but he'd slipped in to buy cigarettes and he'd been in uniform then.

Neither of them had reportedly seen anything unusual on the day of the murder, but they had neglected, most likely in the spirit of uncooperativeness that seemed to come naturally to them, to mention the absence of their tenants at number eighteen. He showed them his badge, told them why he was there and that he would like to speak to them in private. Would they prefer to go into the back?

'We can't leave the shop,' Smith said stolidly.

Joe went to the door and turned the 'Open' sign to 'Closed'. Selling anything from firelighters and scouring powders to humbugs and boiled ham, the shop was no doubt what was known as 'a little goldmine' and a missed customer or two wouldn't be the end of the world. 'Anybody wants anything urgent, they'll come back,' he remarked, ignoring the cluck of indignation from the sister. 'Now then . . . number eighteen. I understand you are the owner, Mr Smith.'

'It's no secret,' Wilfred said.

'Why didn't you tell our officers that, or inform them your tenants were away when they called round – twice?'

'Didn't think it mattered. They couldn't have seen anything anyway, if they were away, could they?'

'It's wasted police time, so I'd advise you to make up for it now. Firstly, what was their name?'

'Morris,' he admitted reluctantly.

'Christian names?'

'Don't know. That's all I needed to put on his rent book.'

'How long have they been gone?'

Wilfred shrugged. 'I don't keep track of their movements. Three or four months?'

'That's a long time. What about their rent?'

'They paid six months in advance. The next's not due yet.'

'Six months?' Joe was flabbergasted, until he thought, well, the rent for a house like that couldn't be much – a few bob a week, maybe—

'Fifteen-and-six,' Smith supplied before he could ask, and in case the sergeant should faint with the shock, added defensively, 'It *was* furnished.' A quick glance at Joe's face and he decided to be more forthcoming. 'It was Old Dick lived there, see, Dick Heath. When he died, I got sick of asking his relatives to clear out the house, but they wouldn't bother, said it was all junk anyway and to give it away if I couldn't sell it. It was better to rent the house furnished than to pay to have the stuff taken away.'

All the same, he must have thought his birthday had come when he succeeded in renting it, Joe reflected: the demand for furnished property in Folbury, even low-grade property like this, was practically non-existent. It was easy to see why no questions had been raised about the absence of someone who was willing to pay that much rent in advance. 'Tell me about these tenants.'

'What do you want to know all this for? They couldn't have had anything to do with that business over the road if they haven't been back for so long.'

'Didn't that strike you as odd? That they'd pay to rent a house and then not use it? Come on, you must have wondered. Where did they come from? What were they doing here? What were they like?'

Wilfred Smith shrugged and was silent.

Eva Smith said suddenly, speaking for the first time: 'They're not from round these parts, they talk lah-di-dah. Swanky.'

Then what were they doing here, living in Henrietta Street? Where the houses were not yet wired for electricity and the lav was outside at the back? Joe was beginning to get a tingle. 'Presumably you have a spare key?'

After several moments' hesitation, Wilfred Smith went into the back premises and returned with one, which he reluctantly handed over. 'I want it back, mind.'

'Thanks, I'll see you'll get it,' Joe said, leaving the shop, not forgetting to turn the sign back to 'Open' again as he did so.

On reflection, he decided not to go into number eighteen before letting Reardon know this further development, and was relieved to find he had already returned when he got back to the station. However, having listened to what Joe had to report, he said rather disappointingly that there was no rush to go back there that day. 'We'll get over there first thing tomorrow. I'd like to have a look-see for myself.'

This time, they went to Arms Green in the car, with Stringer as chauffeur, but at least Reardon's presence in the back ensured a merciful silence from him. When they reached Henrietta Street he was forced to settle his resentful presence with a newspaper when told to wait for them.

Number eighteen had a musty, unpleasant and airless smell when they pushed open the front door. Smith hadn't been wrong in saying he would have had to pay someone to get rid of the furniture in the front room: you could see at a glance it was the sort of stuff nobody wanted today – heavy, dark mahogany Victorian pieces in the front room, probably passed down by the parents of Old Dick, the previous tenant; never expensive, even when new, but solid and well made, though overwhelming and oppressive for present-day tastes. A thick film of dust lay over everything, dead flies littered the windowsill, and a fly paper descending from the gas light was loathsomely black with insect corpses. The kitchen was worse, the smell disgusting. Reardon muttered, 'Bloody hell!' Joe thought the same idea might be crossing both their minds.

With mounting apprehension at what they might find, they began a search of the rest of the house, the two bedrooms, where the wardrobe and drawers were empty of clothes – or anything else – the small, bare attic and the smaller coal cellar. They found absolutely nothing. All signs of occupation had disappeared and it seemed obvious that the house had not just been temporarily vacated, it had been abandoned, most likely in a hurry. A half-eaten and now fossilized sandwich, possibly ham, had been left by the kitchen sink, which might account for the flies. Another fly paper, this time drawing-pinned to the ceiling, hung in here, too. Cobwebs swung across the corners. There was a sour smell of mice. But no dead body, as Joe had half-expected.

'Seems like a wild goose chase.' They had better call it a day.

Joe was already at the front door when he was halted by a call from the kitchen. He returned and saw that Reardon, in a last look around, had spotted a small drawer set underneath the unscrubbed deal top of the kitchen table. He had pulled it open and was rifling through what looked like decades-old, might-one-day-come-in-useful detritus – a miscellany of old keys, bits of wound-up string, odd screws, a broken comb; some thrifty soul had even saved a few old paper bags . . .

He had unearthed what appeared to be a rent book lying amongst the paper bags. On the front cover Joe saw the name Morris: the paid-up rent book, a final confirmation that the tenants had not intended to return. A used envelope with a shopping list on the back fell out as it was opened. He turned it over and pointed to the stamp on the envelope. It was South African, and the postmark was Cape Town.

Joe gave a low whistle, then took a look at the scrawled address. He stared at it for several moments before realizing what he was seeing. Wilfred Smith had obviously heard the name 'Morris' when making out the rent book and his new tenant hadn't corrected the spelling when he had written it down. The envelope was addressed to Wm. Mauritz.

Yet looking even more closely, he saw it was not Wm., as he'd first thought, the usual abbreviation for William, but Wim – though that could possibly be an abbreviation for the

same name. For a moment or two longer, he stared. Wim.
WIM.

'That's what Aston wrote against all those dates, sir. Not
initials for something, it was a name.'

His mind was racing. Wim Mauritz. Foreign. Continental
sounding. Dutch? There were a lot of families of Dutch origin
in South Africa. The original Boers had been Dutch. Would
anyone around here have recognized a South African accent?
Probably not. Joe knew he wouldn't. Anyone originating from
outside the radius of the Black Country was regarded as 'a
foreigner' and their accents as posh. Maybe theirs hadn't sounded
that different to British upper class – 'lah-di-dah', as Eva Smith
had described it.

Reardon listened in silence. 'Well, we won't start counting
chickens just yet, but it's possible we might have a breakthrough.
Could be we've found your Snowman. We need to talk this
through.' He looked at the table, stained and sticky with God
knew what, and the two dusty chairs drawn up to it, and
glanced further round the room, but not for long. His eyes
coming to rest on the unsavoury remains of the sandwich,
green with mould, the obscene fly paper, he made a moue of
disgust. 'But not here. This place is only short of Miss Havisham
in her wedding veil. Let's get somewhere we can breathe, for
God's sake.'

Was the body of the Snowman that of Wim Mauritz? It was
hard to believe now that it could be anyone else. The evidence
was mounting, the 'coincidences' becoming too many to ignore:
an unidentified dead man found with a South African shilling
in his pocket and brass swarf embedded in his boot soles; a
South African, now missing, who had been living in Henrietta
Street with Aston's machine shop only a few strides away . . .

The cumbersome business of tracing this Wim Mauritz
through the South African Police would have to be set in
motion, Reardon reminded himself, to provide the final proof.
Meanwhile . . .

'Three dead men,' he said.

'Three?'

He had drawn his triangle again, this time with Osbert

Rees-Talbot at the top. 'I'm not suggesting that he – Rees-Talbot – was murdered,' he said, digging his pencil on the name, 'but we can't rule him out of the equation. Those loans to Aston. Can you believe his gratitude would extend to paying out for the rest of his natural? Once, maybe, to help him start his business. But then, to start again, after so many years – cash payments, plus the Hadley Piece premises?'

'Which all started after the arrival of Mauritz.'

'Or at any rate after he rented Henrietta Street.' Reardon fell silent. He kept coming back to that strange conversation he had had with Deborah Rees-Talbot about her brother. Sins of omission! It wasn't a concept he'd ever had reason to consider, and he wasn't sure whether to put much credence to it, yet now he kept wondering. Omission, commission. They said, didn't they, that it wasn't the things you had done in your youth that you'd regret in later life, but those you hadn't. On the other hand, Reardon could think of a few things he'd done that he'd prefer to forget. The thought of Miss Rees-Talbot reminded him that he hadn't yet asked her niece if he could see what her father had been working on just before he died.

'Sir?' The sergeant's voice cut into his thoughts. He pulled his mind back to the present discussion.

'Just thinking, Gilmour. How it all leads back to South Africa, when Rees-Talbot and Aston were serving there. Maybe something happened that gave Aston the hold he had over his former officer. If so, it must have been something pretty damning, all things considered. Look at it for a minute. Say the man Mauritz somehow learns about it – never mind what or how for the minute – and comes over here to join in and demand his share, teams up with Aston. The pressure on Rees-Talbot is increased, until finally it becomes intolerable, he's had enough, says to hell with them all and takes the only way out he can see. No more golden eggs – the goose that laid them is gone. No point in Mauritz hanging around after that. But he does. Until he gets himself killed. Murdered and shovelled into the ground.'

'Who by? Aston? And if it was him, why?'

'Falling out among thieves isn't unknown. Except it's only a guess that Mauritz knew either of them. Apart from the swarf on his boot soles, of course. And the fact that they were living practically opposite Aston's workshops. He – and his wife. Now here's a thought – why did she never come forward to say he was missing? Odd, to say the least. Unless she did him in herself.'

'A woman, getting him out there, and burying him at the edge of the woods? Heck, I doubt I'd have attempted to dig a grave with the ground as hard as it was, sir, never mind a woman!'

'She could if she'd had an accomplice. If, say, she and Aston did it together. He had a car, remember, he could easily have driven Mauritz's body out to Maxstead and buried him.'

'Why?' Joe asked again. 'I mean, why Mrs Mauritz? What reason could she have had for killing her husband?'

'Since we don't know anything about either of them yet, there's no telling – but for what it's worth, I'm not inclined to bet on it that she did. For one thing, Mauritz was hit pretty damn hard on the head, several times according to the autopsy, and with some strength. It would depend on the woman, of course. I've seen plenty of women I wouldn't like to encounter on a dark night and Mrs Mauritz may have been built like a prize fighter for all we know. But if Aston did kill her husband, that still leaves the question of who killed *him*.'

'It's not impossible, is it, supposing she knew or suspected it was Aston who'd bashed her husband's skull in, that Mrs Mauritz might have gone after Aston for that? If so, she took her time. Mauritz died before Christmas.'

'Waiting for the right opportunity, maybe.'

It was possible, of course it was. An easy crime for a woman to commit. The woman Gladys Ibbotson had seen running away? *Away* from Henrietta Street. Possibly for ever.

'If that's what happened – but it's a big if. We're guessing, Gilmour. And if she *is* our lady, and she's any sense at all, she's on her way back to South Africa, across the other side of the world.'

He leaned back and his eye fell on this week's *Herald,* which some fool had placed on his desk, open at the exact place Joe had been hoping the DI wouldn't see. Reardon picked it up.

'The police would like to interview a woman who was seen

in the vicinity of the Henrietta Street premises of Aston Engineering at nine a.m. on the tenth of April, the day Mr Arthur Aston was found dead. Mr Vincent Tompkins who was delivering milk, has reported seeing a woman run across the road, causing his horse to rear up and plunge to one side. "Daisy's not a nervous horse, but the woman ran directly in front of her," Mr Tompkins said. "She was lucky I was there to grab hold, or she would have been run down." The woman is thought to have been wearing a brown coat and—'

At this point, a tap on the door was followed by Pickersgill, attempting with some success to push the door open with one hand while carrying in his other two full mugs of tea by their handles and not spilling any. He was just in time to catch the end of Reardon's fury as he flung the newspaper from him. 'What the devil does the woman think she's up to?'

Tea slopped out of the mugs and spread across the desk as the constable put them down too quickly. His face as he spluttered apologies had turned crimson. Reardon gave an exasperated grunt and quickly shoved a pile of files out of the way, while Joe reached for the fold of blotting paper on the desk, jerked his head as a signal for the constable to make a hasty exit, and began to mop up the mess. Pickersgill fled. The telephone rang.

It was Reardon's boss from Dudley, Detective Chief Superintendent Cherry, no doubt wanting to know what progress was being made. As Reardon listened, he mouthed, 'Leave that,' to Joe, who picked up the half-empty mugs, grabbed the offending newspaper, and left the office.

He found the young constable at the front desk, assiduously immersing himself in the night's occurrences noted in the report book, his ears red. He tapped him on the shoulder. 'Next time you think of chatting to Tinkerbell here' – he tapped the newspaper – 'keep your lips buttoned. She's running rings round you, lad.'

He saw his guess had been correct. Pickersgill had turned round, but was looking anywhere except at him, clearly wishing for nothing more than to find a crack in the floor to crawl through. 'Sarge, I . . . Sarge . . .'

'Pack it in before Reardon cottons on. He's not a fool even

if you are. No harm done as it happens, but she ain't worth your job, Dave.'

When he returned to the inspector's office, Reardon had simmered down and was disposing of the sodden blotting paper. 'Clumsy young clot,' he remarked as he tossed it into the waste paper basket.

'He's all right, sir. Doesn't know his arse from his elbow sometimes, but he's OK.'

Reardon grunted a laugh. 'All right, if you say so. Where were we?'

'Maxstead.' Joe didn't mention the newspaper and Reardon had evidently decided to ignore it.

'I fancy I'd like to take to look at where Mauritz's body was found,' he said, adding after a moment, 'You wondered the other day, why Maxstead, didn't you?'

'I suppose I did. Just a passing observation – though actually, if you wanted to bury a body not too far out of Folbury and went in that direction, you'd be hard put *not* to bury it on Maxstead land. The Scroopes own half the county, or very nearly.'

'That's what Micklejohn told me.'

So far, Reardon hadn't seemed to feel it necessary to volunteer any account of his meeting with the man who had been in charge of the Snowman investigation. At the time, Joe, as one of the uniforms at Folbury, had only been co-opted to help with the routine enquiries of the case – but he'd heard a few grumbles from the detectives whom Micklejohn had brought in with him. He sensed there'd been a feeling that the enquiry had been sloppy, that the DI hadn't been keen to push it further when the enquiries had threatened to grind to a halt. He wondered if Reardon had picked up on the fact that he had been a bit too overanxious to wrap it up before he retired. It had been a frustrating case, and Micklejohn quite obviously hadn't been sorry to see the back of it, despite leaving behind him an unsolved investigation.

Reardon said abruptly, 'He believes the Scroopes wanted it hushed up. Was that the general feeling?'

Joe considered. 'A family like that . . . yes, I reckon it was. They just wouldn't have been able to stomach the idea of their name being connected with anything of that sort, would they? Mud sticks.' He was rather taken aback that Micklejohn should actually have said that to Reardon; at the time, he'd dismissed any idea that privilege should influence the matter either way.

'You recall who found the body, Sergeant?'

Cracking a knuckle, Joe searched his memory. 'Wasn't it the gamekeeper, out with his dogs?'

'He wouldn't like being called that, I suspect. Colonel Frith, according to Micklejohn, is Lady Maude's land agent, the chap that administers the estate.'

'Oh? *He* was the one who found him?' Joe had forgotten the name, and not being a country boy, distinctions between gamekeepers and land agents didn't mean enough to have registered with him. Though he'd no doubt they would be important to Colonel Frith. He remembered *him* all right – the chap who'd been with Lady Maude that day when Joe had visited her to tell her the enquiry was being suspended. Stiff sort of fellow, like the dowager herself. Between them they'd made his hackles rise. He liked to think he didn't have the sort of chip on his shoulder some folk had against the gentry, but a cynical question had occurred to him at the time: would the same casual acceptance of the police having been unsuccessful in finding anyone to blame for the murder have applied if they'd failed to catch anyone poaching pheasant or stealing trout?

'I'm glad the matter has been resolved satisfactorily at last,' her Ladyship had said, after he'd told them the enquiries were suspended. 'Thank you, Sergeant, for letting us know. A storm in a teacup after all.'

The worlds of Lady Maude and Joe Gilmour were a long way apart, and he had no desire to close the gap if she could describe any man's death as a storm in a teacup. 'It hasn't been resolved, unfortunately, merely put in abeyance.'

'Oh, quite.'

She had actually looked disconcerted for a moment and it had given him a small satisfaction to know he had shown himself not suitably put in his place.

Reardon said now, after a long silence, 'Hindsight's a wonderful thing. Micklejohn probably did the best he could with what he had. All the same, I can't see it would hurt to have another word or two with those out at Maxstead.' He twiddled a pencil. 'It's a rum do, all this – posh folks at one end of the scale, Arthur Aston at the other, and the Rees-Talbots in between. Not to mention our friends from the other side of the world. What's between them all is what I'd like to know.'

Of course, there was shortly to be a marriage between the Rees-Talbots and the Scroopes, and the obvious links between the elder Rees-Talbot and Aston had been established, but to Joe, any connection between Rees-Talbot's erstwhile batman and the family at Maxstead was as impossible to envisage as Lily's crocheted cushion covers decorating the antique furniture there.

Having obtained from Margaret Rees-Talbot the neatly typed manuscript of the booklet her father had been writing about the Second Boer War, Reardon took it home with him to read that night. It didn't take long, and left him with mixed feelings.

Her father had written of the military engagements he'd fought in, though without specifically mentioning his own involvement in them. The rest of the manuscript was written in an oddly perfunctory way that to Reardon's mind would certainly not rouse any excitement in military historians – or even in a wider public. To most of the world, anyway, it had been a war between the British and the Dutch settlers and, bloody as it was (not only in the fighting but in the enteric fever that had killed more soldiers than enemy guns had), it had been eclipsed in many ways by the infinitely bloodier world war which had followed not much more than a decade later.

It had, however, not been the battles or the extent of the deadly fever that roused Rees-Talbot to eloquence, but the British scorched earth policy that had ultimately ended the war but left the Boer settlers without their farms and driven them from their lands. It had forced their womenfolk to become refugees – after which they were herded into what became known as concentration camps, where the conditions were so horrific that thousands of women and children perished. It was evident where his sympathies had lain, but much of what he had written, even so long after the conflict, would not have been welcomed in Britain, had it ever been published. To have been labelled 'pro-Boer' would have damned the book before it ever saw the light of day.

Rees-Talbot himself had in fact had second thoughts about publishing what he'd written, his daughter had told Reardon, when, not without protest, she had handed over the manuscript. 'Why on earth does my Aunt Deborah think this will be of any use?'

'I can't say that until I've read it.'

And having done so, he still couldn't. It didn't appear to throw any light on anything that might have given rise to Rees-Talbot's blackmail.

> *Dearest Plum,*
>
> *I must tell you what happened yesterday. About five o'clock, I bumped into Felix amongst the crowd who had just come out of the railway station. He was walking towards Alma House and as I was going that way too, I walked along with him.*
>
> *I saw immediately that he looked different – same old jacket and flannel bags, his hair still badly in need of a cut, still sloping along in the same loose-limbed way that made it difficult for me to keep up with him, but I had an odd fancy that he held himself straighter, and he was certainly looking flushed and elated, and his eyes were just blazing. He didn't say anything about where he'd been, or why, and I didn't ask, but after a while I could see he was dying to tell me. We were passing the park gates and all of a sudden he grabbed my arm, propelled me inside and threw himself down on the nearest bench. 'Sit down a minute, I've something to tell you.'*
>
> *He has got himself a job! Yes, really. With the TUC, working in their London offices!*
>
> *I must have looked astonished. Well, he hadn't spent three years at Cambridge reading law for nothing, he said with a grin, though he wasn't expecting to be anything but a dogsbody at first in this new job – or at least, he would be if he could take up the offer by the end of the week. Otherwise . . .*
>
> *His face fell. He might not be allowed to leave Folbury, he*

admitted at last, because he had got himself into a scrape with the police. And so, the whole story . . .

'Though not a word of that must go into that paper of yours,' he said, suddenly recollecting to whom he was speaking, grabbing my wrist tight. 'Promise?'

After a moment's hesitation, I promised – but don't read anything into that, Plum.

He opened a new pack of cigarettes and lit one, which seemed to give him the courage to tell me the details of how the fight had happened. It seems Felix found out that Arthur Aston had been blackmailing his father, went to Aston's house and picked a fight with him. They actually came to blows, but he'd done nothing more than knock Aston down before his wife came in and the fight stopped. I didn't say that I already knew about this from Lily, and that the morning after, Aston had been found dead and, hey presto!, Felix is the chief suspect.

Well, of course, it's ridiculous. I know Felix couldn't have done it, and if the police think he did they have a long way to go yet, but he's by no means convinced they think the same, or that they have finished with him. And as I pointed out to him, it's going to look even more suspicious that he's suddenly decided to take a job away from Folbury.

'What made you go for the job, anyway?' I asked him. 'What made you do it?' I had a good idea, of course, but I needed to hear him say it.

He didn't want to say anything about why he'd decided until I prompted him: 'They tell me you've resigned from your WSG, Felix.' Though resigned seems a grandiose word for simply walking out of the meeting and leaving behind all the waffle and bad feeling. I hadn't been attending their meetings lately – they're a ridiculous waste of time – but I'd heard about the row. 'The group will fall apart now.'

He made a wry face. 'Truth is, it was never much together, was it? Oh, I know, they'll say I'm a traitor to the cause, et cetera, et cetera, but I hope I can do much more good in the end . . . You know Bobby Armstrong's left as well? It was he who put in a good word for me at the TUC. He's going there, too.'

Well, the fact that Bobby was leaving didn't surprise me.

He's a hothead from the Durham coalfields, with a chip on his shoulder the size of an oak tree about working conditions up there — and though I have every admiration for his sincerity, I do wonder how he'll get on at the TUC. He's convinced the union top dogs sold the rank and file down the river over the General Strike settlement.

We talked about him, and the new job, for some time, then I asked, 'Have you told Vinnie Henderson?'

'Not yet.'

'If you want to marry her, don't you think she has the right to know?'

'Well, maybe I don't want to marry her, not now.'

After that, he went silent. I thought he was sulking, but after a while he said, 'I can't make you out, Judy Cash.'

'I can't make myself out, most of the time. I don't know why I do the things I do.'

'All the same, nothing stops you. You always know just where you're going.'

'I must have what I want, if that's what you mean. You know that, don't you?'

It was very quiet in the park, that time of day. Most people were at home, having or preparing their tea. Beyond the gates, I could hear the noise of motor traffic, the rumble of a cart, but in the park there was silence. You could have heard a leaf drop.

'And we both know what we want, don't we, Judy?'

I held out both my hands and after a while he took them, and after that . . . well, you don't need to know about after that, my darling Plum.

Fifteen

The following afternoon, Joe and Reardon were driven out to Maxstead Court. On Joe's previous visit, since there were no buses out this way, he had cycled. It was quite a distance but he had been pleased to find it hadn't taxed his staying powers overmuch. This time, they arrived in style. Given the option, Stringer would have driven down the tree-lined drive and swept ceremoniously up to the front door, but Reardon stopped him short of the house by a couple of hundred yards while he and Joe got out of the car and proceeded on foot down the double avenue of trees towards the big house set four-square in front of them.

The contrast with Henrietta Street couldn't have been greater. This was gracious living. Set in acres of lawn against a heavily wooded backdrop was a grey stone house, scarcely a mansion, but certainly large, flat-faced except for two bays flanking the front door on either side, slightly intimidating behind gravel paths and a parterre of severely geometric flowerbeds, bare of bedding plants as yet, that did nothing to soften the heavy grey outlines of Maxstead Court.

A tall man of soldierly aspect and a dumpy, middle-aged woman dressed in dark colours were standing at the foot of the wide flight of steps to the main door.

'You're the one who's met the dowager before, but let me take this, Sergeant,' Reardon murmured as they neared the couple.

'Right, sir.'

Had she answered the door to him, Reardon would have taken her for the housekeeper or someone employed in some other similar capacity. As it was, she was the first to speak, removing all doubt. It was Joe she addressed, whom she obviously recognized from his previous visit. 'Sergeant . . . Gilmour, isn't it?' she uttered as they got within speaking distance, showing admirable recall; there had been barely a hesitation. 'What can we do for you this time?'

The royal 'we', like Queen Victoria. Come to think of it, she was not unlike that royal personage. She was the same size, the greying hair drawn back into a tight bun, and she had the same unamused look and commanding manner. She inclined her head graciously when Joe introduced Reardon. He had expected a different response when he told her that their business was to reopen a discussion about the dead man found on her land, but she didn't flinch on hearing it and invited them to enter the house.

The man beside her immediately prepared to take his leave, but she detained him. 'Please stay, Giles. This is my land agent, Colonel Frith,' she told Reardon.

'I believe it was you who found the body, sir.'

'I did.'

'In that case, it would perhaps be as well if you did stay. You may be able to help us.'

Frith didn't look too pleased, but evidently saw he had no option, and when Lady Maude led the way inside he followed, stiffly upright. Reardon tried not to let his private prejudice against men who kept their military rank after they had left the army get in the way, though from his demeanour it wasn't difficult to see that Frith disliked taking orders from those he evidently still looked on as the lower ranks.

The wide oak door opened on to a vast, cold and empty hall with a stone-flagged floor, dim portraits frowning down from the upper reaches and a ceiling disappearing into the ether, where every word echoed and reverberated. Fortunately they passed through this into what her Ladyship referred to as the 'snug', a sitting room that perhaps also served as some sort of office. It was amply furnished with books, easy chairs and a desk holding several ledgers and files, a comparatively small room made to seem even smaller by the echoes of Victoriana in the heavy furniture, the crimson wallpaper, and the bottle-green plush covering a round table.

It was all comfortably shabby in the way these old, inherited houses tended to be, but Reardon didn't make much of this; in the present climate many aristocratic families living in country houses like this one were on a downward spiral. He admired the savoir faire that enabled such owners to carry on as usual despite death-watch beetle behind the panelling and crippling debts due to estate taxes and death duties. He couldn't begin to envisage what unimaginable sum it might cost to run and keep up a place like this. A surround of the brocaded wallpaper behind a picture showed considerably lighter than the rest of the wall, plainly indicating that a larger and perhaps more valuable one had once hung there.

Lady Maude seated herself behind the desk and graciously indicated facing chairs, while Colonel Frith chose to stand to attention by her side, his hands clasped behind his back, a remote expression on his face as if to say all this had nothing to do with him.

It was that which made Reardon decide to start with him, but before he could do so, tea for four appeared on a silver tray which the maid who brought it placed on the plush-covered table. As far as he was aware no one had ordered tea, yet here it was as if conjured up by telepathy. Lady Maude removed herself from behind the desk and graciously presided over the pouring as if it were a tea party, though it was just tea, no fancy cakes or cucumber sandwiches, not even a biscuit.

'I have to tell you that there have been further developments, a possible identification—' he began, but was again interrupted before he could go any further when the door was opened by a young man, accompanied by a female fashion plate in a short, rose-coloured dress trimmed with black braid.

'Oh tea, how topping!' she exclaimed, coming forward. 'Binkie, naughty boy, has walked me round the garden until I'm simply *exhausted.*'

'Bit early for tea, isn't it?' her companion asked Lady Maude.

'Not now, Julian. Tea will be at the usual time.' Presumably when the cucumber sandwiches would be served: however mysteriously it had appeared, this tea was clearly not for the family. Lady Maude smiled, but with a steely glint in her eye that clearly indicated a dismissal, yet Julian chose to stay, even when she told him who the visitors were.

Frith saw fit to add, curtly, 'They are here about the body found under the snow, Sir Julian. It seems they now know who he was.'

Reardon opened his mouth to say this wasn't at all certain,

but was prevented when the young woman gave a little gasp and exclaimed dramatically, 'Oh not that frightful business again! Binkie, darling, I feel – I think I may be going to faint.' She leaned on his arm. 'If I could just sit down . . .'

Drooping decoratively, enveloping Reardon in a wave of expensive scent as they passed him, she was led to a seat by a seemingly unconcerned Binkie.

'Here, Opal, drink this.' Lady Maude, equally unsympathetic, handed her the cup of tea she had just poured. To Reardon, she said, waving a hand, 'My son, Sir Julian, and his wife.'

The young Lady Scroope was quite exquisite, in a china doll, porcelain skin, peaches-and-cream sort of way, notwithstanding the plucked eyebrows, sharply shingled golden hair, and a petulant mouth. Despite the faintness, her cheeks remained pink and her slim, delicate hands took the china cup and held it quite steady.

'My wife,' said Sir Julian, 'hasn't been well.'

'So silly. I sprained my ankle,' explained Opal in tragic tones.

She was making a meal of it, Reardon thought, especially since the ankle in question was unbandaged and she was wearing a pair of fancy shoes with three-inch heels. Had she been genuinely shocked by the announcement, was it a diversionary tactic, or simply attention seeking? The latter, probably. She had every appearance of one of those spoilt women who thrived on being the centre of whatever was going on.

As for Sir Julian himself, this fellow with his butter-coloured hair and languid appearance, there was no resemblance whatsoever to his brother, the Reverend Symon Scroope, Margaret Rees-Talbot's fiancé, who had been with her yesterday when Reardon had picked up her father's manuscript. For that matter there was no resemblance to their mother by either of them. He settled down next to his wife as she sipped her tea, with every intention of staying, despite his mother's displeased stare. Cracks beneath the surface, in more ways than one.

Reardon would have preferred to have dealt with Lady Maude and her agent alone. He was as annoyed as Lady Maude by the untimely entrance of the pair and their refusal to take the hint and leave. There was, however, nothing he could do about it but follow her example. She seemed at last to have succumbed to the inevitable. Short of directly dismissing her son, he supposed she could do no other.

She turned to Reardon with a polite smile. 'You must excuse me if I ask that this little talk should be short. We are expecting people in to look at the roof.'

That explained the tea, and who it had been meant for. The arrival of himself and Gilmour had been mistaken by some servant for an expected couple of architects, surveyors, or whoever would be doing the inspecting. 'Not a serious matter, I hope?'

'Serious enough,' she answered with a quickly suppressed sigh and a swift look towards her son, in which he caught a glimpse of a worried woman behind the controlled exterior, and sensed the weight of her anxiety. Nevertheless, he wasn't here to sympathize.

'We won't keep you any longer than necessary.'

'Very well, then . . . although there's nothing more Colonel Frith or I can tell you about that poor man than we could originally.'

'Perhaps not, but new evidence has turned up. We now believe it's almost certain the murdered man was from South Africa. Does that ring any bells? Have you, or anyone you know, ever had any connections with South Africa? You, Colonel Frith, perhaps?' Presumably, because of the South African coin in the dead man's pocket, they had been asked this before by Micklejohn or one of his team, but he saw no harm in repeating it.

'I served there for two years,' Frith said stiffly, 'during the war with the Boers. But I left with my regiment shortly after it was all over, jolly glad to do so, and I have never had any "connections", as you put it, with anyone there either then or since.'

Reardon thought about that manuscript of Osbert Rees-Talbot's he had been reading last night. The majority of British officers who had fought in that war had not directly been part of any decision made by the upper echelons of the army and those retributive actions Rees-Talbot had deplored, except that they had obeyed orders and kept their mouths shut. This was such a man, he thought, meeting the boiled gooseberry eyes, his choleric glance, this soldier with a stiff upper lip. Just obeying orders.

'And you or your family, Lady Maude?'

'As a matter of fact, I did spend some time in South Africa myself, at the time Colonel Frith is referring to, though it was only for a very short while. I sailed out with Lady Randolph Churchill on her hospital ship. Unfortunately, I was taken ill and didn't stay there long.'

'Did you by any chance make friends there, that you might still correspond with?'

'No one special. I came home soon after I recovered, and I married very shortly after that. South Africa was no longer a part of my life.'

'Quite.' Changing tactics, he said suddenly, 'I believe you are acquainted with the Rees-Talbot family, who live in Folbury.'

She raised her eyebrows. 'Certainly. My younger son is engaged to be married to Margaret Rees-Talbot.'

'So I understand. Her father served in the same war. Did either of you know him in South Africa?'

'Rees-Talbot was not in my regiment,' Frith said. 'We never met there, and he died before I could meet him here.'

Reardon asked the same question of Lady Maude. 'Oh, only briefly,' she answered vaguely. 'One met so many people . . . soldiers came and went.'

'In any case,' put in Sir Julian, coming to life, 'what has Margaret's father to do with that man found near the covert?'

Reardon didn't answer him directly. 'He may have been living in the Folbury area for some time before he was killed. His name may have been Wim, or perhaps Willem Mauritz. Does that mean anything to any of you?'

The dowager shook her head.

'And you, Colonel Frith?'

'Never heard of the feller.'

Reardon turned to Sir Julian. 'What about you, sir?'

'Any reason why I should?'

His wife gave a tinkling laugh. 'Goodness, he doesn't sound like the sort of person we would know, does he darling?'

'I should say not,' agreed Binkie. 'In any case, we actually live in London, don't you see, only visiting.'

Which didn't answer the question, but Reardon didn't press it further. Yet despite Julian's smooth, polished appearance, the suit with the fashionably wide lapels, the tie Reardon suspected might be an old school one, the deadpan countenance and the cool manner, he had nicotine stains on his fingers, his nails were bitten to the quick, and he was not a man one instinctively trusted.

There was something here, something going on between some, or even all of them, he was sure, but he didn't think he was going to get much further at the moment. Lady Maude kept her beady stare fixed on him, without blinking, her mind possibly on the coming meeting with her architect. Her son avoided looking at anyone. Giles Frith shrugged and spread his hands. In the silence that followed Lady Maude stood and smoothed down her skirts. 'And now, if you'll forgive me, I must ask you to leave.'

When she was alone once more, the police gone and that disagreeable business with the architect and his assistant about replacing the lead flashings on the roof concluded, Lady Maude forced herself to face the unsettling implications of what had transpired during the police visit. Sitting rigidly upright, her hands folded tightly on her lap, she deliberately took her mind back to the last time she had seen Osbert Rees-Talbot.

It had been a meeting of future in-laws, designed to introduce Osbert to the Scroope family and to show him the ancestral home, though Julian and his wife had pleaded another engagement and Osbert himself had shown little interest. He had sat tight as a drum, creating a distinct feeling of things present but not being said, and making everyone uncomfortable. This was not the young officer Maude had known in Cape Town, spruce in a smart uniform, invested with glamour, sociable – though even then with something reticent about him, it had to be admitted. That day here at Maxstead, Osbert had been so obviously ill-at-ease that she had at last taken pity on him.

'Margaret would like to see the garden, Symon. Show her the new topiary – and while you're there take a look at the goldfish pond if you will and break the ice if it's frozen over. It's cold enough, I'm sure.'

Winter had come early, the afternoon was cold as charity, and the bare November gardens were hardly at their best, the wind-whipped paths devoid of any shelter, but though Symon had met her commands with a speculative glance, he had taken Margaret out without comment.

The door had scarcely closed behind them before Osbert asked, leaning forward, 'There is something I have to know, Maude, that you must tell me. I think you know what it is.'

She had guessed it was the presence of the others which had been inhibiting him, but she had not expected such directness, even though they were now alone. Giving herself time, she stared through the window across the garden. She watched the two young people walking together arm-in-arm, taking one of the ruler-straight paths that radiated from the winter-bare flower beds by the house towards the bank of elms, where crows sat huddled and shivering in the leafless branches. They paused for a moment, standing close together as Symon adjusted the small fur around Margaret's neck, and then suddenly she had begun to run, taking his hand and pulling him until his strides caught up and they were laughing together like children. Maude nodded approval. Symon had always been too much inclined to seriousness.

She continued to gaze across the smooth expanse of lawn, punctuated by specimen trees planted by some Victorian Scroope: a giant hundred-and-fifty-foot sequoia with dipping branches; a cedar, misshapen now after being struck three times by lightning; and a graceful, weeping ash. Beyond, the ground rose to the dense forest.

In the lush, tropical garden of the house where Maude had stayed in Cape Town the trees were tall palms whose branches waved in the hot southern breeze, casting black shadows across the blinding white paths. The grass was scorched by the heat and a fountain tinkled into a marble basin. A white-painted seat; a blaze of proteas and bird-of-paradise flowers. Intense blue skies and Table Mountain in the background . . .

'What happened, Maude?' Osbert repeated urgently. 'Tell me what happened.'

She had turned from the window. 'Isn't it a trifle late to be asking that?' she said severely, and then was shocked into gentler tones by the pain in his eyes. 'Did Hamer not tell you?'

He said nothing.

'Then you'd better prepare yourself for a shock.'

Sixteen

It was still early, and there were not too many customers as yet in the Punch Bowl. Joe ordered his half-pint and looked around, and as he had hoped he might, saw Eileen Gerrity was there, the only woman in the place, sharing a table with a dark, stocky man with the physique of a heavyweight boxer. Neither of them looked pleased to see him when he crossed over to their table.

'Not your usual stamping ground, this, Sergeant, is it?' Eileen greeted him.

'Actually, I don't live far away. Felt like a drink on the way home. But I've been intending to see you, to have another chat about your employer. Do you mind if I join you for a minute or two?'

'Ex-employer,' her companion said pugnaciously. 'The bastard.' To Eileen, he said, 'Who's this?'

'Ron,' Eileen replied warningly. She touched his sleeve. 'He's OK, he's from the police – but do you mind? Just for a minute or two?'

'What?' Ron stared, and looked as though he might be going to refuse to move, but after a moment scraped his chair back 'All right, but don't you go upsetting her, Ginge.'

'What can I get you both?'

'Mine's half a bitter, ta, and she'll have a port-and-lemon.' Ron drained his own glass.

'Don't mind him,' Eileen said, after Joe had brought the drinks from the bar and the charmless Ron, looking bigger than ever, had taken his half to a table where he could keep an eye on them, still glowering. 'He's my brother-in-law. My sister died about a year ago and he's lonely. We keep each other company. I know what he looks like but he wouldn't hurt a fly.'

'It's not the flies I'm worried about.'

'You look big enough to take care of yourself.' She frowned.

'I haven't thought of anyone else who had it in for Arthur, if that's what you're after. Still thinking it might be Frank Greenwood?'

'No, they're both off the hook, him and his partner.'

Not naturally aggressive, Frank Greenwood, as Eileen Gerrity had said, though nervously plucking at his tie, sweating at the thought of being involved with the police. But he and his more belligerent partner, Charlie Bell, had unshakeable alibis. Both had been attending a nine o'clock meeting in the Town Hall to put in their application to have their rates reduced because of the proposed erection of a new bus station, which would hinder the parking of their vans and lorries.

'It's not them I want to talk about, it's Aston.'

'What do you want to know that I haven't already told you?'

'I want to know what sort of a man he was, really. And you knew him as well as anybody.'

She gazed down into the depths of her port-and-lemon as she swirled it around in the glass, saying nothing. After a moment she looked up and said, 'Well, Ron's right in a way, he could be a . . . No, I'm too ladylike, but he wasn't always, and anyway, he was very good to me.'

'But not to his wife.'

She gave him a look. 'You get what you deserve, sometimes.'

'I hear he treated her as a skivvy, didn't speak to her much, kept her short . . . Did she deserve that?'

'Lily Aston,' said Eileen, 'is a bitch.'

Joe was taken aback at the venom in her voice. From her point of view, of course, that might be how it seemed, but it wasn't how Joe had seen Lily. Soured by her life with a domineering, tight-fisted husband; trapped into a loveless marriage from which she felt there was no escape. It wasn't an unusual situation – there were thousands of women like her, unable to see their way out. It needed courage to start afresh at her age, with no money and nowhere to go. 'That's a bit harsh, isn't it?'

'He didn't know what was going on behind his back. At least, what I *think* was . . .' She stopped uncertainly, looking sorry that she'd spoken.

'All right, let's try something else. 'What do you know about the people at number eighteen, Henrietta Street?'

'I know nothing about *anybody* on Henrietta Street. I only work there.' She shrugged. 'I sometimes go into the corner shop for fags, but otherwise . . .' She lifted her glass for another sip of her drink.

'Does the name Wim Mauritz mean anything to you?'

Ruby drops landed on the table as she put the glass down too quickly. 'Should it?'

'He lived at number eighteen. He was the WIM that Aston kept jotting down. Come on, he came to the works to talk to Aston, didn't he?'

He thought she was going to deny it, but after a second or two she said, 'All right. He did come in a few times. Arthur said he was a potential customer but I didn't believe that. They never talked business, see, just general chat.'

'Did they ever mention the name Rees-Talbot?'

'Who?' She seemed genuinely not to know the name, and shook her head again. Then she said abruptly, 'He was the chap in the snow, wasn't he? Mauritz, I mean. The Snowman?'

'What makes you think that?'

A movement from the far table as Ron got to his feet. She noticed and waved him back. Her face looked pinched, the way it had when he'd seen her just after Aston's body was found. She had been fonder of him than she had admitted, hard as it was to see why. He didn't want to upset her unduly, but he wanted to know what it was that she was keeping back. With a shaky hand she took out a packet of Players. Joe lit a cigarette for her and waited for her to answer his question.

'Well, he was South African, wasn't he?' she said at last. 'So who else could it have been? Added to which he'd suddenly stopped coming into the office. The last time he came in Arthur grabbed his hat and coat, said they were going for a drink – and that was the last I ever saw of Mr Mauritz. Not that I was sorry. I didn't like him. Thought himself God's gift to women . . . you know the sort. Good looking, but I thought he was shifty. He'd flirt with anybody – even someone my age.'

'Did you know he had a wife?'

'A *wife*?' Clearly she did not.

'Can't you try and recall anything he and Aston spoke about?'

She thought about it and in the end said reluctantly, 'They were up to something. I don't know what it was, but Arthur didn't want me to know about it. I . . . I think – do *you* think that may have been why Arthur got himself killed?'

'I don't know yet, Eileen.' Joe finished his drink and stood up. 'But thanks for your help. We'll need you to come to the station and confirm what you've just told me.'

'No, no, I can't do that!'

Joe put a hand on her shoulder. 'I'm sorry, but I'm afraid you'll have to.'

'Eileen'll have to do nothing of the sort.' The heavyweight boxer stood there. Joe was half a head taller and several years younger, but he didn't feel inclined to argue with him. He took his hand from Eileen's shoulder and left. He could catch her later, when she'd had time to think over what else she might have told him.

Seventeen

They drove down to Maxstead in a jangling silence, in the yellow Alvis which even Opal, with her madly expensive tastes, had to admit was a huge extravagance. Silent because the lively, noisy twins, normally squashed into the back with their nanny whenever the Binkie Scroopes went down to Maxstead (since their presence was expected – if not commanded – by their grandmother) were on this occasion absent, never mind that she would not be pleased. Jangling because of the monumental quarrel between Binkie and his wife the evening before, when everything that could be said at that time had been said, leaving behind only this great hiatus of what couldn't be voiced.

Money, as usual. 'It's gone,' Binkie had announced baldly.

'What do you mean, gone?'

'Gone, as in disappeared, down the plughole, melted into thin air. Vanished. We are stony broke.'

For a moment, Opal didn't believe him. 'Not . . . not *all* of it, surely?' she asked sharply, her mouth hardening.

'Every last penny. In that so-called dead cert investment that rotter Mauritz put forward. Gone, and him with it.'

Mauritz.

The name had a familiar ring, and though she was sure she'd heard it somewhere before, she couldn't for the moment think where. Things she didn't want to know about never settled in Opal's mind for more than two seconds before taking wing like butterflies. But he must have been referring to That Man. Binkie had always avoided actually mentioning his name whenever he had needed to speak about the stranger whom he – but not she – had met somewhere or other, and who had promised the earth, and whose influence over Binkie it now seemed she had been right after all to suspect and resent so much.

'Well then,' she returned, even more sharply, 'you must get it back from him.'

It was at that point that the sight of his stony face caused her suddenly to feel frightened – no, afraid was the better, graver word. Especially when Binkie laughed harshly and said, 'That might be difficult.'

'You can't mean he's absconded – with our money?'

'I mean Wim Mauritz has disappeared, like everything we once had. To be more accurate, he's dead. Dead and buried, with a hole in his head. But resurrected.'

Opal's stomach lurched as though she'd missed the bottom step. It came back to her, instantly, where she'd heard the name before and what it might mean. This Wim Mauritz, this man with the foreign name, was the one the police had arrived to enquire about when she and Binkie were last down at Maxstead. He was the unidentified man who had been found dead at the edge of the forest . . . the one whom Binkie had denied any knowledge of.

With an intuitiveness not normally given to her, she knew now why he had always forbidden her so fiercely ever to mention That Man in his mother's presence – and why he had also sworn to her, Opal, that he hadn't seen his mysterious acquaintance for months, when all the time . . . Her thoughts were like scrambled eggs as she tried to fit the facts together. She remembered the horrid corpse being found buried under the snow, and the hue and cry that had gone on for weeks and weeks. While Binkie had apparently known who it was all the time, but had kept his mouth shut! That she might have got things wrong in her usual scatterbrained fashion never even entered her head. She needed no convincing – what else could he have meant by 'resurrected'? Her husband had known all along that the stranger found buried under the snow was the man he had known as Wim Mauritz. He had known his name, where he came from, yet during all the enquiries, the appeals for information – even when faced directly with the police – he had kept silent.

There could, even to Opal, be only one reason for that. My God, oh my God!

Whatever his other faults, Binkie was rarely drunk. And he wasn't drunk now, the day after that appalling admission. He loved high-performance cars and always drove well, extremely fast but sure, and his hands were steady on the steering wheel, his foot pressed no harder than usual on the accelerator. All the same, there was a kind of blazing, barely contained rage emanating from him that brought her heart into her mouth, as though they were hurtling at top speed into disaster.

It was a disaster, whichever way you looked at it. Not only because of the money, though heaven alone knew that was devastating enough, impossible to contemplate without panic. But what was even worse than that amounted to nearly the end of the world: that the man Mauritz – the one Binkie had been so sure would be their salvation, whose advice or recommendations he had followed to invest all their money, was dead, murdered. But *no* – the idea of Binkie killing anyone was simply too, too ridiculous. He had refused to speak of it any more last night. She had asked, but not begged – scared, really, of knowing the details.

No one had ever thought Opal clever. All the same, she could see what it all meant, whichever way you looked at it. Last night, realizing what the future might hold, in the end it had all been too much for her. She had finally given way to hysterics and Binkie had slapped her face, cold and hard as he always was when they quarrelled, though he could when he felt like it be so sweet, her Binkie-Boo. Not last night, though. After her hysterics had subsided into hiccuping sobs, and then finally ceased after the glass of brandy he thrust into her hands and made her drink, they had gone to bed, lying as far away from each other as they could, on the very edges of the mattress. He had made a perfunctory apology for having to slap her, though she didn't believe he was really sorry, and he hadn't slept any more than she had, she was sure. And then, this morning, he had announced his intention of going down to Maxstead. Where it had happened. They would both go.

It was a horrible day, grey and still, with lowering yellowish clouds, as if to underline the disaster that had befallen them, a day unlike the glancing April days of the last couple of weeks when there had been sun, showers, daffodils and bursting greenery in the park their windows overlooked, new spring clothes to think about and the social season ahead. Today the sky hung over the earth like a lid, heavy with rain that wouldn't fall. Opal, usually exhilarated by the speed at which Binkie drove, prayed he would slow down.

He hadn't forbidden her to speak to anyone else of what had passed between them. He evidently felt there was no need, knowing she was well aware which side her bread was buttered and what would happen if all this came out. It hadn't been greed, he had said, it had been necessity which had made him so reckless with their money. Just damned bad luck it should have turned out the way it had. But what are we going to do, how are we going to live? Cut back, he said, they would have to cut back. On *what?* The idea of going without anything at all in their luxurious lifestyle was incomprehensible to Opal.

And how would she bear the double-edged sympathy of her friends? '*How too simply awful, darling!*' (*But what a fool, letting himself lose everything . . . although, there but for the grace of God . . .*) His mother would not lift a finger to help, though help of some kind was certainly what Binkie was heading towards Maxstead for – yet surely not to admit to her the idiocy of the actions which had brought them to this pass? The old witch would not say anything, but she would *look.* As if she had always known their marriage must come to this, that it was all Opal's fault. In any case there was every possibility that she *couldn't* help, not with the great white elephant that was Maxstead hanging round her neck – round all of their necks – the source of all this trouble, thought Opal, too muddled, miserable and confused to see anything at all amusing about the image that conjured up.

Anyway, who would want to live in this mausoleum, even if they could afford it, she thought peevishly as the square grey house appeared; they all thought so much of it, but to Opal it was nothing more than a fortress, a prison.

'Oh God, the Reverend's here,' Binkie said, seeing a car he recognized before the front flight of steps, as they emerged from the long avenue of trees that darkened the day even further.

It was barely five o'clock on a spring day, but dark enough to have lights already blazing out from the house, as though the economy Maude preached to her son didn't apply to her beloved Maxstead. Even as Opal thought this, all the lights in the house went out.

Symon and Margaret had driven over to Maxstead that day in the Rees-Talbot family motorcar. It was a comfortable, if not luxurious one that Osbert had bought and Margaret had learnt to drive, simply in order to forestall the possibility of her father having a heart attack by having to submit to the breath-stopping terrors of being driven around by Felix.

They had sat down to a lavish tea, while Symon listened to his mother's news of Giles Frith's pending retirement with mounting anger against his brother. How the dickens would she cope alone, without Frith's efficient management of the estate? He had been a prop and a bulwark ever since Sir Lancelot had died.

Symon held out his cup and saucer for her to refill. A match had been put to the fire and lamps had been switched on to relieve the dark and dismal afternoon, and the one next to Lady Maude reflected a sharp, momentarily dazzling flash of light from the silver teapot. Symon blinked and shifted his glance, and it came to rest on her face. There were lines of worry creasing her forehead, round her mouth, that he hadn't noticed before. He was suddenly aware that his indomitable mother was approaching fifty. Not old yet, by any means, but not immortal.

Once, for the sake of the family, when he was contemplating taking up a career, Symon had briefly entertained the idea that he might take over from where his father had left off, working in harmony with Frith, as Sir Lancelot had done, in default of any interest from the rightful person, Binkie, who had a dog in the manger attitude towards taking on responsibilities along with his inheritance of the title. It might have worked. It was not in Symon to be idle and he knew himself capable enough and indeed felt a strong leaning towards the idea; what he didn't already know he could soon learn, providing he put his mind to it. Family tradition meant a great deal to him, the steady continuation of the ancestral line, though not as much as it did to his mother, who had not even been born a Scroope.

Weighing up the possibilities, he had been forced to

acknowledge it was not a feasible proposition, for him or for any of them, in the ultimate. Estates like Maxstead, families like theirs, the Scroopes, looked increasingly unlikely to have any future in this post-apocalyptic world. Nothing was ever going to be the same after that last war. Tell Maxstead's predicament to the man in the dole queue, waiting for a pittance handout to feed and clothe his family, and hear what he would say about it! His mother shut her eyes to this and Binkie didn't give a fig – all he cared about was that the estate sucked up money like a whale sucked up plankton. Symon knew that although he could have succeeded in keeping things ticking along, sooner or later the axe was bound to fall. The attempt to discuss it with Binkie had ended in a row, and he had tried to tell himself these were decisions it was not up to him to make, though this did not assuage his guilt.

He looked at other ways of spending a useful life and had surprised himself by the career he had been drawn to, never before having thought himself religious. He had excelled in his studies and by the time he was ordained as curate, clearly before him stretched the path towards preferment, with its eventual goal. Here, however, when his thoughts reached the archdeaconry in the cathedral close, he abruptly checked such pleasurable meanderings before they should stray as far as the bishop's palace. Yet he chose to believe that it was not sinful ambition or false pride that drove him, but an inborn conviction that one day he would surely be directed there.

At that precise moment in his thoughts, the lights went out. He gave a long-suffering sigh, put his teacup down and went to seek candles and matches where he knew they would be found, lit oil lamps already primed for such a regular emergency, while reflecting grimly that the unreliability of the electricity supply might be a profound metaphor for Maxstead's precarious existence.

He hadn't lit all the lamps when from the front of the house came a roar and a scrunch of gravel that proved to be the arrival of what was known in the family as Binkie's Yellow Peril. Maude gave a distracted cluck. 'What are they doing here? They were only down a few days ago and— What a surprise! Julian darling, Opal. Lovely to see you, but where

are the children?' she cried, hurrying out to greet her son and
his wife as they came into the hall.

'Oh, they have a little cold, we thought it best . . .' Opal
replied vaguely.

How odd this was. And where was the baggage train that
usually arrived with Opal – the suitcases, hatboxes, trunks,
even if only for a few days? Just one overnight valise for the
two of them. And both of them looking . . . well, Binkie,
always pale, was even more so, and drawn, too, nervously slap-
ping his driving gloves against his thigh. But Opal! Maude had
never seen her so distraught. Her face was white and pinched
under the grey of the velour cloche hat pulled down close to
her ears, and it was obvious she wore no make up at all. She
had quite clearly dressed in a hurry; when she took off her
coat, underneath was a mismatched collection of unsuitable
clothes. Being Opal, all this spelled some dire disaster.

'My dear!' Summoning a kindness she normally found difficult to show to her daughter-in-law, Maude sat her in a chair
near to the fire. Opal held her hands out to the blaze and
Margaret poured tea and handed it to her, with a scone which
she left untouched on her plate.

Binkie ate nothing either, but thirstily drained a cup of tea
and then, immaculate as usual, stood up with his back to the
fire, cleared his throat and prepared to make his pronounce-
ment. 'Rather glad you're here, Symon. There's something I
have to say, and you should hear it.'

Opal's hand flew to her mouth. 'Binkie . . .' she began, but
he stopped her with a dark look. She was terribly afraid he
might be going to confess.

It was too bad Symon was here, with Margaret, too. Opal,
for all her sophistication, didn't know how to talk to him. He
always listened courteously, which somehow made her incon-
sequential chatter and gossip sound too silly for anything. Binkie
said he was a prig, but she supposed he couldn't help that,
being a parson . . . Meanwhile, she couldn't think of a single
thing she might do to stop Binkie. He continued relentlessly.

'It will probably be a shock to you all, but I have decided
to sell Maxstead – if anyone can be found to buy it, that is.
As well as most of the estate.'

Into the stunned silence following this announcement, old Henry, lying at Maude's feet, gave one of those single deep, rumbling barks he sometimes made in his sleep. As if it were a signal, the lights came on again, flickered uncertainly once or twice and then settled down, though no one moved to turn off the now redundant oil lamps.

This was it, Maude thought, feeling the energy drain from every part of her, from her very fingertips; this was what she had been afraid of for so long. 'Why?'

'Because this house is eating money; it costs a fortune simply to keep it standing up, as you all know. Don't worry about yourself, Ma. You needn't move too far. The Bothy will be empty when Frith leaves. It's a nice house, perfectly acceptable for you to live in, without the constant worry this place brings.'

The Bothy, as Frith's Scottish wife had whimsically named it, *was* a nice house, reasonably sized, manageable and pretty, but it's not mine, thought Maude, not the house I love, where I've lived for thirty years and hoped to die.

Symon had his eye on her, knowing what must be going through her mind, but after the first tremble, her lips pressed together in a firm line. She had lost colour, but otherwise seemed quite all right. He suddenly stood up. 'A word in private, Binkie. Not here, come with me. Look after Ma and Opal for now, Margaret, please.'

'I don't think so.' Binkie abandoned his position on the hearthrug and threw himself down into his former seat with every intention of staying put.

'Then think again.' Symon's hand fell on his shoulder, gripping it hard, drawing him upward in spite of himself. Symon was bigger than he was, stronger and fitter, and seeing his expression, the will to resist suddenly left Binkie and he allowed Symon to propel him with some force out of the room, along the corridor and into what had always been called the garden room, an untidy repository for flower vases and baskets, gumboots and mackintoshes, deck chairs, and plants being nursed by their mother on the windowsills. It was cold, and a tap over the sink in the corner dripped intermittently.

'Right,' Symon said, letting him go, but still facing him. 'What's all this damned nonsense about Maxstead, and Ma?'

'Maxstead has nothing at all to do with you, and Ma will be taken care of.'

'Maxstead has everything to do with me. Come on, spit it out or I'll knock your blinking block off. And take that smirk off your face.'

The juvenile threat had come from nowhere and colour ran up under Symon's skin even as he heard himself utter it, but his eyes darkened ominously. Binkie, finding it hard not to grin, didn't notice this, nor his brother's clenched fists. 'The last time I heard you use that sort of language was when you were sixteen.'

When they had been good friends, easy with each other. And here you are now, a reverend gentleman in a dog collar, though let's not be fooled by that, Binkie thought, now very much aware of Symon's scarcely controlled rage. In truth, Binkie had written off his younger brother when he had chosen a vocation that was to him incomprehensible, relegating him to the ranks of the God-botherers. Only now did he see his mistake. Attempting to show sangfroid, he raised an eyebrow but said nothing more.

Symon turned from him in disgust and perched himself on the edge of a scruffy old wooden table, his folded arms holding in his anger, while Binkie, taking the opportunity to distance himself by exhibiting more nonchalance, sank into an old garden basket chair and threw his leg over the arm.

'You've got yourself into some sort of scrape again, that's obvious. What is it now?'

The tap dripped monotonously while Binkie picked up and examined an old yellow pigskin glove relegated now for use when pruning roses. A minute thorn was embedded in the thumb and he spent some time trying to remove it with his fingernails. Symon leant forward, snatched it from his hands and tossed it to the floor. 'Well?'

There wasn't much use in prevaricating. He knew Symon of old. Once he had his teeth into something, he was like a terrier with a rat. Tell him, then. But not everything . . . just enough.

He shrugged and said in an offhand way that he'd made some ill-advised investments which had failed, that he had debts which there was no prospect of covering, and that the only solution was to get rid of encumbrances.

'Encumbrances? That's how you see Maxstead, is it? And Ma? Is she an encumbrance as well?'

'I've told you, Ma will be OK. I'll see she's all right.'

'She'll be happy, packed off to The Bothy, no doubt. That's what you think?'

'She will be when she ceases to have to worry about this place. It's the only way,' Binkie added, beginning to feel desperate.

'What sort of investments?'

Binkie shrugged.

'Come on, you've never been a speculator before, you're not made that way. What the devil made you risk everything? Who got you into this?'

In his mind Binkie ran through a list of those old school friends of his who were successful in the money business, those he might lie about: bankers, stockbrokers, whom he might better have consulted than the disreputable – and with hindsight, plainly untrustworthy – Wim Mauritz, and then realized that was no good. Symon knew most of his acquaintances almost as well as he did. They'd all been to the same school; they'd grown up with many of them. 'You wouldn't know him. He was nobody.'

'*Was?*'

When the two brothers had disappeared they'd left behind them a silence. Nobody seemed to be able to find anything to say, or even want to. For something to occupy herself with, Margaret went around turning off the oil lamps, then returned to the couch where Opal was sitting, nervously twisting her engagement ring, a lovely marquise-set fire opal surrounded by diamonds. Margaret had never imagined it would be possible to feel sorry for her prospective sister-in-law, but she did.

'My dear,' Maude said then, 'why don't you go upstairs and lie down for a little while? I'll have them bring you some hot milk and whisky. If you don't mind my saying so, you look as though you might be in for a cold, like the babies, and I'm sure you could do with a nap.'

Horrid as the hot milk sounded, Opal was astonished by

the unexpected kindness, at the same time feeling an undreamed of stab of admiration for her bossy old mother-in-law, dimly sensing how much greater a blow to her this terrifyingly unexpected situation must be than to anyone else. The ring bit into her palm as she twisted it. They had said opals were unlucky when she and Binkie had chosen this. Unlucky Opal! She felt tears coming; she had a thumping headache after not sleeping last night, and would have liked nothing better than to go upstairs into the room that was always kept ready for them and weep and weep, or better still lie down and sleep for hours, but she was too afraid of what was going on between Binkie and his brother.

'Oh, goodness, no thank you,' she said brightly to the offer. She stood up. 'Where have they gone?'

'Into the garden room, I believe,' replied Lady Maude, attuned to all the sounds of the house. 'But Opal—'

Opal left the room. She walked along the passage and opened the garden room door. Both men turned towards her as it opened.

'Go away, Opal,' Binkie said immediately.

She took another step inside and closed the door behind her.

'Opal, my dear, I think Binkie's right. Leave this to us.'

She knew from the atmosphere that Symon must have got everything from Binkie already, even though he spoke kindly to her, just as his mother had done, as if to a child who didn't understand these things. And though she didn't, not at all, it suddenly annoyed her intensely to know they all thought her such a brainless thing, nothing but a social flibbertigibbet, incapable of deep feeling. Drawing herself up very straight, she said, 'Binkie had nothing to do with the murder of that man Mauritz—'

Binkie sprang up out of the chair as if he'd been electrocuted and grasped both her wrists, tight as handcuffs. '*Shut up, Opal!*' His eyes were not sleepy and hooded now, they were wide open, and this time as she looked into their grey-green depths she was frightened, really frightened, something she had never thought possible of her own husband. 'Not another word, you little fool. Not – another – word!' he repeated, enunciating each word separately. 'Do you hear me?'

'That's enough,' said Symon, stepping up to them.

They all three stood in the centre of the shadowy room, looking at one another, as at last the threatened rain began in a sudden crashing deluge. Then Binkie let go of Opal's wrists and sank back into the chair, his head in his hands. Symon went back to the table and again perched there with his arms crossed, looking stern and accusing and yet, Opal felt, in a funny sort of way, oddly reassuring. There seemed to be nothing more to say, and the sound of the rain drilling on to the paving outside made the silence within all the more intense.

'Well, what am I going to do, Reverend?' Binkie asked at last, looking up.

'You're a bloody fool, Binkie,' answered the reverend forcefully. 'But that doesn't mean you don't know damn well what you have to do.'

Eighteen

The following day, Reardon received a telephone message from Maxstead Court, requesting his immediate presence over there, concerning the matter they had previously discussed. Could this be a breakthrough, coming, as it so often did, through someone deciding they'd be better off telling what they knew? He made a thumbs up sign to Joe, but replied very politely indeed that if Sir Julian wished to speak to him, he would be here all morning at the police station in Folbury.

Now they were gathered in Waterhouse's office, where there was enough room for the four of them: Sir Julian Scroope, Reardon, Gilmour, and Waterhouse himself, who had chosen to keep a silent watch over his domain from the background.

'You told us you didn't know Wim Mauritz, Sir Julian.'

'Well, yes. I do rather think that's what I may have led you to believe.'

Reardon waited.

'What it is, I seem to have got myself into a bit of a fix through him,' Scroope drawled, shrugging his shoulders and not quite looking at any of the police officers from under his hooded lids, though if he was overwhelmed by such a police presence, that was the only way he was showing it. 'He was an embarrassment to me, don't you see? To be more accurate, he took me to the cleaners, as they say. Scarcely something one wants to make public knowledge, hmm?'

'Do I understand you are making a confession?'

'If you put it that way, I suppose I am.' Prepared for this, he answered with a consciously rueful smile. 'But by God no, I didn't kill him, if that's what you're thinking. The bastard – if you'll excuse me – was dead and buried, then found, long before I ever knew the extent of just what he'd done to me. Mind if I smoke?'

Reardon glanced at Waterhouse – it was his office – and

received a nod. 'If it's going to help you tell us the truth, go ahead.'

Julian spent some time extracting a cigarette from a mono-grammed silver cigarette case, lighting it and then offering the case in a general direction. Everyone else declined. 'As a matter of fact, I find it rather a ludicrous notion,' he observed lazily, 'that I should be thought capable of killing *anyone*, much less someone of that size.'

Reardon inspected the man sitting in front of him, a slight man in well-tailored country tweeds, a soft Tattersall checked shirt, knitted silk tie. The no-doubt hand-made shoes shone with a deep, ox-blood polish. His cuff links were black, square-cut onyx and his hands were narrow and shapely, though disfigured by the nicotine stains and bitten nails. He was inclined to agree with Scroope's estimation of himself: he did not look like anyone who could overpower and kill a muscular man of more than six feet, much less dig a grave for him in half-frozen ground. Always supposing, Reardon thought, allowing himself a passing touch of humour, that he would even have known where spades were located at Maxstead Court. On the face of it, Sir Julian Scroope, baronet, wasn't a likely killer . . . but Reardon had known more unlikely ones, and above the bril-liantine scent of his slicked-back yellow hair, he could also smell the scent of fear.

'It would help if you were to start at the beginning and tell us what you know about all this, Sir Julian. First, how did you meet Mauritz?'

'Well, actually, it was at Maxstead.' Fortified by the cigarette, he sat back, crossing his extended legs at the ankle.

'Maxstead *Court*, I suppose you mean? The house? What was he doing there?'

'He had come to see my mother.'

A quick look passed between Reardon and Joe, who was sitting at the end of the desk, his notebook open, pencil at the ready; Lady Maude, too, had denied ever having met Mauritz. 'When was this?'

'Oh, some months ago,' he answered vaguely, and then suddenly became more communicative. The fellow had come uninvited, he said, and in fact had been rather forcibly escorted from the house by himself, at his mother's request. Once outside, they had exchanged heated words, Sir Julian warning him to keep away from Maxstead. But far from leaving, Mauritz, undeterred, had suggested they try to talk more sensibly and resolve the situation. They could do so more comfortably if they went to sit in his car . . .

For some reason Sir Julian had agreed to do what Mauritz asked, and after a while the conversation had indeed taken a more amicable turn. In fact, one thing leading to another, it had ended up with Mauritz putting a proposition before Sir Julian, offering to put him in the way of some insider information regarding the flotation of shares in a newly formed South African copper-mining syndicate. 'About which, he assured me,' he finished bitterly, 'there was no risk involved, otherwise, well . . .'

'Otherwise you would not have agreed,' Reardon finished drily.

'I would have thought twice, certainly.' They had met two or three times after that, he went on, when the Julian Scroopes were down at Maxstead, and negotiations for buying shares in the company, though proceeding slowly, were, Mauritz had assured him, going well.

'How did you contact him? Presumably you had his address?'

'No. He telephoned me to arrange our meetings. In a pub called the Fighting Cocks, on the other side of Arms Green.'

Reardon knew it – noisy, anonymous, crowded, not a place where strangers would be remarked upon. 'When was the last time?'

'Early December. He said he would report back to me after the Christmas holiday as to how things were going, give me some indication of when I might expect some return. He'd promised he would take care of everything, and I have to say he impressed me enough to trust him implicitly. I'd told him how many shares to buy and handed him a cheque and – I'm afraid that was that.' The urbane mask slipped, his face suddenly twisted with held-in fury. It crossed Reardon's mind that he wouldn't like to be on the receiving end of Scroope's temper.

'You heard nothing more from him?'

'Nothing. Nor had I any idea how to get in contact with him. He simply disappeared – until he turned up dead. By that time I was worried sick about what was to happen to my investment. I'd actually engaged a private investigator to see what he could find out, but he didn't hold out much hope. Rightly so as it turns out,' he added bitterly. 'Just a few days ago, I learned there was no company, no mine, nothing, that every brass farthing of my money was gone. To be frank, the whole bloody thing had been cooked up in that damned rogue and swindler's imagination. And now he's dead and my money's gone with him.'

There was a comprehensive silence when he had finished, his cigarette long since burned to ash. He lit another, with hands that were no longer quite so steady.

You had to wonder how anyone, given his advantages of birth and education, could be so incredibly gullible, stupid and – yes, selfish, in believing all that, in not taking into account the possible consequences to his wife and family. Though as far as Reardon knew, none of those things were confined to people of one class. Greed, pure and simple, had made fools of more than he.

'Did he ever mention his wife?'

'His *wife*? Mauritz? No, never.' Scroope's eyebrows rose disbelievingly. 'Somehow, it's difficult to imagine him as being married. Why?' A ray of hope suddenly lit his face. 'You think there could be any chance—?'

'No. I should imagine she's back in South Africa by now.'

'God, yes, I suppose she must be.' He looked bleaker than ever.

'Let's go back to when you first met him. You omitted to mention why it was necessary for you to "escort" him from the house, as you said you did?'

'Ah, well.' He shifted uncomfortably in his seat. 'To be frank, he was threatening my mother.'

'Threatening? Really? How?'

'Perhaps that's a bit strong, but he wouldn't take no for an answer when she . . .'

'Go on.'

He took time to think before answering. At last he said,

'He seemed to have believed . . . The fact is, he seemed to think she knew about something or other that had happened when she was in South Africa, though she told him plainly enough she didn't know what he was talking about. She could hardly be expected to remember everything that had happened twenty-five years and more ago after all. He as good as told her she was a liar. At any rate, that was what he implied.'

'What sort of event, or happening, are we talking about?'

'I really haven't the faintest idea. I only came into the room halfway through the conversation. He had this old photograph with him of a group of people, out in the country somewhere. He was pointing to some young woman that he said was my mother, but she denied it absolutely. I could see he was upsetting her. She became very agitated, and asked him to leave. When he still persisted, that was when I told the blighter to get out, and helped him on his way.'

'And you still want us to believe that although you were so angry with him and turned him out of the house, you got into his car with him and let him persuade you into parting with your money in some shady deal?'

'To begin with, it didn't sound shady. I have an expensive wife, many commitments. A house like Maxstead Court is a millstone . . . it seemed worth the risk. It was only when his body turned up that I knew I'd been duped.'

'Yet you didn't think to come forward and tell us who he was.'

He shrugged. 'You don't believe me.' He ground out his second cigarette.

'Oh, I believe you, as far as it goes. Trouble is, it doesn't go far enough. Why, I ask myself, should this man whom your mother had dismissed and you had personally seen off the premises, suddenly offer you this seemingly golden opportunity? I'm intrigued.'

A faint line of sweat appeared on the baronet's forehead. Out of habit he fished for his cigarette case but this time didn't open it. His self-confidence was deserting him, the supercili-ousness had been wiped from his face to be replaced by another expression Reardon couldn't at first identify, until he recognized it as just the sort of look his new mongrel puppy had given him when she'd chewed his library book. Hangdog, they called it, appropriately enough. Shame.

'This is where it gets difficult.'

'Take your time.'

'He said quite openly to me that he didn't believe my mother when she said she didn't recognize herself or anyone else in the picture. To be absolutely honest, I wasn't so sure either – the lady doth protest too much and all that – but that was my mother's business, if she chose not to speak of it.' He paused, then went on, speaking very rapidly. 'Fact is, he said he could put me in the way of making a bit of money if I could find out from her what the truth was.'

Joe's pencil snapped. The tiny sound was like a pistol shot. Reardon said, deliberately expressionless, 'And did you manage to do that?'

'You don't know my mother.'

'What about Mauritz? Did he give you no more to go on?'

'I rather think he was fumbling about in the dark himself. When she had asked him who had given him the photo, why he had come to her, he clammed up and wouldn't say.' He looked anywhere but at the other men in the room. 'But after he and I had talked, well, he said he would live in hope and that if I could get some information for him, he would keep his promises regarding the mine.'

'He bribed you to get information from your mother.'

'That's a nasty way of putting it. But in fact she wouldn't say a thing.'

Reardon's opinion of Lady Maude rose. 'Presumably that wasn't the end of it. What happened next?'

'Oh, well, later I remembered that when Symon – my brother – got engaged to Margaret Rees-Talbot, it had turned out that her father and my mother had actually met before, in South Africa during the war.'

'You told Mauritz that?'

'I did actually. Nothing wrong with that, was there?' He was beginning to bluster. 'Margaret's father might have been able to help where my mother wasn't able to.'

Reardon bent his head and jotted a note on his pad. 'Well,

Sir Julian,' he said at last, 'it's a sorry story. I hope you may sort your affairs out before long.'

He half rose from his chair. 'I can go now?'

'We'll need your signed statement first – and I fancy Sergeant Gilmour has something he wants to ask.'

Joe sprang to life. 'What sort of car was Mauritz driving?'

'Black four-door Morris Oxford, newish,' he replied with an alacrity that revealed an intimate acquaintance with anything on four wheels. 'Low priced, but not bad, considering.'

Considering its comparison to the price of the yellow Alvis in which he'd arrived at the station, no doubt. No wonder the baronet was short of funds. No wonder he'd allowed himself to be taken in by promises that no one with any sense would have believed for a second.

'That's it, that's Aston's,' Joe said, and Reardon turned to Scroope, asking him if he knew who Aston was.

'Aston? Never heard of the feller, who is he?'

'Arthur Aston, owner of a small light engineering works in Arms Green.'

'Should that mean anything to me?'

'I don't know, sir, I thought perhaps you could tell us. He had certain connections with Wim Mauritz.'

The baronet sat up. 'He was one of Mauritz's associates? Does that mean there's still a chance of getting my money back?'

'I'm afraid not. Arthur Aston is dead. He was murdered, too.'

Nineteen

Lady Maude sat at the piano, playing desultorily, just something to occupy herself with while she waited for Inspector Reardon to arrive. She was not doing it well, but then she had never had the right touch. She hit the notes correctly, as would anyone who had conscientiously practised her scales in childhood in order to attain a social accomplishment, but she knew Sir Lancelot had been right when he had teased her as having no true ear for music. Besides, Piers had been the musical one of the family, and the piano, alas long unplayed, needed tuning.

It didn't help that her fingers were cold in this little-used, unheated drawing room which overlooked the garden, where the fire was seldom lit nowadays through reasons of economy, not even today when the skies were again sunless and overcast. She had chosen to receive the inspector, not in the family snug but here in the blue and white drawing room, resplendent with gilt and mirrors, blue brocade upholstery, silk-panelled walls and the heirloom Aubusson carpet. It would not have been her first choice for the forthcoming interview but the maids were busy turning out more appropriate rooms elsewhere and in any case she had an odd fancy that this formality might help to keep the emotion out of what she had to say. Unaccustomed to dealing with such feelings, she had no intention of letting them get out of hand.

She closed the piano lid, rubbing her fingers together. I'm out of practice, anyway, she thought. Like the piano, I'm out of tune – with myself and everything that's happening around me.

Such a short while ago, she had written to Addie Dunstable *yesterday, our lives were going along in a regulated and uneventful manner, if not, even then, free from the continual worry about Maxstead. But worrying about Maxstead, as you know, Addie dear, has been an established fact for so long that one has grown accustomed to it, like ever-present indigestion, I fancy – unpleasantly there in the background, but something one has to accept because there seems to be little to be done to alleviate it permanently. And now look at us: people we have*

never heard of, dead people, intruding into our lives. A son who has
brought us face to face with ruin, brothers who are at loggerheads – or
to put a kinder slant on that, who are not seeing eye to eye . . .

It was a letter destined never to be sent. She had torn it up,
thrown it into the fire and watched the flames consume it,
knowing she could not share such frightening thoughts with
anyone – thoughts that led, inevitably, to Binkie's decision to
sell Maxstead. It was a form of self-pity and she must not –
she *would* not – allow herself to indulge it.

Closing her eyes, trying to blot out terrible forebodings, she
felt rather than heard the distant reverberation of the heavy knocker
on the front door. She just had time to compose herself before
old Stanton showed him in, the detective inspector with the
scarred, unsmiling face, but one which, she was inclined to hope
and believe, hid a more sensitive nature than it led one to expect.

She hoped, in fact, that it was because he didn't wish to
inhibit her from speaking freely that he had come alone today,
on the premise that one policeman was less intimidating than
two. She waved him to a chair, choosing one for herself that
had its back to the light.

She had decided beforehand to surprise him by taking the
initiative, and she began immediately he had taken his seat. 'I
believe you might have guessed why I asked you to come here,
Inspector.'

It was indeed she who had requested the meeting, and
though he had fully intended to see her again after the interview with her son, he hadn't felt it appropriate to request her
to present herself at the station, as he had Sir Julian. 'Guessing
isn't what we're paid to do in my profession, my lady.'

She smiled slightly. Her fingers drummed on the table beside
her until, becoming aware of it, she quickly folded her hands
on her lap. They were square hands, and small – fingers too
short for the piano; she had never been able to span an octave
– and she did not want him to notice how rough they were,
the nails trimmed very short. Gardener's hands – certainly not
a lady's. She took a deep breath, tried to recall the prepared
phrases, and as she began to speak prayed he would not notice
how difficult she was finding this.

'I have spoken to my son, Inspector, and we do not need,

I think, to go over what passed between you regarding his unwise investments with . . . with the foreigner, Mauritz, as I understand his name was. On the other hand, I now believe I owe you an apology for not being entirely frank with you about that person when we spoke before.' She hesitated only a fraction and then went on firmly, 'I am prepared to do what I can to help you now.'

'Thank you, Lady Maude. Any help you think you can give us would be greatly appreciated.'

'We at Maxstead are as anxious as you are to get to the bottom of all this.'

'Indeed.' He hoped that was true.

They were interrupted by a smiling maid who came in with a graceful silver coffee service on a tray, and there was silence between them while the girl poured it out and offered thin almond biscuits before leaving them alone once more.

That apology had cost the lady a good deal, Reardon was willing to bet, as he nibbled the biscuit. If her offer of help was genuine, it made him feel more kindly disposed towards her, and willing to give her as much background information as he thought wise regarding Mauritz. When the door had shut behind the maid, he briefly outlined what they had discovered about him, and his probable links with a man named Arthur Aston. Her brows rose enquiringly at the last name, but he decided it was not necessary to elaborate that particular point. Her stiff, formal manner of speaking – natural to her, or due to nervousness, or possibly just to remind him of his place, he hadn't yet determined which – was catching. He heard himself saying when he had finished, in a way that didn't sound like himself, 'I understand Mauritz made himself unpopular by coming here and probing into some occasion, or happening, that occurred when you were visiting South Africa some years ago.'

'Visiting? That is not precisely what I was doing there. It was wartime, you understand, the South African war, and I had gone out there on Lady Randolph Churchill's hospital ship, hoping to nurse our wounded soldiers. However, I was taken ill and had to stay behind in Cape Town while they sailed on to Durban. It was a bitter disappointment to me, but in the end had certain compensations for a very young woman such as I was then. When I was pronounced fit enough, I was able to enjoy the many distractions and amusements Cape Town had to offer, which would not otherwise have been the case, before I left for home.'

'It's my understanding that Mr Osbert Rees-Talbot and his brother were two of the army officers serving out there.' In view of her apology, he didn't remind her that she had evaded the answer to this question about them before. 'I understand he was injured and spent some time in hospital in Cape Town. So I suppose it was very probable you associated with them there?'

A small porcelain clock on the white marble mantelpiece emitted a silvery chime, and the crystal drops decorating two vases either side shivered very slightly. 'I did,' she admitted stiffly after a moment or two.

'Very pleasant to meet up with old friends, I dare say, neighbours from here in England.'

'I had never met either before I left England. I was still unmarried and living at home with my parents, mostly in town and only occasionally at our home in the country, which lies some miles to the west of Folbury, so the number of people I knew, friends from this part of the world, was limited. The Rees-Talbots and I did not move in the same circles. In fact, we actually met for the first time in Cape Town when Captain Rees-Talbot – Osbert – was convalescing from injuries. He returned to his regiment shortly before I went back home. That was the extent of our acquaintance.'

'Which presumably you renewed after the war?'

'No, not at all. Our paths did not cross again.'

'Perhaps I misunderstood. When we last spoke you told us one of your sons is engaged to the late Mr Rees-Talbot's daughter?'

'Yes, indeed, Margaret is shortly to become my daughter-in-law, I am happy to say, but their meeting was nothing to do with family friendships or connections. Young people nowadays do not expect their parents to concern themselves with making matches for them, as we did.'

'I suppose that's true.' That sort of thing had never been part of Reardon's working-class upbringing and thank the good Lord for that. He waited a moment before saying carefully, 'About Cape Town. I'm afraid I have questions to ask, personal questions . . . I'm sorry if they should be painful.'

'I understand. Carry on.'

Without any more hesitation, he plunged straight in. 'Was there, by any chance, any sort of . . . attachment at the time, between you and either of the Rees-Talbot brothers?'

She stiffened, but met his gaze directly and answered readily enough. 'We went to the same dances and parties, I found them both charming, and very amusing company as I have said, but I assure you there was never anything remotely romantic about our meetings.'

He tried to imagine what Lady Maude – stocky, plain, grey-haired – would have been like as a girl. Although she could never have been a beauty, in the chocolate-box, Gibson-girl prettiness popular in her youth, she would have had vitality, he was sure, that spark of liveliness in her eyes that was, in the end, more attractive and lasting. But no, not in any circumstances could he imagine Lady Maude flirting.

'Sir Julian told us that when Mauritz came to see you, he was anxious to question you about an old photograph he had with him. You told him quite definitely that you didn't recognize anyone on it, which he saw cause to doubt. What do you think he was hoping you would say?'

'As to that, I remain as much at a loss as you, Inspector.' She fixed him with her sharp, bright stare, head a little to one side, probably hoping to disconcert him, he felt, until he decided she was actually assessing him, weighing him up. After a moment she seemed to come to a decision and picked up a book on the small table beside her. Underneath it lay an old, slightly faded snapshot, which she slid across to him. 'The photograph he had was another copy of this. How it should have come into his possession I have no idea. When I asked him where he had obtained it he refused to say. The girl there' – pointing to a rather dim corner of the picture – 'is me. It was taken one day when a large group of us took a picnic out to a well-known beauty spot by Table Mountain, where the views are magnificent.'

'Yet you denied that when he showed it to you.' He could see why she'd hoped she could get away with doing so. The girl she had indicated was sitting in the shade of a large tree, with the result that the picture of her was too indistinct to give any unmistakable impression, and Mauritz would have had no grounds for challenging the truth of what she said.

'If he had been plainer and less secretive, told me honestly what he hoped to gain by questioning me, I might have been more forthcoming. One does not take kindly to unlooked-for probing into one's private affairs. And there was also something very shifty about the man that I did not like.'

'What about the other people in the picture? Were either of the Rees-Talbot brothers there, by any chance?'

She placed a hand on the coffee pot, and finding it still hot asked, 'More coffee?'

'Thank you, no.' He waited until she had poured one for herself before repeating his question. 'The Rees-Talbots were not there?'

'No, they were not,' she answered firmly.

'I see. Lady Maude, do you remember any particular, untoward incident that occurred when you were in Cape Town?'

'*Untoward?* Unpleasant, you mean? My dear inspector, we were at war with the Boers. Incidents of an untoward, not to say distressing nature were happening all the time.'

'I'm not necessarily referring to the fighting. I was thinking of something different, something that might have happened to people you knew personally. Scandals, rumours going around?' He thought carefully before adding cautiously, 'Particularly regarding either of the Rees-Talbots?'

She drew herself up and sat very straight. 'I believe you are in danger of overstepping the mark, Inspector.'

'I'm sorry, but that's something that can't always be avoided. You must see I have to ask you these questions if we're to get to the bottom of this matter. We have reason to believe, you see, that Mr Osbert Rees-Talbot may have come under pressure before he died regarding some occurrence when he was serving in the army there.'

He could feel the frost from where he sat, and feared he might have lost whatever sympathy had been generated between them. It had been a mistake to imply that any breath of scandal – however far in the distant past – could have touched the family of her future daughter-in-law. In that world in which she moved, such a thing would reflect itself on the Scroopes and would have to be avoided at all costs. Social snobberies like that were a far cry from life as he – and almost everyone else, he suspected – knew, but just because they were beyond his experience didn't mean they didn't exist.

After a while, a trifle less coldly, she said, 'I take that to mean Mauritz had been pestering Margaret's father too?'

Reardon might well have thought this of Mauritz, had those payments been made to him, and not to Aston. He had come to believe that they must have been working in collusion, but he was not, however, about to befog the issue by bringing Aston into this discussion with her Ladyship. Perhaps he had already gone too far. She was sharp, quite intuitive, and Aston or Mauritz, it was not going to take her long to put two and two together and reach the conclusion that Osbert Rees-Talbot had been hounded into taking his own life, with all that would mean to the Scroopes. Either way – past or present scandal – they would see themselves as being allied to a family tainted with disgrace, ridiculous as that was. They might, he thought, be living in a Jane Austen novel.

Yet even while he was thinking this, she said something which made him decide that he may have been doing her less than justice.

'My son – Sir Julian, that is – has been a fool,' she said bluntly. 'And we do not yet fully know what the consequences of that will be. I love him as a mother, but I speak as someone who is not easily deceived. I tell you, whatever the man Mauritz had done, Julian could never have committed murder on him. Not even,' she added with a sardonic trace of humour, 'if it was to save his own life.'

She stood up, a signal that the interview was over, and he followed suit. He towered above her but did not feel he had the advantage. 'Thank you for talking to me, my lady. I have a small request before I leave. May I borrow that photograph, please?'

She hesitated only fractionally before pushing it across the table. 'Very well.' Suddenly she asked, 'How old was that man?'

'Mauritz? It's believed he was in his thirties.'

'I thought younger, but then I am a bad judge.'

Could it possibly have been relief he heard in her voice?

Twenty

Making regular reports to his superintendent was necessary but awkward. An afternoon meeting had been fixed up, too early for Reardon to knock off for the day afterwards, yet late for getting on his motorbike, riding to Folbury and then back home again, when he'd sworn to snatch time to take Ellen to the concert she'd been looking forward to for weeks. Hopefully, he might just be able to make it.

It was the sort of thing you had to take in your stride. DS Cherry was a good boss, a competent and experienced officer, a colleague of long standing. At the moment he was, as he put it, up to his eyebrows in paperwork, but it was only a matter of time before he decided to put in an appearance at Folbury: Reardon had a reputation for not working by the book, and Cherry kept a watching brief. Especially now. Though Cherry himself had had reservations about the decision to suspend the Snowman case, he too had his bosses and he'd had to bend to the prevailing wind; he must be feeling chuffed now that his doubts had been justified, despite the lack of convincing suspects as yet for either murder.

He listened to the account of Sir Julian's admissions and what had passed between Reardon and Lady Maude the previous day with a lengthening face. 'Tread softly there, Bert,' he warned. 'One step out of line and we'll have the chief constable, the high sheriff and God knows who else on our backs.'

Not to mention the press – that dainty, irritating little creature, Judy Cash, in particular. Before it was suggested they might need more men on the strength, Reardon grasped the opportunity to put in a general good word for the back-up he was getting in Folbury, and in particular to praise the work Gilmour was putting in. The sergeant was out to impress him, of course, knowing that backing from him would speed up his transfer, but Reardon had early marked his potential, even as far back as when he'd worked with him on the Broughton Underhill case. He was impetuous on occasion, but he was capable, as well as being ambitious. When he'd developed the necessary protective carapace he'd be even better.

Ambition, in Reardon's own experience, was a double-edged sword. He himself had disappointed Cherry by refusing further promotion to chief inspector after his marriage. Satisfying to the ego, no doubt, but although the downside to life for *anyone* in the detective branch was that it too often cut into your personal life, he had no desire to be swamped with paperwork on top of that, desk-bound, with less and less opportunity for the sort of work that had made him want to be a policeman in the first place.

Back in Folbury at last, having divested himself of his motorcycle leathers and helmet, he found Joe scrutinizing the photograph Lady Maude had lent him with a magnifying glass.

'Well, I wouldn't have recognized the old girl from this, sir,' the sergeant remarked, 'and you say she denied either of the Rees-Talbots were on it, but still . . . this fellow here' – he jabbed a finger at a young man lounging on the grass – 'you know, Lily Aston has a picture of Osbert that belonged to her husband, taken with some other officers. I wouldn't like to say for certain, but I wouldn't be all that surprised if this was him, though I'd like to have another look at Lily's picture and compare it with this. Can you give me half an hour to go and persuade her to let us borrow it, sir?'

He was off like a shot, almost before he'd been given agreement, bagging one of the police bicycles to pedal off to Cherry Avenue. Standing at the window and watching him go, Reardon frowned. If Gilmour's suspicions proved correct, if the two men in the photos did prove to be one and the same, it followed that Lady Maude had been lying. Again.

And she had almost convinced him.

When Lily Aston opened the front door Joe was immediately struck by the emptiness of the narrow hallway. There was room to pass now that the cumbersome, laden coat rack which had previously hindered progress had disappeared. All that remained was a coat, a hat and a raincoat hanging from pegs on the wall.

He couldn't help noticing a difference in Lily, too. She was not looking at all well, cradling a bandaged hand against her body. She became flustered when she saw Joe's eyes on her, and her unbandaged hand went to her hair. Maybe that was what made the difference, Joe thought doubtfully. It sat in rigid waves either side of her parting, and he wasn't sure that it improved her appearance, but if she thought it did, perhaps that was all that mattered. The way women felt about their hair was an unaccountable mystery. Maisie had been talking about getting hers bobbed, though it was her best feature, long and thick and a glossy dark brown, and he didn't understand why she was so anxious to get rid of it. 'Don't suppose you do, but you don't have to spend hours washing it and waiting for it to dry,' she'd retorted. True, but he hated the idea of it disappearing at a few snips of the scissors.

Lily was willing enough to let him borrow the picture of the group of officers she had shown him. 'In fact you can keep it,' she said in an offhand way. 'It's no use to me. The major wasn't *my* friend after all, so it doesn't mean a thing to me.'

It was an enlarged photo that had been framed, and not heavy, yet he noticed the wince as she attempted to lift it from the wall. 'Here, let me. What's the matter with your hand?'

'Thanks. It's my thumb – that cut I got from the key when I was unlocking the cupboard to get the desk key out for you. It's gone wrong,' she said resentfully. All his fault, of course, that she'd had to open the cupboard in the first place! 'Been giving me gyp.'

'You want to get it seen to.'

'Oh, I got some stuff from the chemist.'

'Shouldn't you let the doctor see it?' He hesitated, then said carefully, 'You don't look well, you know.'

'I suppose I'll have to if it doesn't get better, but it'll be all right.' She stared at him. Two hard spots of bright colour had appeared on her cheeks. She said challengingly, 'I know I don't look so good, but it's not my thumb. You haven't noticed I've had my hair waved, have you?'

'It's . . . very nice.'

'No, it isn't. It's awful. And my new shoes don't fit properly, either.' And without warning her face crumpled and a bewildered Joe was leading her to a chair, where she sat weeping, sobs heaving her skinny frame, her fingers raking through her hair. He was nonplussed. He didn't know what else to do, apart from patting her shoulder awkwardly, so he just waited until presently she regained some control of herself. 'Well,' she said, scrubbing angrily at her face with an already soaking handkerchief, 'made a right fool of myself there, didn't I?'

'Mrs Aston, I mean it,' Joe said. 'Your hair looks quite all right.' And it did look better than it had, looser now that she'd mussed it up. 'Anyway, that's not what's upsetting you really, is it? All this has been a nasty shock and you're bound to feel like this sometimes.' He was shocked himself at the ideas that were suddenly coming to him, unbidden. And he knew he was being less than adequate, devoutly wishing some woman – even that pesky reporter – was here to help her. 'Shall I make you a cup of tea?'

'No, it's not tea I need. I know you mean well, but you'd best be on your way.'

He could only do as she asked. Some people were not easy to help.

Reardon was talking to Waterhouse in the DI's office when he got back, so he had to wait. He undid the brown paper and string that had wrapped the picture and laid it on the desk, but his thoughts were now on something else entirely.

Well, Lily, after all.

Lily, looking ill and grey, nursing her bandaged hand. It must have been a nasty cut she'd got from that key. A *key*? He took out his own bunch of keys and jiggled them on his palm. None of them looked sharp enough to inflict a cut. You were more likely to hurt yourself on the sharp ends of the split ring itself. They were the devil to open sometimes in order to remove a key. Was that what Lily had been doing? Because the little key to the desk he had asked for was on her husband's officially missing ring with all his others – including the one to the foundry?

That coat hanging from the peg in the hall was a brown

tweed mixture – and the woman Gladys Ibbotson had seen running away had been wearing a brown coat. Aston had dropped Lily off that morning on his way to the garage to leave his car. Easy enough for her to have walked over to Henrietta Street for some reason rather than do her shopping, and then followed him into the foundry.

He could all too easily imagine what could have happened then: taking a God-given chance . . . giving him a shove when his back was turned . . . holding him down with her foot, the dominated dominating, at last. Such an ignominious death, even for an unlikeable character such as Aston had apparently been. Could Lily's resentment have pushed her so far to the edge that it no longer mattered? And why now, after putting up with him for all those years? Was it just a case of the worm turning? Or had something else triggered it off?

Well . . . The hat on the other peg, for one thing. It was a man's hat, a soft grey trilby. Aston had famously worn a bowler, rain or shine; it had made him a familiar figure to the residents of Henrietta Street, though only by sight. Most of them had never spoken to him.

'*He didn't know what was going on behind his back,*' Eileen Gerrity had said. And hadn't she also said that Mauritz was capable of flirting with any woman, whatever her age . . . even Lily Aston? She wasn't by any stretch the kind of woman you'd dream of flirting with, though presumably Aston had once found her so, enough to marry her. But I've never seen her other than when she's upset or ill, Joe reminded himself charitably. I don't know what she can be like, really. She could have hidden depths, be sentimental enough to keep some token of her lover, such as that hat, just as his own mother had treasured his father's dressing gown and kept it hanging on the bedroom door until the day she, too, died. He saw it now, a dark plaid with a frayed collar, surely the subconscious memory which had started all this speculation?

A new lease of life, it must have seemed to Lily, if Mauritz had led her to believe there was some future with him. She was easily led – look how she had been persuaded to trust Judy Cash. It was all speculation, but if that *was* what had happened – and if Aston had killed Mauritz and Lily learnt about it . . . what better motive for killing him than revenge?

Joe sat still for a moment then looked at his watch, pushed his chair back and rushed off in search of Stringer. Eventually he found the driver with his feet up on a desk, dunking ginger nuts in his tea. 'Quick, I need the car. I need to be at Henrietta Street before half past five.'

Stringer looked offended. He was here to take orders from Reardon, not Joe Gilmour. Who said *he* was authorized to order the car just when he wanted? He picked up another ginger nut. Then nearly lost his balance as his feet were lifted off the desk. He decided not to argue.

Joe caught Eileen just as she was putting her coat on. 'I won't keep you. Just tell me one thing. Was Lily Aston having an affair with Wim Mauritz?'

Startled, she paused in the act of picking up her handbag, then laughed. 'Well, I'd hardly call it an *affair* – though she might have seen it that way. I told you, he gave any woman the glad eye. I reckon he couldn't help it.'

'Where did they meet? You told me your boss didn't socialize with his customers.'

She looked away, then shrugged. 'Well, maybe he did in this case. OK, OK, yes, he sometimes used to invite Mauritz home for supper.' She looked doubtful, perhaps having heard of Lily's meals. 'Or maybe just a drink.'

'You didn't know he was living in Henrietta Street?'

'Who, Mauritz? Here, you mean? You can't be serious! His sort, living in this street? Nobody lives here that doesn't have to.'

Reardon was waiting for him when he got back. 'Took your time, didn't you?' he asked impatiently. It wasn't like the DI to have his eye on the clock, but it was complicated to explain that he hadn't just that moment come back from Lily's house.

'Sorry, sir, but—'

'Is that the photo, then?' Reardon interrupted, suddenly catching sight of Lily's picture lying face downwards on the desk.

'Yes, sir, but there's something else first.'

'Something else? Like what? All right then, carry on, but make it quick.'

Lily and her situation depressed Joe. He was sorry for her, but he'd no choice. If she'd killed her husband, then . . .

'Right, sir.'

Reardon looked at his watch but settled to listening without making comment, not even when Joe had finished. 'That's theory, not proof,' he said at last. 'You're running away with yourself, lad. Where's the evidence? How did she know Aston had killed Mauritz? And if she did, why did she keep quiet? Why did she wait all this time before taking revenge? Why kill him at all, in fact? If she'd shopped him, that would have been enough to get him out of her life, all right.'

Reardon had never put much store by Lily's guilt. And put like that . . .

Joe felt like a raw rookie. Why hadn't he kept his mouth shut until he'd thought it through? 'She *did* lie about Aston never bringing customers home, sir – Mauritz in particular. Well, they both lied about that, Eileen Gerrity as well as Lily – but I think in Eileen's case it was because she won't let herself believe Aston might actually have been a murderer. She may still have some feelings for him – more than likely the only one who has!' Reardon was drumming his fingers impatiently on the desk now, but Joe went on, 'Anyway, Lily seems to have been dazzled by Mauritz. He fancied himself as a ladies' man, and I think maybe *she* lied about knowing him because she knows she'd been taken in. More or less as Eileen believed.'

'That may be so, but how convinced are you that she's *capable* of murdering her husband? She's evidently neurotic, but would she go that far?'

Joe didn't think Lily neurotic, just someone at the end of her tether. Reardon hadn't seen her sobbing. 'I don't honestly know.'

Reardon considered him, then closed his eyes, giving the impression he was doing some complicated summing up in his head. When he opened them again, it seemed as if he might be interested after all. 'It's a *possibility*, of course. No more than that. All right, we'll go and see her again. Not that I think there's anything in it. But for now, let's concentrate on this other thing.' He turned the picture the right way up and laid it flat. 'Any luck?'

'Still not sure.' Reardon placed the photograph borrowed from Lady Maude alongside and Joe indicated the officer Lily had said was Rees-Talbot. 'I wouldn't lay bets on them being the same chap – the small photo's not all that clear, and all these officers with their slouch hats and moustaches tend to look alike, don't they? All the same—' He broke off suddenly.

'Gilmour?'

Joe was staring at the photograph received from Lady Maude with a bemused expression, all thoughts of Lily banished from his mind. Why hadn't this been obvious before? Reardon followed his pointing finger and took a closer look.

'See what I mean, sir?'

He frowned, not at first seeing what Joe had seen, but after a moment or two comprehension began to dawn. They stared at one another in silence as the kaleidoscope shifted and reformed into a different pattern, and all of a sudden, things began to take on another, altogether different focus.

'Well, well. Good work, Gilmour.' He sighed, then said, 'Give me a minute. I'll have to let my wife know our plans have changed.'

He picked up the telephone as Joe left the office. So that was why he'd been so tetchy. It occurred to Joe that making those sorts of telephone calls was going to be part of his future too, some day, if he was lucky. And part of Maisie's to receive them.

Twenty-One

'I can't deny it's come as a shock, meeting you again, Hamer, after all these years, though I would have preferred it to be in happier circumstances. However, this disagreeable business with Julian has gone on quite long enough. It's a miserable affair and I'm glad to see *someone*' – Lady Maude nodded graciously towards Margaret and Symon – 'has had the common sense to do something about settling it once and for all. Maybe now the rest of us will find some peace of mind.'

Hamer Rees-Talbot, a large, tweed-suited man, looking slightly out of place in the formal, elegant drawing room, smiled slightly. 'You haven't changed, Maude.'

But *he* had, she thought. Still as handsome, his figure upright and trim, but his many years as a senior army officer, his wide experience in both peace and war, had given him an authority that had certainly not been apparent in his days as a freewheeling subaltern, when he had taken his pleasures and his obligations lightly. A young fellow well-liked by everyone, he had never needed much to keep him happy outside his duties – little more than a horse to ride, some shooting, and pretty girls to amuse himself with.

She suspected he had been trapped by astonishment into agreeing to come over here with Symon and Margaret when they'd motored across to Malvern, where he was now living in retirement with his new wife in what she had heard spoken of as a cosy villa – no doubt stuffed with elephants' feet stools and Benares brassware, probably manufactured in Birmingham, shipped out to India and then sold as authentic. She doubted Hamer would have known the difference, or cared if he had: he had never been the aesthetic sort. Golf, the company of the widow he'd married, a good dinner and a glass or two of port to look forward to every evening, and he would be a happy man.

In actual fact she was wrong on several counts, but especially about Hamer's reasons for allowing himself to be persuaded into making the journey to Maxstead. Margaret had given him little explanation, only that it was something to do with Lady Maude and the time he'd spent fighting in South Africa. He hadn't known Maude Prynne well out there, though well enough to admire the spirit that had taken her there in the first place, and the fortitude with which she'd borne her disappointment at not being allowed to continue with what she had clearly seen as her patriotic duty. Because he had believed that the sturdily independent girl he remembered must really need his help if she had requested him to come and see her after all these years, he had allowed himself to be driven over here today without much demur. All the same, his antennae had twitched. He had a nasty feeling about what was to come. And only a few minutes ago he had discovered it was not her idea at all that he should be brought here, but that of his niece and her fiancé, Lady Maude's son, the padre. She had seemed, in fact, more surprised than he was, though she had recovered herself remarkably well.

It was only now, having partaken of cups of tea and scones with strawberry jam, that they were getting down to brass tacks. 'I'm sorry, Uncle, if you feel you're here on false pretences,' Margaret began. 'I'm afraid you'll think this has all been very devious, but I thought you wouldn't come unless . . .'

He considered it damned devious, if the truth be known, but he was not the impatient young man he had once been, and was prepared to wait until he found out what was going on before voicing any opinions. He was fond of his niece, and he felt she wouldn't have brought him here for nothing. She had had a lot on her plate lately, one way or another . . . and as far as he could gather, Felix hadn't been much help there, a thought that caused him a nasty twinge of conscience. Hamer had been uneasily aware for some time before his brother's death of the disagreements between Felix and his father, but had not felt it his place to interfere, especially in the delicate circumstances that existed between himself and his brother. Well, Ossie was dead now, and perhaps the time had come to step in himself, *in loco parentis,* as it were. A Cambridge graduate, clever young devil, Felix should have left all that left-wing claptrap behind in his student days. A spell in the army would

have put paid to it. Never did any young feller any harm that
Hamer had ever seen.

'Well . . .' Margaret began hesitantly. She certainly wasn't
herself. Not the bright, happy girl he knew.

'Margaret, my dear, Symon will tell this,' Lady Maude intervened, turning to her son for support. 'He's more used to
explaining difficult things.'

Hamer had in his time presided over numerous courts martial
and he now listened judicially while Symon, after giving his
mother an ironic glance at this role she had assigned him, gave
an admirably succinct account of the recent events which had
involved his elder brother, Sir Julian (apparently known as
Binkie) with some chap from South Africa who had got himself
murdered. South Africa! His apprehensions deepened. The
trouble was, Symon went on, that the police didn't yet seem
prepared to dismiss his brother from their enquiries entirely,
though Binkie had had nothing to do with the victim, other
than unwisely investing in some shady scheme that had been
put forward and gone the way of all such schemes.

'Are you saying they actually suspect him of this murder?'

'I can't believe so, or they wouldn't have let him go, surely.
But it seems they're still not quite satisfied – very likely grasping
at straws. Until Binkie came forward, they didn't seem to have
much to go on.'

'How did he get himself mixed up in all this?'

'The chap who was murdered was some scoundrel who
persuaded him to part with money – got him to invest in a
South African mining company which didn't exist.' Symon's
reply sounded deliberately neutral, revealing no indication of
his own opinions on the matter.

'Who was he, eh? Apart from being a bit of a rogue?'

'Who, indeed?' asked Lady Maude. She had grown slightly
flushed, and Hamer began to think she was perhaps not as
much in control of herself as he had thought. 'If you can tell
us that, it may justify your having been brought all this way,
Hamer . . . Oh, please forgive me, I suppose I should give
you your rank! It's *Colonel* Rees-Talbot now, I believe?'

'Yes, but Hamer will do, Maude,' Hamer said gruffly.

'Very well.' He had forgotten she had a very sweet smile,

not unlike that of her son, though neither of them appeared to use it much. 'I must ask you this: did you know anyone in Cape Town called Mauritz?'

'No one in particular, that I can recall. It's a common enough name in that part of the world.'

'Wim Mauritz, this man called himself. He came here with a copy of a photograph – one taken when we all went on that picnic near Table Mountain. I can't show you my own copy – the police have borrowed it – but you'll remember that day, and the de Jager girls, Sophie and Bettje?'

He knew for certain now where this was going and felt lowered by the knowledge. They were all looking at him. Margaret's fingers were locked together. Already desolated by her father's death, this was going to be a further blow, which he devoutly wished he could spare her, while knowing now that he could not.

'You must remember Sophie and Bettje?' Lady Maude repeated. 'They were very attractive girls. I stayed with them at their house in Cape Town.'

'Yes, of course I remember them.'

'I knew you would. I venture to say you were very much taken with Bettje, were you not?'

'We both were, Osbert and I. More than a little. Half in love with her, in fact. She was – enchanting.'

'And also quite a silly girl, at times.'

'We can all be foolish when we're young.' There was no backing out of it now. He harrumphed, then squared his shoulders. 'Yes. There was a bit of trouble . . . you must know about that, Maude, you were there.'

'I know what was being whispered while I was there. It was what happened after I left that I know nothing about.'

'Nor I – I was back with my unit before you ever left the country. Osbert, too – and almost immediately wounded again, more severely. Losing his arm, in fact. As soon as he'd recovered sufficiently he was sent home. Cape Town was behind us, and neither of us ever saw it again.'

'But did you not hear any of the stories – the gossip? There were so many officers, in and out of Cape Town, and such news travels fast.'

'Not until three years later, I swear, long after South Africa. Some fellow from another regiment I met when I was serving in India . . .' He stopped, took a breath, and then went on rapidly. 'You obviously know that Bettje had a child, Maude?'

From outside came an unearthly shriek. Hamer, startled, swung his gaze to the window, though none of the others in the room appeared to notice. It wasn't until, through the corner of his eye, he saw a flash of impossibly exotic blue, limned against a dark hedge, that he realized it was nothing more than a peacock strutting across the lawn, stopping to spread its tail and display its finery.

It had provided a distracting moment. Lady Maude waited until the sound had died down before speaking. 'I did hear the rumour that she was expecting one,' she answered slowly at last. 'I didn't know whether to believe it or not, but it was obvious that something was wrong in the family. The de Jagers, the mother and father, went about tight-lipped, and poor Bettje wasn't allowed out without supervision. I left for home about that time, and though I wrote to them when I reached England, thanking them for their hospitality, they never replied. I have always wondered what happened to Bettje.'

Hamer spread his hands. 'According to this chap I met – Browne, his name was – the parents washed their hands of her.'

'That doesn't really surprise me. They were extremely strict.'

'Yes. Well, I regret to say, this chap Browne looked a bit askance at me when he told me all this, obviously thinking I was responsible. Can't blame him too much. I'd escorted her around pretty frequently, and I must confess I had a bit of a reputation with the ladies at that time' – Lady Maude raised a wry eyebrow – 'but he'd got the wrong end of the stick.' He stopped and looked down, inspecting the immaculate toecaps of his polished shoes, and when he looked up, his face was crimson. 'The wrong Rees-Talbot, don't you see.'

Margaret gave a small, inarticulate sound.

'My dear,' Hamer said sadly, 'I know, I was shocked, too. I wrote to Ossie immediately, asking him if it was true and if so what he had done about it, but, well . . . the upshot was, he wrote back that even if it was true, it was nothing to do with him.' He stopped and cleared his throat, and then, looking straight ahead to avoid meeting anyone's eyes, he went on, 'I couldn't believe that, you know. Bettje was a frivolous young minx, but I know she was in love with him, or thought she was, and he – well, it was so obvious how he felt about her I'd backed down myself in his favour. And I was certain there was no one else around at that time. But by the time I heard about the child and wrote to him, Ossie was back in England, married, with a wife and family, didn't want complications. It was in the past and best forgotten, as far as he was concerned, no need for him to intervene after all this time.' His shoes occupied his attention again until at last he looked up, saying, 'I thought it a bad show, to tell the truth, and it caused a rift between us. We didn't write or communicate for years. You wouldn't know about all that, Margaret, you were only a child. It was your Aunt Deborah who persuaded us to patch things up later, after a fashion, but things were never the same between us.'

'What happened to her – to Bettje?' Lady Maude asked.

A moment or two passed before he spoke. Clearly he was having difficulty in finding the right words. 'The worst,' he said finally. 'I'm sorry to say, Bettje, poor young thing . . . she died. If what they say is true, I'm afraid she took an overdose of laudanum or some such.'

'And the child?' Margaret asked in a choked voice.

'Her sister had married and took the child in, m'dear – her sister Sophie. It was taken care of.'

There didn't seem anything more anyone could say. It was hard to credit, harder still to bear, but the facts spoke for themselves. Her father, Major Osbert William Rees-Talbot, DSO, had not acted like the officer and gentleman he had always held himself up to be – or even as any honourable man should. He had branded himself as a moral coward and it had eaten into him all his life. And in the end, had his cowardice come back to haunt him?

'So this man who came over here to England and obtained money from Father – threatening him, I suppose, was . . .' She stopped. It was impossible, just yet, to allow herself to voice the inevitable conclusions that were forcing themselves on her:

a stranger, a man called Wim Mauritz, and what he must be to her, and to Felix, personally. Had Osbert met him? She closed her eyes to shut out the image – and immediately another came to her. 'But it wasn't him those cheques were made out to, it was Aston.'

Hamer gave a startled exclamation. '*Who* did you say?'

'Arthur Aston. He was Father's batman at one time. He must have known about all this. Father had been making cheques out to him . . . that's what the payments to him were all about, they must have been!'

'Lance Corporal Aston? Oh yes, I remember him. Amateur boxer, saved Ossie from Johnnie Boer once, but I never took to him much. Always one like him in every company. Knows everybody's business, where to get you anything you want, as long as you ask no questions. Threatening, was he? Just let me have a few minutes with him!'

Symon said quietly, 'Colonel Rees-Talbot, the man is dead. He has been murdered too.'

The silence went on so long it was almost an intrusion when Margaret spoke. 'But Felix . . .' she said, through stiff lips. She knew now that the blood could and actually did run cold; she felt icy, to the very pit of her stomach. Images and ideas flashed before her like a series of moving pictures: Aston, murdered . . . Felix's fight with him the night before he was killed, after Felix had just found out that Aston had been blackmailing their father . . . But what if he had not *just* found out? What if he had known *before* then? What if he had heard more than he'd told her about that overheard conversation of their father's with Aston? What if he had known about this man, this Mauritz – *and had learnt who he was?* It wasn't difficult to see where that might have taken him.

She didn't know how long she had sat there, frozen into immobility, but suddenly found Symon was pressing a tumbler with brandy in it into her hand, closing her fingers around it, guiding it to her mouth. He must have left the room and brought it in without her noticing. She gulped obediently, swallowed, and the fire of it immediately began to warm her.

At that precise moment, the door was thrown open and, without ceremony, in burst Major Frith.

Red-faced and with his usually smoothly brushed iron-grey hair dishevelled, he took two quick strides into the room. 'There is no need to panic, my lady, but you must all leave the room. Don't rush, but move as quickly as you can.'

'What? What is it, Giles?'

'There's a fire,' he answered, stating what was becoming increasingly obvious, second by second. Acrid smoke was beginning to drift from somewhere further along the corridor outside, unaccustomed noises and shouts, the sounds of panic, were issuing from the back quarters.

'Where is it?'

'Never mind that!' ordered Hamer, automatically assuming control and marshalling them out into the corridor behind Frith, at the same time as Frith shouted over his shoulder, 'Not that way, can't get through the hall! Follow me, this way, out at the back.'

Having left the house by way of the kitchens, the women assembled on the front lawn, along with some of the older servants. Margaret left Lady Maude in the care of old Hanson and the housekeeper, and went to help the rest to carry out what they could, anything that was deemed valuable. The fire was raging in the snug, and by now the hall was alight, the flames licking towards the green baize door that separated it from the kitchen quarters. Anything that would hold water – buckets, bowls, saucepans – was being thrown on to the flames, which barely hissed as they swallowed it up.

'The fire engine's been sent for, my lady,' Stanton tried to reassure her. 'And the Colonel's organizing water being drawn from the big pond.'

'They'll never get here in time,' Lady Maude said, visualizing the miles of winding lanes and rutted roads that lay between here and Folbury.

There was nothing to do but stand helplessly and watch Maxstead as it blazed to the ground.

Twenty-Two

The town's fire engine passed them, clanging its bell and heading out of the town just as Stringer was drawing the car into the side.

'Are you sure this is the right address, Gilmour?'

'It's the one they gave me, sir.'

They left Stringer to find a place to park the car where he could wait for them. 'Near as possible,' Joe reminded him. Reardon had scarcely spoken since leaving the station, wrapped in his own thoughts.

Castle Street was a busy side street running between Victoria Road and the market, but it was mostly small shops, some of them with premises above. Although it was getting towards the tail end of a bustling market day, the shops were still full: a queue of late shoppers snaked out on to the street from inside a pork butcher's whose pies and faggots were famous beyond Folbury, a mouth-watering smell of hot roast pork issuing from its door, while a few steps further along came the nutty smell of wholesome bread. Joe's stomach growled. It might be some time yet before supper, and he was hungry – even for supper supplied by his aunt.

In the greengrocer's they were headed for, the proprietor was too busy weighing out potatoes and onions to give them more than a cursory glance before calling over his shoulder that the flat above the shop had a side entrance, then straight up the stairs, green door at the top, only one, can't miss it.

It was indeed the only door off a square landing at the top of scuffed, lino-covered steps, with a passionate tenor rendering of '*You are my heart's delight*' coming from behind it. A second knock was needed before eventually the door was opened.

For a split second nobody said anything. Mutually taken aback, they all stared. Finding his voice, Joe announced their business.

'Well,' said Judy Cash. 'Well, I suppose you'd better come in.'

'You do get around, Judy, don't you?' Joe remarked,

exchanging a look with Reardon as they followed her down a short, narrow passage. She didn't seem to think his comment worthy of a reply. What the devil was she doing here, Miss Christmas Tree Fairy? She appeared quite at home, the skirt of her bright green dress swishing confidently as she danced lightly in front of them.

They reached another door at the end of the passage where she stopped abruptly with her hand on the knob, the glass slave bangle high on her bare arm glinting in the light of the one unshaded electric bulb in the ceiling. Momentarily hesitant, revealing herself more shaken than she had appeared, she murmured, 'Go carefully, won't you? It's not what you think.'

Reardon digested this enigmatic statement, making no comment. In return, something flashed in the depths of her eyes. Perhaps it was the colour of her dress that made them seem catlike, almost golden green.

She turned the knob. As the door swung open, the woman kneeling on the floor beside a half-packed suitcase looked up and then froze, as if in a tableau, a folded skirt lying across her outstretched palms, like a priestess making an offering to some deity.

The day was beginning to fade and in the uncertain half hour before dusk began, the north-facing room was full of shadows. All the colour seemed concentrated on the rigid figure of Vinnie Henderson, kneeling motionless before the suitcase in a red jumper, with her bright gold hair loose around her face. Slowly and with great care she placed the skirt in the case, shut the lid and stood by the fireplace, her hand resting on the mantel. Behind Reardon, Judy switched on the light and the room was revealed in all its tawdriness, a shabby little bed-sitter that had seen better days, as had the furniture, a gimcrack collection assembled no doubt to make rented accommodation from what had once been a bedroom. Sugary as golden syrup, the throbbing tenor continued to pour his heart out.

'It's the police, Plum.'

'Yes. We've met before, haven't we, Inspector . . . Sergeant?'

'Leaving us, are you, Miss Henderson?'

Vinnie had quickly recovered from whatever shock their

entrance had given her. 'Actually, yes,' she replied easily. 'What brings you here?'

As the love song reached louder and more passionate heights, '*Your life divine . . . brings me ho-ope anew . . .*', he gave the standard formula: 'We've reason to believe you can assist us with our enquiries and we'd like to have a word with you – if you'll please turn that music off.'

Judy went to the gramophone in the corner and lifted the arm, but not gently enough; the needle screeched across the record and Richard Tauber groaned to a dying fall. 'Ouch! Sorry.'

'Have a seat, gentlemen – if you can find one. I'm afraid we're in a bit of a mess.' There was indeed hardly anywhere in the room that wasn't strewn with clothes and other possessions, presumably waiting to be packed. 'What is it you want? Why are you here?' Vinnie repeated.

'I'd very much like to know the same thing,' intervened Judy Cash, briskly sweeping books to the floor from a high stool and perching on it.

Joe settled for propping himself against the table while Reardon pushed aside a pile of clothing on the sofa. 'I think we might well ask the same thing of you, Miss Cash,' he remarked mildly.

'It's Judy,' she said, slightly irritated. 'Well, in case it had escaped your notice, this is actually my home.'

'Yours? The King's School gave this as Miss Henderson's address.'

'So it is – for the present,' Vinnie said. 'When I gave in my notice I naturally had to give up my live-in accommodation there. My friend Judy offered to put me up,' she added with the wide, bright smile Reardon had been so taken with.

Her friend Judy?

The incurious person at the school who had answered Joe's polite request for her address hadn't thought it necessary to say that leaving her job as the headmaster's secretary had involved Miss Henderson in a change of address – or indeed that she had even left her position there at all.

'But before living at the school, you lived at number eighteen Henrietta Street.'

'Henrietta Street? Where's that? No, sorry, I've never lived there.'

Reardon smiled. 'Well, you know, I don't think that's true, is it? I believe you *did* live there for some time, Mrs Mauritz.'

An odd look crossed her face, to be replaced almost instantly by one of barely controlled amusement as she caught Judy Cash's eye. Reardon had long since acquired immunity to this sort of levity through interviewing countless witnesses who thought it clever to know something the police didn't. But neither of them were to know that, and she sobered instantly when it became clear that neither he nor Gilmour shared their amusement. 'Mrs Mauritz? What on earth gave you that strange idea? You've surely got the wrong person if that's who you're looking for.'

She had barely uttered two words when they had met her previously, during the interview with Felix at Alma House, when she had come into the room with a vase of spring flowers and been prevailed upon to stay. Now, hearing the clipped vowels as she spoke, he took it to be the South African English that Eva Smith had put down as 'swanky', though it wasn't all that noticeable and he didn't think he would have remarked on it had he not been looking for it.

'Tell me, Miss Henderson, why are you leaving?'

'Oh, I'm afraid I'm a footloose sort of person,' she answered carelessly. 'I soon get bored with living in one place, you know? Folbury's just hunky dory, I've enjoyed living here, but it's time to make tracks for home.'

'And home is South Africa?' Another look, secret and complicit, passed between the pair. Their relationship intrigued him. 'For both of you, I take it?'

'That's right.'

'And you've never made it known to anyone that's where you were from? Not even to your friends, the Rees-Talbots?'

She shrugged, avoiding his eyes. 'They never asked.'

What about Felix, the young man he had previously assumed she was attached to? Weren't young lovers supposed to be desperate to know every last detail about their beloved? She had probably lied to him, inventing an imaginary past to satisfy any curiosity he might have had. Yet he had an odd fancy, despite the flippancy, that she might have regretted the deception, as if she might be sad at the way things were turning out, that she had hoped they might have been different. In fact, neither woman was as casual as they were making out, however much they tried to appear so.

He went back to his previous question. 'Sergeant Gilmour here has interviewed witnesses who can prove that a man named Wim Mauritz lived at Henrietta Street. The same witnesses will be able to identify the woman who claimed to be his wife. He was from South Africa, too, which seems an unlikely coincidence – unless you can explain what you are doing over here, for instance, and why you're now leaving so suddenly?'

'You don't have to answer that, Plum.'

'Let Miss Henderson speak for herself.'

Vinnie Henderson – or Mrs Mauritz – or *Plum* – replied composedly, 'Well, I don't know where you've got all these ideas from, but I certainly wasn't married to that man, whoever he was. I'm not married to anyone.'

All this time she had remained standing, her elbow propped casually on the mantelpiece of the small black cast-iron fireplace in which a sulky fire smouldered. Presently she lowered herself with apparent nonchalance to the hearthrug where she sat with her feet curled under her. He had noticed an odd thing: each time she spoke, it was preceded by a glance at her friend, almost, you might have thought, as if she were seeking guidance – or even permission. He would not underestimate either of them, but the feeling that it might be little Judy Cash who was the dominant personality in this room didn't altogether surprise him.

In fact it was she, cool as water, who now demanded of Reardon, 'Is it too much to ask again why you're here? And what gives you the right to interrogate my friend like this? As far as I can see, she's done nothing to warrant it.'

'Good question.' Reardon slipped a hand into his inside jacket pocket and pulled out the photograph Lady Maude had produced. Both pairs of eyes were drawn to it, but for the moment he kept it turned face downwards in his hand. 'Before I answer it, we first need to talk about Arthur Aston.'

'Oh, your latest murder?' Judy came back maliciously. 'Unsolved, like the last?'

'Neither unsolved for much longer, I hope.'

'Really? Well, it's good to see the police recovering from their inefficiency at last.'

'That's not a word I would use.'

'I don't suppose you would, but a murdered man is found, and nearly two months later you still don't know who did it. And now another one, equally unsolved. I'd say that was inefficient, wouldn't you?'

'I'm not interested in bandying words. This isn't a game. We're investigating two murders and I need some answers from both of you.' He was annoyed with himself for being drawn and let a moment or two pass before saying abruptly to Vinnie Henderson, 'I'd like you to take a look at this photograph, please, and tell us who you recognize.'

She held it steadily, taking her time, then shook her head.

'You see no resemblance to anyone you know?'

'You don't have to answer that!'

He silenced Judy with a look, her feet twisted around the rungs of her seat, not so much a fairy now as a wicked gremlin perched on a toadstool.

'It's all right, Judy.' Vinnie scanned the photo but in the end shook her head. 'The way these people are dressed, this photo must have been taken before I was even born. Why should I know any of them? Who are they?'

'I was hoping you might be able to tell me. What about you, Judy?'

'No.' She scarcely looked at it before returning it.

They were both lying, he was sure, and Judy Cash was beginning to irritate him seriously. 'Look here, it's been a long day, and I'm not prepared to waste any more time with either of you. Perhaps you might be more accommodating if I asked you, both of you, to accompany us down to the police station. We have a car waiting.'

Neither of them answered. Some tense, unspoken communication was passing between them, almost a battle of wills. At last Vinnie gave an almost imperceptible shake of the head and unwound herself from her position on the floor. Unconsciously echoing Judy's words at the door, she said, 'To begin with, it isn't what you think—'

'For God's sake, Plum! Are you crazy?'

'It's OK. I know what I'm doing.' She began again, 'Nothing turned out as we expected. You see—'

Judy jumped off her stool so quickly it fell over behind her on to the floor. 'Take no notice of her! She doesn't know what she's saying. Her wits have gone haywire.'

But Vinnie looked entirely sensible, an odd, stoical look on her face as she opened a drawer in a rickety sideboard and took out a writing pad, tearing off a wad of sheets, folding them in two and offering them to Reardon. 'There's nothing for either of us to be afraid of, Judy. It's for the best.'

Judy, however, sprang forward, snatched the papers from her and would have tossed them into the fire, had Joe not grasped what she was about to do and intercepted her, grabbing her wrist until she let go and the pages scattered loosely and harm-lessly to the floor in front of the hearth.

Reardon bent and gathered them together. 'What's this?'

'It's a letter to the Rees-Talbots . . . Felix and Margaret. It's not finished yet, but I think it'll tell you all you need to know.' She faced Judy. 'Burning it wouldn't have solved anything.' To Reardon she said, 'Since you know so much, there's no point in not telling you.'

A sound came from Judy that might have been either an exclamation of temper or a dry sob. She jerked her wrist from Joe's grasp, stalked to the window and turned her back on the room, looking out over the street. Every line of her narrow back expressed outrage.

Reardon glanced briefly through the neat but closely hand-written pages he'd picked up. He didn't much fancy reading what might turn out to be a confession, here under the silent scrutiny of three pairs of eyes, even if one pair did belong to Gilmour. On the other hand, he knew he had as yet nothing against either of the two women to warrant an official inter-rogation. 'You can both remain silent while I read this,' he told them, 'or I must ask you to come down to the police station. It's your choice, though in any case there'll be more questions after we've read this, and statements to make, I dare say. Which is it to be?'

Judy spun round to face him, taut as a bowstring. 'Does that mean me, as well?'

'Yes, Miss Cash. It does.'

'Are you arresting us?'

'Not unless you resist. At the moment, you're merely helping us with our enquiries.'

She turned back to the window as Vinnie said, 'Please read the letter.'

Dear Felix and Margaret,

Events have compelled me to leave Folbury suddenly. This is not a good way to tell you, after all your kindness, but I could not bring myself to do so in person. I know you'll feel I have behaved badly, and believe me, I have felt badly about deceiving you – as well as having to leave without saying proper farewells. I have good reason for this, as you'll see when you have read this letter. I deeply regret having done what I have done – the reper- cussions have been more than any of us bargained for. Bear with me if I begin with a long preamble. I'm writing it in the hope it will help you to understand, if not to forgive . . .

I was born and raised in South Africa, something I believe no one here has guessed up until now. I never knew my mother – or only as an elusive shadow that darted across my mind at unexpected moments, quick as the blink of an eye, impossible to catch, but bringing with it a feeling of being held, close and warm, and then leaving me with an immense sadness.

I didn't realize that fleeting shadow was a memory of my mother – not then, not until I had been living with Tant Sophie and Oom Cornelis Joost for most of my thirteen years, when Tant Sophie, in a moment of temper at my refusal to accompany her to one of her prayer meetings, told me I was not their child, but her sister's. I had never had any reason to suspect they were not my parents. Up until then, but never afterwards, I had always called them Mama and Papa – but I was not unduly upset when Sophie told me; in fact I soon realized it was something of a relief. It explained why I had always felt so different from them, why we had never been able to connect.

I suppose I had imagined it had simply been an accident of birth that I had been landed with the parents I had – dutiful but distant, concerned with their own lives and especially, in my uncle's case, his exporting business . . . or in recent years, to be more precise, its failing, since the European demand for elephant tusks, lion skins, ostrich feathers and native artefacts was falling

*off considerably. We were not well off, but I was never actually
deprived of anything – except affection. As an adult, I came to
realize that perhaps it was an inability in either of them to show
any such emotion, rather than a deliberate withholding of it, but
when my younger self saw my friends and the fun and laughter
they had with their families, I used to feel curiously empty, and
envious, while not knowing what it was I envied.*

*My uncle and aunt had no children of their own. I never found
out whether she minded this or not, but now I fancy resentment
and jealousy of her sister played a good part in her attitude towards
me. She had done her Christian duty, taking me in when my
mother died, but I was not, and never could be, her own child.
She cried a good deal, Tant Sophie, a woman who felt circumstances
were always against her: she had married a man who had fallen
on hard times . . . he was forever preoccupied with his business
troubles . . . she had been forced to accept an infinitely less affluent
lifestyle than the one in which she had grown up and had had
every reason to expect would continue . . . I was an ungrateful
and uncooperative child. This last was true enough quite often, at
home, but at school, where I was happy, I pleased my teachers, I
was popular and had plenty of friends.*

*The red leather family photo album that held so many
memories for Sophie and sat prominently on top of the gramophone cabinet was scuffed, its pages grubby from being thumbed
through so many times, marked with the tears that constantly
fell on it. I used to think I might have cried too, if I had been
married to Oom Cornelis, who was a farmer's son from near
Pietermaritzburg, an uncommunicative man with a strongly
developed streak of Voortrekker Christian pig-headedness.*

*'Is there a photo of my mother?' I asked on that momentous
day she told me who I really was – when I had got my breath
back, that is. I'd never paid any attention to the album before,
having no desire to look through anything which could cause so
much misery to anyone.*

*She opened the album and showed me the photographs then.
Dozens of them, on the ornately decorated and gilt-edged pages
of thick card. I was amazed to see how pretty Sophie had once
been, though she could not hold a candle to her sister, Bettje,
in my opinion. Even more amazing was how happy and smiling*

everyone in those pictures was – except for my grandparents, whom I saw for the first time: he, Titus de Jager, a tall, stern-looking man, and she prim and proper with a buttoned-up mouth. But it was Sophie's younger sister Bettje, my mother, who held my attention. She wasn't beautiful, but even through the dim sepia tones of those faded old photos, I could see she had a smile that hinted at mischief, she looked like a girl who would be full of fun and bubbling with happiness, the exact opposite of her sister, my aunt. I knew I should never get my fill of looking at her.

But, duty done, Sophie closed the album. 'Well, now you know. You came to us when she died, and that's all there is to it,' she concluded, reaching for yet another of the indigestion remedies she was always swallowing.

Who was my father? Where was he? Was he dead, too?

But those were questions she would not answer, and the album itself revealed nothing of him. There were stiff, formal pictures of Tant Sophie outside the church in her wedding finery with Oom Cornelis, but none of my mother as a bride, or even of me as a baby.

'Where are her wedding pictures?' I persisted.

'She wasn't—'

She broke off and pressed her lips together. Clearly, she could have bitten off her tongue, but it was too late. Young as I was, I knew then that my mother had been what Tant Sophie and the respectable ladies at her church called a Fallen Woman.

It did not make my longing to know more about her, and my father, any less. The red leather album became as important to me as it was to my aunt. I pored over the pictures of Bettje, trying to see any resemblance to the face I saw every day in the mirror, but it seemed to me I looked more like Sophie, one of those indefinable family looks that are passed down.

The next year, when I was fourteen, I entered a competition run by the local paper for its younger readers. The subject was 'Old Cape Town' and I won the first prize, which was to have my piece printed in the paper. Greatly impressed by this, my aunt persuaded my stubborn uncle to let me have lessons in shorthand and typing, like my best friend Judy Cash, something I'd been hankering after for some time but which he'd adamantly opposed. I had already decided that was the first step towards something I knew I could do, for which I would need shorthand skills. I had no wish to be a journalist, like Judy, but I fancied the next best thing to being a successful person in business, nearly impossible for a woman, was to become secretary to a highly successful man.

But though I gained excellent qualifications and was able to command a reasonable salary when I went to work, time went on and I still hadn't succeeded in getting right where I wanted to be. I was tempted to think that perhaps men might have a point in believing women don't have the necessary intellectual capacity to compete with them on equal terms. But Judy was shocked to the core when I spoke like this, and lectured me about even allowing myself such backward thoughts, never mind expressing them. We had every right to believe we were the equals of men, she said, possibly their superiors. When it came to men like Wim, I could not but agree.

Willem. Willem Mauritz, always known as Wim. Who was he really, apart from an adventurer, a chancer, a younger cousin of Sophie's?

I had known him always as an occasional visitor to our home. The only time I ever saw Sophie really animated was when he arrived on the doorstep, always unannounced but confident that a bed and three meals a day would be available to him for as long as he chose to stay. Which of course they were. What he did for a living was anyone's guess – but it must have been a precarious existence; he would turn up at the house and stay there until something else of glorious promise appeared on the horizon and took him off again. But this time he had stayed away so long, without a word to say where he was, or even letting us know if he was alive or dead, that I believe Sophie had almost ceased to believe he would ever come back.

'Where is she?' he asked when I opened the door to him.

This time he was too late. Tant Sophie had died a few weeks before, of a perforated stomach ulcer which might have been detected earlier had she ever consulted a doctor about her chronic indigestion. I suppose her death must have affected me because I missed her – even the tearful turning of the pages of the photograph album. She had been a sour and undemonstrative woman, but she had taken me in, motherless and fatherless. In her own way, she had done her best for me – and for my mother, when she'd been left in the lurch.

He had wicked black eyes, Wim Mauritz. There was nothing else remarkable about his looks, but he was the sort of man who was said to charm birds off trees – and most women into his arms – and he knew it. Even Tant Sophie was not immune, though to her, who had known him since he was born, he was still a delightful, delinquent child who could be forgiven any mischief. I was not one of those who were charmed, however. I knew he was wild and I suspected he was a liar. I did not trust him.

He took it for granted that he would still be allowed to stay, even though Tant Sophie was not there to kowtow to all his needs, and the weeks went by, and there he still was. We were sitting on the stoep one breathlessly hot evening, watching the sun go down, an ineffable South African sunset in a brandy-coloured sky, when something prompted me to ask him if he had ever known my mother.

He swung round to stare at me. 'Of course I knew your mother!'

'I don't mean Sophie, I mean Bettje.'

'Oh. Oh, well, I knew her too,' he replied after a moment. Perhaps he had never noticed that I had stopped addressing Sophie as 'Mama'. In fact, I had avoided calling her anything at all when I could.

'And my father?'

He shook his head.

I had this photograph which I had found tucked away in one of Tant Sophie's drawers when I was clearing out her things after she died. I went to fetch it, a snapshot taken some years ago, obviously at a picnic. A rather sophisticated picnic with an awning in the background and a table laden with food and several young men and women sitting about in various poses. My mother, Bettje, in a straw boater, a leg o'mutton-sleeved striped blouse and a long skirt, was arranged on the grass, and a couple of young men lounged beside her. One was propped on his elbow, raising his glass to her, the other smiling down at her. She would never, I knew without being told, have been *short of admirers. I handed the snapshot to Wim. 'You're not there, but you might recognize the young men with Bettje.'*

'No, I'm not in the photo,' he agreed, scanning it. 'I must have been still in the schoolroom, not deemed old enough to join in such jollifications. And I'm sorry, I don't recognize the chaps with Bettje, or anyone else for that matter.' He looked at it again. 'Except maybe that one there.' He indicated a small, dark-haired girl sitting to one side, her face a little blurred, and peered closer. 'Yes, I'm sure that's the English girl, I remember her. She'd been ill and stayed at the de Jager house for some time, but she went back to England. She was a lady.'

'A lady?' Then I saw what he meant, one of those English titles. 'Lady what?'

'Lady Maude something or other. I don't remember her last name.'

But I knew where I could find out. Later, when he had gone and I was alone, I took out the red photo album and turned the thick card pages and found the picture I wanted. Another old-fashioned wedding group, this time labelled in Sophie's careful handwriting: 'Maude's wedding'. Protruding slightly from behind the formally posed photograph was a yellowed scrap of paper which I hadn't thought to bother with before. Slits in the page held the photo in place. Easing the friable folded paper out carefully from behind and spreading it open, I saw it was a newspaper cutting of a British society wedding: the marriage of Lady Maude Prynne and Sir Lancelot Scroope of Maxstead Court, Worcestershire.

When I told my uncle I was quitting my job and going to England for an indefinite period, he put forward none of the objections which he normally made on principle to any plan that didn't come from him. He actually seemed relieved, and I soon learnt why: I had saved him the trouble of explaining to me that he intended to get rid of the house and what was left of his business and return to his native Natal. I would not now be on his conscience – if such a thing had indeed been troubling him. We could neither of us pretend that we were sorry to be parting; there had never been any spark of understanding between us, not to say love.

He didn't ask me why I wanted to go to England and I

didn't tell him, but he did however ask me how I was going to live there without any money.

'I have a bit saved. It won't last long, but I can get a job over there.' With my qualifications, I didn't anticipate having any trouble finding a position. Being one of the new career girls might even be easier in England.

'Well,' he said awkwardly, 'there'll be something for you when the house is sold. Not much, but it's what your aunt would have wanted.'

I was touched, despite my earlier feeling, and for the first and last time in my life, I kissed his cheek, astonishing both of us. He grunted. 'Take care, then. England's a long way to go on your own.'

I told him I shouldn't be on my own. 'Wim's going with me.'

He did not look reassured, any more than I had been re-assured when Wim had suggested it. But in the end, it had made sense. For a start, he had been there before and knew the ropes, he said, not really surprising me that his wanderings had taken him so far. His life when he was away from Cape Town had always been a closed book. For another, I was actually quite nervous of what I proposed to undertake and would be glad of some support, even from Wim. As I expected, I found I should have to lend him the money for his passage. I mentally said goodbye to it, though he swore he would pay me back. Like me, he would find work when we got there.

It didn't take Judy more than five minutes, when I told her what I was going to do, to decide she was going to come along with us, too.

'No, I don't want you in on this.'

'Yes, Plum. I'm going with you.' Plum is her little joke on my real name, Victoria, which I couldn't pronounce when I was very small. I called myself Vinnie and it had stuck, until Judy decided she liked Plum better. It's not something you actually welcome, a silly nickname like that, but the pun amused her and I didn't mind too much. We've known each other since our first day at school, when we were put into adjoining desks and became inseparable.

Although I love her, I have to admit she's a very controlling person, and likes to think she can sway me to her way of *thinking. I don't contradict her as a rule – arguing never gets you very far with Judy – but by appearing to agree with her I can sometimes manage to turn the tables and get my own way. She ignored what I'd said about not wanting her with me. 'You need looking after, Plum. Or you do with Wim in tow,' she added darkly.*

They didn't like each other and I could foresee trouble ahead. On the other hand, if Wim became difficult, or suddenly got tired of the whole project and drifted off to something more interesting that beckoned (which I knew was more than possible), I could think of no one better to have with me than Judy. She was alight with enthusiasm and determination for what she saw as a new project, even at the expense of abandoning her hard-won position on The Cape Argus. *She wasn't exactly their star reporter yet, but it was her avowed intention to get there some day, and she was already well on the way.*

She laughed off my objections. 'Experience, darling Plum, wider experience. It's all grist to the mill.' In any case, she went on, she was almost sure she would be able to persuade the editor at The Argus *to take a series of articles of her impressions of England and the English. Or even a regular column – 'Our reporter in England'. Or something like that.*

In the end I gave in, which I suppose was a foregone conclu-sion. I told myself that in any case, as a journalist she would know better than I how to go about ferreting things out – as Wim would too, for that matter. Admittedly, there are circumstances when a man is useful – even a man like Wim.

'And the rest of it?' Reardon asked fifteen minutes later as Joe finished reading the last of the pages which had been passed on to him. 'What else were you going to tell them?'

'What else? Oh, how should I know? I just wrote what came to me and that was as far as I'd got . . . what does it matter?'

'Like it or not, I'm afraid it matters a great deal, Miss Henderson.' Her name was in fact unlikely to be Henderson. Was it Joost, the name of her aunt and uncle? Or even her mother's name, de Jager? Not Mauritz, at any rate. 'You – and your friend – have had strong connections with a man who has been murdered. And sooner or later you're going to have to tell us what you know.'

Throughout this time, Judy had remained where she was, motionless in front of the window, though the street below had grown quiet and held little interest now that the shops had mostly shut, the shoppers gone home and it was dark but for the street lamps. What he said made her at last turn her back on the window. 'Bullying tactics will get you nowhere,' she said coldly.

Reardon was too old a hand to let that sort of thing bother him. 'Well, Miss Henderson?'

'I don't know where to begin.'

She did indeed look confused and upset, but how much of it was play-acting, how much was real? It would be a mistake to underestimate her, though she showed none of Judy Cash's aggressiveness. Even as he thought this, Judy walked over to where she sat on the sofa and knelt at her feet, whispering something and taking her hand. The nails of her own hands were bitten to the quick. Vinnie submitted passively. He wondered if it was an apology on Judy's part, though she seemed no less angry. How could the other one not sense the barely controlled emotion, feel the heat of it under the skin of the woman kneeling at her feet?

His patience was running out. 'All right, we've now established that you came to England in search of your father, and we've dispensed with the fiction that you didn't know Wim Mauritz. Right? So let's go back to the beginning. You found work here, both of you, when you arrived . . . There's a lot would envy you that. Jobs aren't easy to find in the present climate. You were lucky.'

'Luck had nothing to do with it, in my case,' Judy retorted, stung. 'I came with a recommendation from my editor in Cape Town. The *Herald* happened to have a vacancy and they jumped at me. Vinnie had to wait a bit longer for the job at the school. It paid peanuts for someone with her qualifications but she could live in.'

'And until then you lived with Mauritz at the house on Henrietta Street, whether as his wife or not. Don't deny it, we have witnesses,' he reminded her.

For several moments she was stubbornly silent, then at last she admitted it. 'He'd heard it was up for rent. At first, it seemed better than the rooms we'd taken when we first came here – well, anything was. Judy already had this place, so I went with Wim . . . We decided just two of us would arouse less comment than three, especially if we said we were a married couple – and for the same reason we agreed never to meet up with Judy,' she added, studying her feet, not wanting to admit to what such secrecy implied.

'Presumably he heard of the house through Arthur Aston?' He expected her to say she didn't know who Aston was, but she nodded acquiescence. 'Tell me, how did your friend Mauritz come to know him?'

'Oh . . . they just happened to meet.'

'Happened? *Happened?*'

'Well, he said it was luck, but of course it wasn't, not entirely. He'd been hanging around Alma House watching who came and went for a long time—'

'Just a minute. How did he know that was where Rees-Talbot lived?'

It took her some time to think of an answer. When she did, it didn't appear to add much to the facts already on record: Mauritz had called on the Lady Maude of the wedding photo, she had been uncooperative but Mauritz had made a deal with her son, Sir Julian, who had given him a pointer towards Osbert Rees-Talbot and where he lived. But then she went on to say that he had noticed Aston going to the house several times and in the end had followed him to a pub, where they struck up acquaintance . . . 'Something Wim was very good at,' she said, her mouth twisting. He had got Aston talking and heard him refer to Osbert Rees-Talbot as 'the major', and it wasn't long before he knew he'd struck gold. 'But meeting him,' she finished bitterly, 'was just the worst thing that could ever have happened. Together, the two of them ruined everything.'

'I always said it was a mistake to have Wim Mauritz with us,' Judy intervened sharply. 'He was no good, only in it for himself.'

'I know now. It was just plain stupid on my part.'

Considering her opinion of Mauritz, Reardon thought this

was very true – at the very least she had been naive, refusing to see he'd accompanied them halfway across the world for nothing except hopes of his own gain. On the other hand, Reardon didn't believe Vinnie Henderson, any more than Judy Cash, was naive. 'Exactly how did they ruin everything?'

'By pairing up and demanding money – which was truly the last thing I wanted.' Reardon's mental eyebrows rose: what else had she expected? Their meeting, she went on, might have been a 'coincidence' that had been arranged by Mauritz, but luck had certainly entered into it when he'd discovered that Aston had always known, or suspected, the outcome of his former officer's affair with Bettje de Jager. He had in fact made use of what he'd learnt all those years ago to extract a substantial loan for himself when he was starting up his business. It had been easy. The major, already guilty, was soon convinced that a word or a hint dropped here, a whisper there, could have been enough to turn his family life upside down, not to mention besmirching his reputation as an upstanding citizen. Aston had been canny enough, however, to realize that the Rees-Talbot purse was not bottomless and that his victim might at any time baulk at paying out and decide to face up to the consequences, so he had neglected to repay the heavy loan and put no more pressure on Osbert. Until he needed his agreement on the Hadley Piece business, Reardon reminded himself. And then Mauritz had come on the scene, bringing with him Osbert's unacknowledged daughter, when the blackmail stakes had been raised regardless.

'Which had never, ever been my intention! I didn't want money,' Vinnie repeated, suddenly passionate. 'I did not! All I wanted was to get some acknowledgement from my father that I existed, to be part of his family. To have some sense of who I really was!'

Reardon was willing to acknowledge there might be some basic truth in this, yet he was sceptical about the money. And wasn't there, after all, a certain ruthlessness about the way she had gone about insinuating herself into the good books of the Rees-Talbot family, and even perhaps into the heart of Felix, while knowing any attraction he felt for her was doomed from the start?

'If recognition was all you wanted,' he said dryly, 'I wonder you didn't simply make yourself known to your father.'

'I've told you – I had to be sure how he felt, first. He might have refused to believe me. I had no proof, nothing.'

She had only been a child when she had fancied she had no likeness to her mother. But had she looked in a mirror lately?

'He died before I could pluck up courage to approach him. But . . . but he knew anyway, and that's why, when Felix . . .' She left the rest unspoken. 'Well, anyway, I'm convinced he knew.'

He must have been blind if he hadn't. The striking resemblance to her mother – and those blue eyes, now tear-filled, so like Felix's, which must have come through Osbert himself. He had known the truth was facing him at last, and what he had chosen to do was kill himself . . .

'You stayed on, though, after he was dead,' Joe put in.

'There was still the family. I thought perhaps . . . I was desperate that we might . . . but then things became difficult with Felix.'

'In what way?' Reardon asked.

'It doesn't matter.'

'I'm afraid it does, you know.'

'Well, he'd convinced himself he wanted to marry me. Of course he didn't know who I was – and anyway, I knew it didn't go very deep.' She looked at Judy for help, but Judy was looking resolutely away. 'Besides,' she added in a low voice, 'everything had fallen apart and I was responsible. If I had never come to Folbury, my father would still be alive. You think the family would have welcomed me, opened their arms, if they knew about me? I had to go home.'

If she was acting, she was doing it very well. So perhaps she did have regrets, maybe she *was* sorry for the events she had set in motion. On the other hand, there had been resentment in that letter she had written. Hadn't she written that her mother had been 'left in the lurch'?

Judy leaned forward, picked up the poker and jabbed angrily at the fire, which responded with a little burst of smoke but nothing else. She threw it down. 'So now you've got the sordid truth, maybe you'll leave us in peace, Inspector.'

'Not, I'm afraid, until you've both told us what you know about Wim Mauritz's murder.'

Despite what Judy had just said, he was sure they had been aware this must come, after what had just passed. But he hadn't expected the sudden capitulation, though to deny any knowledge of it, to say nothing, wasn't a realistic option now. Neither woman was slow to see that. Very likely it was a relief, to Vinnie at least. The last hour had taken its toll on her. She looked dramatically tired, her head drooping, dark circles round her eyes. She was a young woman who, in her own opinion, had gone through a harrowing experience, and there was yet more to confess – but from which of them?

It was Judy Cash who spoke first. 'Wim didn't want to go back home,' she began abruptly, 'he wanted to stay in England, though not in Folbury. Fair enough, but we both agreed to tell him that the least he could do before he left was to give back his share of the money they'd got from the major.'

'To which I'm sure he agreed immediately!'

Vinnie said angrily, 'Of course he didn't. Being Wim, he thought we were mad. So we decided we had to do something about it.' She hesitated, but only for a moment. 'There was no question of opening a bank account here, so he kept it hidden at Henrietta Street. I went back that night to get it from him.'

'*We* went back,' Judy said. 'We went together. It was very late, nearly midnight, but when we got there he was still out. Luckily, they'd had an extra back door key cut and Vinnie still had it. We daren't light the gas, so we had to fumble about in the dark with a torch.'

'But I knew where he'd hidden it,' Vinnie said, 'in an envelope, taped behind a wardrobe.' Now they had started talking it was going along almost like a well-rehearsed script. 'There was precious little left – I should have remembered what a gambler he was – but it was better than nothing. We were halfway down the stairs with the torch when the front door opened and he came in. He was in a state.'

'Drunk?'

'No, he'd had a few but he wasn't drunk, not bad enough that he didn't see us. It was a freezing cold night but he'd no hat and coat on. His face was streaming with sweat as though he'd been running. I had to make up some story about having left something behind in one of the drawers. I wasn't sure whether he'd believe me, but he was too full of what had just happened to him to bother about why we were there. Once he'd got his breath back, he couldn't wait to tell us his tale.'

'Go on.'

Judy said, 'It was farcical, really. Well, *he* found it amusing. He'd been having what you might call a cosy half-hour with Lily Aston at Cherry Avenue, when her husband came home unexpectedly. Luckily he wasn't undressed, but he'd had to leave his hat and coat behind when he fled through the back door.' He was still laughing about it when we heard a car draw up outside and there was Aston, bursting through the door. He had Wim's coat bundled up under his arm and he threw it at him, then without any warning at all he punched him and knocked him down flat. He wasn't really hurt, though. He just lay there, looking up at Aston, grinning. Then he said, 'You've forgotten my hat, old boy.'

Joe said, 'His hat?'

'I think that was what did it, the sneer. Aston went berserk. He grabbed the poker out of the stand and just smashed and smashed it down on Wim's head, until . . . until . . .'

Vinnie covered her face with her hands, and Judy was shaking, her voice barely a whisper. 'It was all over in a few minutes, but it was awful, absolutely terrible. We tried to pull him off, but he was like an ox.'

'What happened then?'

'He just told us to get out – and after what we'd seen, we didn't stop to argue. There was nothing we could do for Wim – anybody could see he was quite dead.'

'And Aston? What did he do?'

'Nothing. He just stood looking down at him. There was blood and . . . stuff, on the hearthrug . . . and I suppose elsewhere. He must have cleaned everything up and put Wim's body in his car after we'd gone.'

And then driven out towards Maxstead, until the most likely place to bury him was found. Sheer luck for him that it had been so late at night, that none of the neighbours had seen or heard anything they thought suspicious, or hadn't thought it worth reporting if they had.

The silence grew heavy. 'So that's it?'

'You don't believe we're telling the truth, Inspector.'

In actual fact he was inclined to believe them, though the chances of proving it or finding the evidence were slim. Aston's car would have been thoroughly cleaned, probably several times. The hearthrug would have been disposed of – there was Aston's furnace handily nearby – and the poker cleaned, too, a heavy great thing, he recalled, standing on the hearth at number eighteen, in a weighty cast-iron stand fashioned from a wartime shell case. And the perpetrator himself was now dead.

'Go on, please. I'm waiting to hear the rest of it. Arthur Aston killed the man in a jealous rage, two of you actually saw him do it, and I'm wondering why you didn't see fit to report it.'

Neither said anything, which didn't surprise him. The instinct not to get involved applied to most people, even if they had nothing to fear, unlike these two, who still had a great deal to hide, he thought.

'All right. I think you didn't report it because you were afraid that if Aston was charged with killing your friend Wim, he wasn't going to keep silent about the connection you two had with him. And that might prevent you from leaving the country, as you were planning to do – that was what you needed the money for, you never intended to give it back to the Rees-Talbots, did you? But there wasn't nearly enough to get you back to South Africa. So you stayed on, working until you had enough for your fares, I suspect, saying nothing, and he might have got away scot free, if he hadn't been murdered himself.'

'Not if the *Herald* had anything to do with it,' Joe said. 'Not the way they kept on about Mauritz's killer being found. Beats me why,' he added, looking at Judy.

They let her think about that.

'When somebody you know has been killed, you don't look at it that way,' she said at last. 'Wim was all sorts of a pain in the neck, but he was a sweetheart compared with Aston. He wasn't *evil* – he didn't deserve to die. I didn't see why an animal

like Aston should go unpunished. But what I was writing in
the paper didn't seem to be making any difference to him
being found, and the enquiry was petering out.'

'And then, of course, came Aston's murder.'

'I was pulled off that story. I only did the first couple of
pieces before Butterworth insisted on taking it over himself.
So . . .'

While Joe was making a mental apology to Constable
Pickersgill for thinking he'd been giving away information – it
was Butterworth, the editor, with his police buddies! – Reardon
finished the sentence for her. 'So you took care of his punish-
ment yourselves.'

'*What?*' exclaimed Vinnie.

At the same time, Judy burst out, 'My God, you people
have a one-track mind! I was actually going to say, so the time
had come to leave Folbury.'

'I can't bear the place any longer,' Vinnie said. 'Everything.
It started out as nothing more than wanting to find my father,
but it's become a nightmare.'

Reardon suddenly recalled the unfinished remark she had
made about Felix and his father. 'Did Felix know about the
relationship between you and his father?' he asked her.

She flushed angrily. 'Of course he didn't! And he still doesn't.'

'Then he didn't know *why* his father was being
blackmailed?'

He saw they understood immediately what he meant. If
Felix had known the real reason, it would have provided him
with a far stronger motive for killing Aston than the one which
had made him confront the man at his home.

Vinnie said in an exhausted voice, 'I've told you. He has
no idea who I am – and he didn't kill Arthur Aston, if that's
what you're thinking.'

Reardon had been feeling tired, too. But they still had
their statements to make before either he or Joe could go
home, and in view of what he knew was still to come, that
was a luxury they couldn't afford. He looked at them, sitting
there, still holding hands, and said deliberately, 'It looks to
me as though there's every indication that's exactly what Felix
Rees-Talbot did.'

A silence fell between them all until at last Vinnie spoke, so low he hardly heard her. 'Nobody killed him. It was an accident.'

Judy said, 'Plum . . .'

'You seem very sure. Tell me how you know.'

'Because,' she said, taking a deep breath, 'I was there.'

Judy closed her eyes and sat as if turned to stone.

'I went to back to the house that morning, to number eighteen,' Vinnie said, 'and waited until he arrived for work.' She stopped, then took a deep breath, and went on rapidly. 'He went straight into the foundry and I followed him in. He was thumbing through some sort of book, a ledger or something, running his finger down the columns. When he turned round and saw me, he looked simply astounded, as if he'd never expected to see me again – I would swear he had almost *forgotten* the whole thing. I spoke to him about returning the money to Felix and he pretended he didn't understand.'

'Are you sure?'

'Of course I'm sure,' she said, almost angrily. 'I was there, wasn't I?'

'I mean, are you sure about the money? You didn't go there believing he would return it, any more than Wim would have done, did you? You wanted it for yourselves to enable you to get home, or you would go to the police about Wim's murder. It was the sort of threat he'd understand, being a blackmailer himself.'

He thought she might burst into tears, that Judy Cash would come at him like a spitting cat, but neither happened. There was another long silence before she spoke. 'You can't know what it's been like, ever since Wim died. It's been horrible, horrible. Trying to forget it, as though nothing had happened, though nobody missed him, nobody except Aston knew he was dead. And then his body was found . . .'

'We'll come to why you neglected to come forward with information later. Carry on with what happened when you went into the foundry.'

'He turned his back on me and began writing in that book. I tapped his shoulder and he swung round and took a step towards me and pushed his big, fat face into mine. I put my hand up and he jabbed it so hard with his pencil the point broke. He leant forward, raising his fist, and I knew he was going to hit me. I'd just time to step aside as he was bringing his arm down. He fell forward into that big heap of sand and just lay there, winded. I was petrified.'

'Didn't you even try to turn him over to see if he was all right?'

She recoiled. 'I couldn't have touched him! Anyway, he was just winded by the fall. I didn't want him to come after me again, so I got out, as fast as I could.'

'After you'd held him down to make sure he wasn't breathing.'

'No! No, how can you say that? Why would you think that?'

'There was a bruise on the back of his neck, as if a shoe or something similar had been planted there.' But, he reminded himself, Dr Dysart had said it could just as easily have been caused by that fall across the brass fender when Felix had knocked him over.

'Well, I didn't do anything like that. I just left as quick as I could.'

'Picking up the keys and locking the door behind you.' Not the actions of someone in a blind panic, though certainly someone not thinking straight. 'And a woman in a brown coat was seen leaving the foundry, and almost being knocked over by a milkman's horse.'

'Well, that wasn't me! I never saw any milkman – and I certainly don't have a brown coat.'

He didn't doubt it. It would long since have been disposed of, like the keys, which were probably down a drain somewhere.

So, just when they had started to wonder if either of these cases had a cat in hell's chance of success, here it was, a result for both. So simple, cut and dried, presented on a plate, that it was hard to believe it could be true, that it had almost escaped their grasp.

Perhaps it wasn't that simple. They had a result, but how much could be believed? Confessions meant nothing without proof, and where was that?

There was a long way to go yet.

Twenty-Three

Folbury wasn't a town that came alive at night – apart from a few pubs that were rowdy at times but even then were hardly dens of iniquity, and the Town Hall Rooms which doubled as a cinema and dance hall, and youths horsing around on street corners. Otherwise, folk mostly kept to their own homes.

They were walking through the quiet, gaslit streets, not with any particular objective in mind, but close together, Maisie's arm tucked through Joe's, their fingers entwined.

'What's going to happen to those two girls, then?' Maisie asked.

'They won't get off scot free.'

'They helped you find Mauritz's killer, didn't they?'

'True – but they were witnesses to what had happened, not to mention keeping his identity secret after he was found. That'll go against them. There's something called perverting the cause of justice, or at least hindering the police in their duties. And it's not certain yet about Aston's death.' Which was true. Reardon was by no means convinced by Vinnie Henderson's version of events, any more than he himself was, but he felt sure it was only a matter of time. Joe didn't really want to talk about any of it. He'd had enough the last two days, while the two women were being questioned. 'Want some chips?' he asked, twitching his nose as the odour of fish and chips drifted along from the lighted, open doorway of a shop a few yards further along an adjacent street.

'Not unless you do.' They walked a further few yards in silence but she wasn't put off. 'I can't get over it,' she said. 'Everything, but especially about that girl Vinnie, and their father. Margaret's going to take that badly.'

'Not to mention Felix. Hard cheese to find your girl is actually your sister.'

'Oh, I shouldn't worry your head about him. It was the other one he used to take out into the garden after those meetings of theirs.'

Joe thought about it. 'D'you reckon?' he said at last. 'Well, she gets up my nose, but every man to his own.'

'We shan't see her at Alma House, anyway. No more of those meetings, thank the Lord, now he's got this job in London.' She paused. 'Hark at me! What am I saying? There won't even *be* any Alma House, not for the Rees-Talbots anyway, nor for me, of course, when Margaret gets married.'

'Still over at Maxstead, is she?'

They turned the corner and walked towards the bridge over the river. 'She's staying with Lady Maude. Bit of a battleaxe, I've heard, but the fire must have been an awful shock for her'. She spoke sympathetically, but her thoughts were still on the same track. 'She won't like it, you know. Margaret, I mean, about Felix and that girl from the newspaper.' She sighed. 'Well, we don't all of us get what we like, do we?

'Some of us do, if we're lucky.' There were benches overlooking the river, all of them deserted since there was nothing to see but the street lamps shining on the dark water flowing swiftly beneath and a distant view of the town's gasholder, black against the far-off reflected red light from distant fires of forge and furnace.

He drew her to a seat. 'Speaking of which, Maisie . . .' He took a deep breath. 'Reardon told me my transfer will be coming through soon. How would you fancy becoming the wife of a detective?'

She looked straight ahead and said nothing. The gasholder seemed to have a compelling attraction. It wasn't the response he had hoped for and he turned her face towards him. 'Maisie?'

'Are you asking me that because of what I've just said – that I shan't have a home when they've all gone? I can always go back to Mum's, you know – or even stay with Lily. She'll be glad of that till she gets her bearings.'

'But that wouldn't be half as much fun as living with me, would it? Oh, come on, Maisie,' he said as she still didn't answer his question. 'It isn't because you don't *want* to marry me, is it?'

She turned her face towards him, suddenly full of laughter. 'If you don't know the answer to that by now, Joe Gilmour, you're not going to make much of a detective.'

★   ★   ★

Margaret looked around for a more comfortable seat but there were none out here in the garden – and precious few indoors either, at Maxstead, she thought, with a half laugh. It was such an uncomfortable house it was difficult to understand Lady Maude's passion for it. Perhaps one should try to see it as she did, not as a burden but as an unchanging testimony to a long and honourable family tradition. Yet how could you do that, and not feel that losing it was a personal tragedy?

Overnight, Symon's mother had turned into a grey shadow of herself, a woman of fifty who looked seventy. She was occasionally breathless when she spoke, and much less like a plump thrush now. She had a deflated look, almost as if the will which had kept her going had departed, sucking air from her body with it.

It was the sort of subdued, grey day which induced such depressing thoughts. It might rain, or the sun might break through, she thought, as she watched Heaviside and the garden boy busy planting geraniums. A day that encouraged heightened moods, a day much like the one on the day of the fire.

The shattering events of that one day were constantly with her. Not only the fire, but what had come before and after it: the revelations about her father – most of all, that – and the paralysing fear that had so suddenly come to her, that Felix might have known more than she thought and taken his resentment to an extreme not to be thought about. And then, Vinnie . . .

Vinnie. Vinnie and that girl, Judy. What was to happen to them following the revelations of the two murders wasn't clear, but afterwards . . .? Felix and Judy . . . The way he was sticking up for her. 'That won't last,' she'd told Symon, though more in hope than conviction.

'Probably. But that's Felix's worry, not yours. Isn't it, Margaret?'

He was right of course, and she had resolved she wouldn't interfere, that Felix was as he was. She expected too much of people, as she had of her father. If you put someone on a pedestal, they were bound to topple sooner or later. It was something she had to cope with on her own. Symon had been the rock she had leant on, but he had more than enough to cope with in other directions, and Binkie, typically, was being no help.

The fire had not been as bad as it might have been, all things considered – bad enough, but by no means a complete disaster. They had fearfully watched it taking hold, envisaging the whole of Maxstead going up in flames, powerless to do anything about it, praying for either the fire engine to arrive from Folbury, or the miracle of rain. In the event, the fire engine arrived within half an hour and the rain not at all. It had been due to the combined efforts of her uncle and Major Frith, organizing with military efficiency a chain of buckets and hoses from the large pond, that the flames hadn't spread any further.

The snug had been completely gutted, the floor above was presently unsafe, but where it had spread out into the hall it had amounted to little more than the loss of a few of the ancient hangings and a good deal of scorched and ruined panelling. It had left a grey, greasy residue like some scabrous disease over everything and the sour, acrid odour pervaded the entire house. Many of the gloomy ancestral portraits of men and women who had played their undistinguished but worthy part in its history were now unrecognizable, but they hadn't been destroyed. Like Maxstead Court itself, they would survive.

Symon and his mother were talking and viewing the damage when she went in – or rather Maude was talking and Symon was listening, with a brooding look on his face. Margaret took a seat nearby, next to the narrow window by to the door.

'Confounded electrics!' he commented when Maude eventually came to a halt.

She sighed. After a moment, she said, 'No, my dear, it wasn't the electrics. Well, it might have been but I don't think it was. You see, just before you arrived, I'd been working on the kitchen accounts in the snug, and the day being so dark I'd had the oil lamp lit – the one on the tall stand, you know? When I left the room, old Henry followed. He's so blind he's always bumping into things and I thought I heard something, though I wasn't sure. I was in a hurry and didn't go back to find out. If I had, all this might have been avoided. It was all my fault. I simply can't remember whether I turned the lamp off or not—'

'What time did you leave the snug?'

'Oh, just before luncheon, I don't remember the exact time.'

'Then it couldn't have been the lamp that started it. It wouldn't have taken all that time for the fire to get such a hold. It must have been an electrical fault.'

'Must it?' The relief that spread across her face seemed out of all proportion, but he understood it when she said, triumphantly, 'Well, of course – I've said it before and I'll say it again. Electricity! Nothing but a fad. What is wrong with a good old-fashioned lamp? Kinder, too.'

'But not always safer, Ma.'

Symon exchanged a gratified look with Margaret, acknowledging that Lady Maude, despite the dubious logic, was already sounding – and even looking – more like herself as a smile spread across her face. She almost seemed prepared to argue Symon's point, but then changed her mind, though she had clearly not given in entirely. 'Yes, well. Perhaps when we have had the snug – and the rest of it – redone, we should place the lamp in a less vulnerable position.'

'I don't think so.'

'You don't?'

'That's not the answer, long term. It's time we faced practicalities.'

For a long time, she said nothing, searching his face, and then she stumped across to where Margaret sat near the doorway and seated herself in a curious, red leather hooded chair, once a seat for servants who kept watch over the door. It had escaped the worst of the effects of the fire and had been one of the things to be properly cleaned up, its cushion replaced. Her face, hidden in the depths of the hood, couldn't be seen. 'You've come round to Julian's way of thinking. You think a little fire like this will mean the end of Maxstead, don't you?'

'For the Scroopes, perhaps yes. Maybe it's time. But dearest Ma, there *is* life beyond Maxstead.'

'Life at The Bothy I suppose you mean?'

'Only if that's what you consent to.'

There was silence from inside the chair but then she inched herself forward so that she could look around. Her gaze wandered from one to another of the blackened portraits hanging mournfully above the scorched panelling, faces water-streaked as if they were grieving for the grandeur that had once been Maxstead's. 'Blasphemous fables,' she murmured at last.

'What?'

'Dangerous deceits and blasphemous fables. False pride. Isn't that what your articles of religion preach against?'

'Ma,' Symon replied, choking back a laugh, 'You're astonishing, sometimes. But you've got it all wrong. What you've just quoted has nothing to do with pride. It refers to the sacrifices of the Mass.'

'Pooh! Well, the Scroopes have never been short on pride, false or otherwise, and I am about to astonish you more. Margaret, my dear, stop gazing out of the window and come over here and listen to what I have to say.'

Margaret hid her smile, did as she was bid and stood by the chair. 'It may surprise you both to know that I *have* been thinking, long and hard, about what's going to happen here. Let us face facts and agree that there is no possible way Julian could ever be considered a fit custodian of Maxstead – even if he could be brought to consent to such. But he has at least made a decision, and perhaps for once in his life it's the right one.' She drew a deep breath. 'We should talk about The Bothy, and what will happen when Frith goes. I've given it a great deal of thought and I believe it might be possible that the house could be made presentable . . . with some of the furniture from here, that is. As for its garden! I can make something better of it. That woman Ailsa Frith has never taken to it and it's a perfect disgrace, the way she's let it grow wild. She'll be much more at home amongst the heather and the thistles.'

The contrast of the seedling foxgloves and delicate ferns, the pale primroses and other woodland plants that had drifted from the surrounding woods into the garden of The Bothy, and the scarlet geraniums Heaviside was even now planting outside Maxstead's front door made Margaret blanch a little, but her Ladyship was in full command once more.

'What an opportunity! You and Margaret, Symon, shall come with me to inspect it and see if you don't agree. Now, I think, don't you?'

Lightning Source UK Ltd.
Milton Keynes UK
UKOW04f0804181117

312895UK00001B/35/P